A PSALM FOR LOST GIRLS

KATIE BAYERL

speak

SPEAK
An imprint of Penguin Random House LLC
375 Hudson Street
New York, New York 10014

First published in the United States of America by G. P. Putnam's Sons,
an imprint of Penguin Random House LLC, 2017
Published by Speak, an imprint of Penguin Random House LLC, 2018

THE LIBRARY OF CONGRESS HAS CATALOGED THE G. P. PUTNAM'S SONS EDITION AS FOLLOWS:
Names: Bayerl, Katherine, author.
Title: A psalm for lost girls / Katherine Bayerl.
Description: New York, NY : G. P. Putnam's Sons, [2017].
Summary: "Determined to protect her sister Tess's memory,
Callie da Costa sets out to prove Tess wasn't really a saint and finds
herself pulled into a kidnapping investigation"—Provided by publisher.
Identifiers: LCCN 2016027798 | ISBN 9780399545252 (hardback)
Subjects: | CYAC: Sisters—Fiction. | Saints—Fiction. | Death—Fiction.
Mysticism—Fiction. | Kidnapping—Fiction.
Classification: LCC PZ7.1.B38 Ps 2017 | DDC [Fic]—dc23
LC record available at https://lccn.loc.gov/2016027798

Speak ISBN 9780399545276

Printed in the United States of America.

1 3 5 7 9 10 8 6 4 2

Design by Eric Ford.
Text set in Garamond Premier Pro.

The one she left behind

I've had enough. My sister is dead. These people are crazy. Right now, *I* feel crazy. I ignore the silence at the altar, the buzzing fans and the wide eyes that follow me down the long granite aisle. Ma's angry yelp.

"Is that the sister?"

"What's the matter with her?"

"A real wild one, they say."

I press forward until the wooden doors swing open with a bang. Outside, the sun blazes hot, blinding. I teeter on the steps.

What's wrong with me? Miracles are supposed to be *good* things. Miracles make people *happy*. A little girl survived something horrible. I should be happy for her, for her grandmother, for all of us. For you, Tess. Instead I feel like I've been gutted all over again, my chest torn wide.

No one ever talks about this side of sainthood, do they? They ask what the saints can do for them, but no one ever asks a girl if she wants to be their savior. They definitely don't ask her sister.

OTHER BOOKS YOU MAY ENJOY

Amy Chelsea Stacie Dee	Mary G. Thompson
Catalyst	Laurie Halse Anderson
Conversion	Katherine Howe
The First Time I Drowned	Kerry Kletter
Imaginary Girls	Nova Ren Suma
The Sacred Lies of Minnow Bly	Stephanie Oakes
Saint Anything	Sarah Dessen
Shelter	Harlan Coben
The Sky Is Everywhere	Jandy Nelson
Still Life with Tornado	A. S. King

Where there are prophecies, they will cease; where there are tongues, they will be stilled; where there is knowledge, it will pass away . . . And now these three remain: faith, hope, and love. But the greatest of these is love.

—1 Corinthians, 13: 8–13

She's alone now, and it is dark. Tall houses slant inward, their doors locked and windows yawning. Beneath the whir and click of electric fans, the people of New Avon sleep.

The girl's feet move as quickly as they can, which is not much more than a shuffle. They scrape the sidewalk's jagged edges, bumping, jarring, each step a shot of pain. She feels something else too. Something gentle. Kind. It calls to her in the darkness. She sees herself seated on the sun-baked steps, hears the hiss of an open hydrant, the shrieks of children running up the block; mamas calling, home waiting.

Her throat sticks, and the ground tilts. She stumbles, arm folding. Even as the pain rocks her, the girl remains silent. She considers staying here forever. Or at least until morning. Then the people will fling their doors open, rub their eyes, and discover her here, a crumpled doll.

Unless. What if?

Slowly, painfully, she lifts herself to her feet, gripping arm to chest, feeling the hot pulse of it against her ribs. Just a little farther is all she needs to go. Just. A little—

One more step, and a light appears. Candles flickering, shadows splashing. A photo. There are flowers too. A teddy bear. Is that bottle filled with water? The girl licks her lips.

The face in the photo whispers something. What? The girl leans in to listen, but the hushed words are swallowed by an ache that begins at her skull and spreads swiftly downward. Her knees buckle, then her ankles.

She locks eyes with the girl in the photo, lets a small prayer form on her lips.

Help.

1.

I go to all the services at first. I listen to grandmothers, shop-keepers, and schoolkids testify. I stand by my smiling, weeping mother to accept the hugs and offerings. Watch an entire city light candles beneath your giant portrait. I let them do this.

To you, my sister.

But it's been a long, hot summer, and I don't know how much more I can take. My fibers are stretched thin, my insides shredded. Everyone looks at me, impatient, like I should be okay by now, damage contained. Four months have passed since early April. That's almost eighteen weeks since the ambulance, yellow lights whirling, took you away. One hundred and twenty-four days of me without you. And either they don't understand grief or I'm more screwed up than we thought, Tess, because somehow each day bites deeper than the one before.

The last thing you said to me was, "Where's the toothpaste?"

And the thing before that? Those words I said before I slammed the door, an extra-loud snap to make you flinch (Did you flinch, Tess?), well, those are the ones I prefer to forget.

I suppose that's the problem with last words. You don't realize what they'll be until it's too late.

Instead, I like to replay a different conversation, something you told me a long time ago. Would you remember it now? It had been another ugly day at school, the sort that was common back then. I was at the top of my class in those days, a fact that made nobody happy. You sat me on your bed and told it to me straight: "Other kids will bring you down, Callie. It's the way things go. We're lucky, though. We don't need them because we've got each other. Sisters are forever."

The way you said it, I knew it was true: we'd stick together, best of friends, till the very end.

Of course, we didn't know then how it would happen—that first incident two years ago, June, a voice that came out of nowhere, telling you things we couldn't explain. Strange messages that got surprised looks as soon as you said them aloud. People started coming to you, seeking answers and healing. Their stories soon piled one upon the next: a woman cured of cancer, a family reunited, a bullet lodged safely in a rib. Anywhere else these things would've been chalked up to luck, Tess. To fate. To good doctors, maybe, or poor aim. But the people of New Avon had another explanation . . . you.

The first time they called you a saint, we looked at each other, shook our heads, and asked, really?

I mean, *really*?

"Yes, really," they said, nodding brightly. (Or creepily, depending on your point of view.)

You and I exchanged another glance. Creepy, we decided. Definitely creepy.

It only got weirder. During your sophomore year, believers poured from every crack and crevice of this city, drawn to you like cockroaches to a sticky feast. It wasn't just the Portuguese grandmas and Jesus freaks either. There were old people, young people, smart people, dumb people. Okay, if we're being honest, mostly dumb people. Really dumb. As in, *If I rub this doorknob that she touches every day, will God take away all my troubles and make me rich and beautiful?* Uh, let's see. I'm going to go with a big fat no on that one. The people of New Avon are as cash-strapped and ugly as ever, Tess. A truly pitiful bunch. All that's changed is our doorknob, which has acquired an impressive shine.

"I don't know why they think I can help," you told me one night after the crowds left.

"Maybe it's like when you're a little kid and you wish on a star," I said. "Maybe they just want to believe in something."

You nodded, but your eyes stayed cloudy. "What if sometime they pray to me and they realize I can't help? What happens then?"

"Tess. No one ever blames a star when their wish doesn't come true."

I thought my reasoning was solid. Which it was, until it wasn't. Until that little girl went missing and prayers became useless. I guess that's all it takes—one disappointment—for it all to come undone.

Your most loyal believers say it was all meant to happen this way, that even the failure of your big heart was the work of God. When they say that, I do my best not to vomit up my own organs. Because honestly. Since when do people celebrate a seventeen-year-old dying of a freak heart attack? Since when is an undetected birth defect a *gift from God*?

I'll stick with science, thanks. God can keep her lousy gifts.

One small problem: When you're sixteen years old, what you believe is basically irrelevant.

This Sunday, like every Sunday since this whole thing started, Ma drags me to church. We arrive a little late and make our way to our usual spot in the second pew, a Tess-sized space between us. It's a hot morning, muggy as only August can get, and the seats are packed. (Funny how many people found their way back as soon as they heard you were dead.) Around us, parishioners fan themselves with prayer cards, even the most pious among them beginning to droop. Not Ma. She holds her head high, glossy curls styled for the throngs that will greet us afterward. My spine aches just to look at her.

There's no one to nudge, though, no one to share that secret eye roll that would soak up my irritation. So it just sits there, growing more salty.

You should've heard Ma last night, Tess, going on about white flowers or pink, almond cake or sponge. What sort of turnout should we expect for your birthday memorial? she wondered. Should the parish consider ordering incense sticks in bulk? Would enough people come?

I tried to be calm, patient. Ma must be grieving too, even if she has a strange way of showing it. "Tess hated pink," I reminded her. "She hated attention. *Incense gave her allergies!!!*"

So much for calm. By the end of it, I probably looked like one of those cartoon characters with pitchforks in her eyes, smoke coming out her ears, hair turned to corkscrews. Ma stabbed me back with pitchforks of her own, hazel-gray and extra-sharp.

I deflated and went to my room.

Because there's no point, is there? If our own mother doesn't remember how much you hated incense, there's nothing left to say.

The organist strikes a note and a rustle spreads through the pews. We stand and flip to the first psalm. It's one of the sad ones, the type you're supposed to sing softly, lip-synching recommended. Ma belts out the opening bars like it's a show tune.

I hear your muffled giggle, follow its round notes upward, where dozens of angels perch along the arches, their mouths frozen open like they can't believe this shit either.

Ma elbows me in the ribs. "Cut it out," she whispers. "This is the important part."

I bring my gaze down from the ceiling. *You say that about every part,* I want to growl back. (It's true, Tess. You know she does.) But around us, people are watching and Ma's eyes flash danger. I clench my mouth shut.

Father Macedo has stepped to the front of the altar. "Brothers and sisters, I have an unusual departure from today's Mass." His gaze drifts across the congregation, resting for a second on Ma and me. It's one of those moments, right before a glass hits the ground. You see it happening, falling so slowly, and you know if you just reached out you could catch it, but your arms are frozen. The thing keeps falling.

The priest unclasps his hands, and the words scatter like shards.

"*Missing child.*

Early yesterday.   Injured but alive.
Abducted six months ago . . .   No sign of who . . . or why . . .
    Neighbors found . . .   unconscious . . .   head trauma . . .
beside a shrine."

There's a long silence and then, as the pieces click together, murmurs rise from the pews. *Could he mean . . . ? Is it really . . . ?*

He means one of your shrines, Tess. He means they found that missing girl: Ana Langone.

Father Macedo continues. "This morning before Mass I received a call from the hospital. It appears that a little over an hour ago, quite unexpectedly, the child awoke."

My insides catapult upward, knocking against my throat. This is it—the moment they've all been waiting for. One word bounces from pew to pew, a question at first, then louder, gathering courage. *Miracle? Miracle. It's a MIRACLE!*

Father Macedo waves his hands, attempting to calm the crowd. He's saying something about tests and time, but it's impossible to hear him. I can't breathe. There's no air, only thick clouds of incense. My eyelid has gone spastic. I push past Ma, tumble into the aisle.

I've had enough. My sister is dead. These people are crazy. Right now, *I* feel crazy. I ignore the silence at the altar, the buzzing fans and the wide eyes that follow me down the long granite aisle. Ma's angry yelp.

"Is that the sister?"

"What's the matter with her?"

"A real wild one, they say."

I press forward until the wooden doors swing open with a bang. Outside, the sun blazes hot, blinding. I teeter on the steps.

What's wrong with me? Miracles are supposed to be *good* things. Miracles make people *happy*. A little girl survived something horrible. I should be happy for her, for her grandmother, for all of us. For you, Tess. Instead I feel like I've been gutted all over again, my chest torn wide.

No one ever talks about this side of sainthood, do they? They ask what the saints can do for them, but no one ever asks a girl if she wants to be their savior. They definitely don't ask her sister.

In the distance, the harbor glints brilliant blue. Rooftops stagger downhill to meet it, tiered and spiny, like the teeth of an open-mouthed beast.

I kick off my church shoes and run.

2.

Hold on. Slow down. What did Father Macedo say exactly?"

Danny lowers all six feet of himself onto the wooden steps, and I fold down beside him. The air is still, no salty breeze to cover up the smell of frying onions from a nearby apartment. The sun sucks moisture from every pore, shrink-wrapping my skin against bone.

I'd assumed the others would be here by now. None of my friends are churchgoers, and Mrs. Delgado works so many jobs that the house is pretty much always parent-free. But when I arrived a few minutes ago, the house was quiet and Danny appeared at the back door alone. We stood there for a long moment, me with sweat gathering along my lip, realizing he'd still been sleeping, and Danny looking at me like it was the first time he'd seen a girl get out of breath.

I blurted the whole miracle mess in a single gasp.

Now we stare at his small, shriveled yard, and I try to put

the fragments back in some kind of order. The facts go like this: Six-year-old Ana, my across-the-street neighbor, disappeared in late January. No trace, no suspect. The thing is, in a city like ours tragedies happen all the time, rarely causing the media to blink. But something was different this time. Maybe it was Ana's sweet face or the fact that her grandmother recently moved in from the suburbs. Or maybe it was Tess. Her reputation was at its peak—two years in, hundreds praying to her weekly. The prayers now shifted to finding Ana. The atheists and snobs had a field day, poking fun at these backwards fools with their old-world beliefs. It became a sore point with Bishop Landry up in Boston. (The only *real* city around here, according to some people.) The bishop was not on board with some teenage prophet from a tiny, half-forgotten mill city turning his diocese into a punch line. There'd been a blowup between him and Father Macedo about it earlier in the fall. Unclear who won.

In any case, whatever it was—the timing, that little face, or the irony of a bunch of poor folks thinking God gave two shits about them—Ana Langone's disappearance became a massive story overnight.

In New Avon Kidnapping, God Named Chief Investigator
While Police Beg for Tips, Locals Head to Church

As the days dragged on, the headlines grew more barbed: *Faithful Fumble as So-Called Saint Fails to Deliver.* They were real assholes about it. And while I agreed with them on principle (I mean, honestly, who thinks praying is going to solve a crime?), I hated what it did to Tess. She barely slept as the weeks dragged on and . . . well, I don't need to tell Danny what the pressure eventually did to her. He knows that part as well as anyone. There is a reason after all that his face is so pale these days, eyes more like murky mugs of coffee than the cups of warm tea I remember. I'm not the only one around here with a shattered heart.

"They found Ana near one of the shrines," I tell him. "Now she's awake, and they think it's because of Tess."

"Wouldn't it have been a better miracle if they'd found her six months ago?"

I squint at my friend. He's a smart guy, though you wouldn't know it to look at him. With a thick brush of dark hair and rumpled t-shirts that smell faintly of detergent and his mother's cigarettes, Danny Delgado is one of those quiet people who are easy to overlook, definitely not the sort of guy you'd think Tess would choose for a boyfriend. Even I couldn't believe it when she first told me. I'd been hanging out with Danny and the others for a year by then. He'd never once asked about her, and Tess never once mentioned him. (To be fair, I'd hardly mentioned Danny either.)

"I guess the miracle's that she survived," I say. "Father Macedo said something about head trauma. She was unconscious when they found her. A bunch of people got together to pray after the ambulance left, and when they heard she woke up—voilà: miracle."

Danny stares out at the yard, his throat muscles working like he's choking on a thought. "You don't believe she's a saint, do you?"

I almost laugh. "God no. Do *you*?"

He looks at me then, probably surprised that I care what he thinks. And okay, here's the messed-up part: He doesn't know that I know all about him and Tess, how they met in her homeroom last September (Tess, still a junior, and Danny, a second-time senior), how he walked up to her at the Cranberry Festival a few weeks later, offering her the stuffed whale he'd won, or how as the night drew to a close, he shyly asked permission before leaning in and kissing her like she was a regular girl.

Tess was up half the night replaying it for me, overcome with giggles. Danny was my sister's first love and a surprise on so many levels. *When every guy around thinks you're a junior Virgin Mary, it kind of kills your prospects,* she used to moan. For some reason, Danny didn't care about the saint stuff. Maybe he'd spent the first part of high school too stoned to notice. Whatever it was, the two of them were goners from the get-go, so in love that whatever strangeness I could have felt about it vanished immediately.

So yeah, it's a little weird that he and I never discussed it, but Tess swore me to secrecy and what can I say? I'm not one for bringing up sticky subjects with my friends.

Danny clearly isn't either. I poke at his elbow. "C'mon. Do you? Think she was a saint?"

He shrugs uncomfortably, then lowers his head, shakes it. "I'm not really a God person is the thing." Small cough. "Don't tell my mom I said that."

This time I really do almost laugh. Danny's too busy picking at his thumb to see my face, which is good, because it's probably messed up how happy I am to know I'm not the only one with a God/mother problem.

Danny frowns at his ripped-up finger. "I guess the part I don't get is how any of this matters. It's not the first time they called something a miracle, is it?"

"Why am I freaking out now, you mean."

"Well, yeah." Danny peers at me sideways, but he doesn't have to worry. I've done the crying thing. For weeks I cried, an ocean's worth of tears. I'm a parched shoreline now. He couldn't squeeze a drop out if he tried.

"Because now Tess is dead."

"Oh." Danny glances away, swallowing. "Right."

Crap. That came out too harsh, even for me. I try to think how I can explain it more gently. How would Tess explain it?

"The stuff that happened while she was alive—the voice, people praying to her, saying she cured their cancer and whatever—none of that's as important as what happens now. Not to the Church anyway. It's this weird rule, but only miracles after death count toward Vatican-level sainthood."

I've done my research. One so-called miracle sets the process in motion. Two, plus the Pope's stamp, and it's official: Tess da Costa becomes Saint Teresa of New Avon.

"And you really think this one could count?"

"If what they're saying holds up. A little kid survives abduction plus head injuries? It's the stuff miracles are made of."

"But . . . how would they prove it? Like, how do you prove something's a miracle?"

Excellent question. Even better: How do you prove something's *not*?

Danny picks up a pebble, rolling it thoughtfully. His hands are big like the rest of him, square nails, ragged at the tips; his shoulder is so close that I can feel the heat coming off the cotton, a few degrees warmer than the air. I think about dropping my head and telling him everything—about the arguments Tess and I had in those final weeks, how things have been since she's been gone. No one to talk to, thoughts rocking around like tumbleweeds. It's so heavy sometimes, my head. Also, my arms, my shoulders, my feet.

"You miss her a lot, don't you?" he says.

My chest squeezes. "Of course."

Danny doesn't say what I know he's thinking: He misses her too.

He looks miserable, almost as bad as I feel, and maybe my exit from church knocked something loose because suddenly this little dance we've been doing seems absurd.

"You don't have to hide stuff from me, Danny. Tess told me about you. You must've realized?"

His pebble clunks to the ground. "I guess I know now."

His dark eyes flicker upward. How *much* do I know, they ask, skittish.

Answer: Most things, but not all. And neither of us wants to get into all that.

We fall quiet. It's probably not surprising how awkward this is, given how things used to be. I wonder, does Danny remember it the way I do? It was only last summer that everywhere we went we ended up sitting side by side, closer than strictly necessary. It wasn't a crush, exactly. (I never even told Tess.) It was something, though. Gravity played with us back then, two bodies caught in a new kind of orbit, while our friends looked on slyly, waiting for the collision.

But it never happened. And I'm not mad about it. Honest to God. I'm just a little . . . fuzzy on how things changed so quickly.

"Does anyone else know?" he asks.

"Nah. And I hid her journals, so you're good."

Danny's jaw falls open. "Tess kept a—"

"Calm down. No one's read them, even me. And what's the worst that would happen if they did? I always thought it was ridiculous that she kept you a secret."

"She had her reasons," he says quietly.

"Her reasons were crap. Do you know she made me pretend you were looking for *me* that time my mom caught you in the yard? I mean, so what if Ma knew? So what if people talked?"

"Callie, did she tell you—"

"People can be such assholes." I grab the fallen pebble and chuck it across the yard. "That's what scared her, wasn't it? That they'd judge her? But no person can be perfect, not all the time. Not even a saint."

Danny has a strange expression on his face.

"What?"

He shakes his head. "It's nothing. Just promise not to tell anyone, all right?"

He looks truly worried about this secret of his. I wonder what exactly Tess said to him. A shadow flits overhead, and I follow Danny's gaze upward. The sky is so huge, so sunny that it's been leached of all color, faded almost to white, like it's lost all sense of how a sky should be.

"Don't worry," I say. "Your secret's safe with me."

From the Journal
of
Tess da Costa

January 30

Last night it snowed. It snowed and it snowed and it snowed. It was one of those storms that turns the world so white that, pretty soon, the ground becomes the sky. When we wake up, they've announced it: snow day. Normally, that would be a happy thing because, well, <u>no school</u>. But no school also means no D. No school means sitting in the apartment all day listening to Callie and Ma needle each other about the proper way to fold socks. One of these days I'll tape them so they can hear how ridiculous they sound.

Ma, pulling hair & waving sock: When you fold them over, they stretch out of shape!

Callie, waving sock & pulling hair: When you <u>don't</u> fold them, I end up with only one sock!

They've always been like this—a pair of bristling charges, yanking toward opposite poles. Me, the neutral zone that keeps them from flying apart completely. In the past couple years, it's gotten way worse. Most days I don't mind playing my part. They're both funny, especially when they don't mean to be. Also, I love them more than anything in the world, even when they're being total nutjobs.

As Ma begins a third demonstration of her sock-rolling technique, my patience flickers. They'll go on like this for hours if I don't step in with some little distraction—a calming word or, better, a well-timed joke—but you know what? Sometimes this apartment is too small for all that. Sometimes I don't have any sock jokes left. My phone pings and I tell the warring parties I'm going to read in the shed, that I'll be back in an hour to see who's left standing.

Yup. Yup. Sure. Fine, they both say, too busy staring each other down to notice that I don't have a book. I pull on my coat, Ma's boots, and Callie's frumpy hat (did mine elope with the sock?), and close the door quietly.

Outside, the cold air tingles. The street is filled with shrieking kids, the little ones all fat and wobbly in their bright-colored hats and mittens, the older ones blowing on raw hands, reaching for the next snowball. A faint sound murmurs but is drowned out immediately by an enormous yowl. Rudy has spotted me. I press my hands to the slobbery first-floor window, give him a look that says, Not today, my puppy love.

No. I'm the one who's getting rescued this time.

D beeps the horn so gently no one notices but me. His car, a sporty blue thing, practically an antique (not in the good way), has been carefully scraped clear of snow, all but the passenger-side window. He's so thoughtful, my D, leaving me a frosty cover. I come closer and rub away a small circle, blow him a kiss. His smile stretches to Idaho.

I glance around to be sure nobody's looking. But it's just a bunch of kids and snow-covered cars and an old utility truck, probably here to knock snow from the wires. Another soft sound breathes in my ear like a sigh or a voice preparing to speak. I swat it away.

Not now. Please. An hour is all I need. Just one hour without voices or prayers or anyone's problems. Just one hour, please.

The car is toasty inside, heat blasting against my throat. D guides us along slowly, tires slipping in and out of snowy ruts. The whispers grow louder, but I ignore them, chattering something to D. I don't even know what I'm saying, but he's nodding, attentive, like it's the most brilliant thing he's ever heard. He's a very good listener, my D.

We don't go far, just to the Greek restaurant on Woodside Ave, the one that's forever empty and Callie suspects is a front for something else. The parking lot is immaculate, perfectly plowed for all the nonexistent customers. D pulls off to the side, and I go quiet.

BEWARE, says the voice, more clearly now. BEWARE THE ANGEL. (Agh. What does that even mean? Just one hour. I can't even have that?) Frustrated, I yank off my hat, and D's mouth curves upward.

Uh-oh. I flip open the mirror. It's as I suspected: a curly girl's nightmare. I try to smooth down the frizz & fluff, but D pulls my hands from my head.

I still can't believe a girl like you would pick someone like me, he says.

I frown. What do you mean? I'm just like anyone else.

Not true, he says. You're not like anyone. You're—

He's staring at my frowny lips, bites his own, hesitating. The next second, we're mouth on mouth and jackets are flying and there's no knowing what D really thinks I'm like. We kiss until the icy window melts and then fogs up again. We kiss until I'm dizzy and fizzy and have forgotten all about crackly voices and grumpy sisters and stretched-out socks.

By the time D drops me back at home, my head has settled, thoughts gone still for the first time in days. The shrieking kiddos have all been tucked inside, and the sun has slipped behind the apartment buildings, leaving a pure blue light.

The first phone call comes as I'm warming my hands by the stove.

A child. Missing.

It's Ana Langone, Ma says. Did you see her when you were out there?

I panic then, think hard, trying to picture each bundle of color, which hat belonged to which face, but all I can remember is D's hands as they slipped under my sweatshirt, chilled at first and then, suddenly, shockingly, hot.

Sorry, I say. I can't . . . I didn't . . . see.

Callie gives me a sideways look, and I feel my cheeks go warm. She knows exactly where I've been, but I know she'll never tell.

Ma comes up beside me, peering into my eyes. Maybe you heard something? The voice, she means.

I shake my head. BEWARE THE ANGEL, that's all it said. It didn't make sense, Ma. It never makes sense! Did I miss a sign?

I sound slightly hysterical, and Ma tries to pretend she's not disappointed. Before she can ask another question, Callie steps between us, suggesting we turn on the news. She laces her fingers through mine as the three of us stare at the screen. There are no updates about Ana. When the phone rings again and Ma goes to get it, Callie squeezes my hand, whispering, You didn't do anything wrong, Tess. You weren't out there to babysit.

I squeeze her hand back. My little sister. When the going gets rough, she always knows what to say.

Callie and Ma decide to join the search party, and Ma suggests that I stay behind to keep a watch on things. Maybe you could say a prayer too, she says.

Callie rolls her eyes and says missing children are found when people look for them, not by praying to invisible spirits. Ma tells her to have a little respect.

The two of them clatter down the stairs, squabbling, and I watch as their flashlights wink across the sidewalk, drifting down the block. When their lights are gone, I sink to my knees, hands folded, and look out the window into the deep dark sky.

Dear Lord, I say, please help this lost child. Help her find her way home.

3.

"Did someone say *secret*? I like secrets."

Danny's cousin Karen has planted herself at the base of the deck, gripping the largest iced coffee the world has ever seen. With her unprocessed hair, unsubtle t-shirts (today's: *Yes, I Was Born This Awesome*), and fondness for black rubber jewelry, Karen is the opposite of most of the predictable girls in this city. Most of the time I'm glad to see her.

"Oye, though, for real. Secrets are my specialty," she tells Danny and me. "Steamy scandals. Juicy detalles. My lips are zipped, so tell me what you got."

She mimes throwing away the key and I roll my eyes. This girl. She's the reason I started hanging out with Danny and them to begin with. First week of my freshman year when the saint rumors had just started and the whole school was buzzing around me, trying to figure out whether holiness is genetic, Karen plunked herself down next to me at lunch and started ranting about urban negligence and the dubious items our administrators dared to call food. She held up a sloppy joe, letting it splatter to her plate as proof.

At the time I wasn't sure if she was refreshingly honest or slightly unhinged, but one thing was clear: Karen Pérez didn't give a shit what I—or anyone else—thought of her. I decided I liked her immediately.

"C'mon, kids. I ain't getting any younger. Sexier, possibly. If you can imagine *that*." She flicks her long black ponytail and pops a scrawny hip.

"Back off, Karen, it's none of your business," Danny says, an edge in his voice. Only a slight one, though. Danny's terrible at standing up to people, especially his cousin.

Karen's brows do a little dance. "Aww, c'mon, primo! Tu business es mi business, verdad?" She bounds up the steps, pausing at my feet. "Callie? C'mon, tell me what's good."

"It's not—"

Danny shoots me a nervous look. As if I'm the one we have to worry about here. I've kept his secret from our friends since last October. I'm not about to crack now.

"It's honestly nothing," I tell Karen. "Just let it go."

"Mmm-hmm." She takes a long drag from her drink, nodding in a way that means she doesn't buy it for a second. "I see how you want to play. I bet it's nothing a little truth or dare won't get out of you. Vámonos. Challenge: accepted."

It takes a full minute for my eyes to adjust to the gloom inside. With its wrecked plaid couches, faux wood paneling, and vague smell of mushrooms, Danny's basement is the never-never land of New Avon, a place where time stands still and teenage burnouts never grow up. Carlos and Amanda appear a few minutes later, like bugs from the woodwork, her in skintight jeans and enough eye goop to paint a house, him with the same Red Sox jersey he wore yesterday and a hungover squint. Will Carlos ever get his shit together, I wonder. Will Amanda discover the limit to how much mascara the human eyelash can hold?

We settle into our positions—me, Danny, Amanda, and Carlos sprawled out on the balding carpet, Karen perched on the mini-fridge—and just like that, we're playing another marathon round of truth or dare. As always, I take all the dares.

Carlos comes up with the first one: "Callie, I dare you to chug that beer without taking a breath."

Me: "Done."

Karen: "I dare you to run to the corner store and back . . . with no bra on."

Me: "No sweat." (And no boobs to speak of, anyway.)

"C'mon," I tell them. "I want a good one this time." They've gone easy on me since Tess died, which I mostly pretend not to notice.

Amanda: "I dare you to call the Sisters of Mercy and pant like you're having wild sex."

Me: "Yawn."

I've done that dare so many times even the nuns are bored with it. But Callie da Costa doesn't turn down a dare, even a tired excuse for one, so I dial the convent and pant dutifully into the phone. I even throw in a bark this time. When I'm through, I hold up the receiver, and on cue, Carlos growls, Amanda howls, and Karen throws in an earsplitting yelp.

I don't tell my friends they're barking into an answering machine, that Sister Lucretia and the others are at church right now, plying the after-Mass crowd with stale danishes and empty blessings. Ma is there too, chatting up the deacon and the other importants, probably apologizing for the scene I caused earlier. *Teenagers,* she'll say. *Who knows what they're thinking?*

Beer swirls in my stomach. I drop the phone into its cradle, swipe my hand on my skirt.

Danny's been quiet since we came inside, picking at a thinning patch of carpet. Behind him, the boxy old television flickers on mute.

"Callie," Carlos proclaims, "you are awesome."

"The awesomest," says Amanda. "I wish I had guts like that." She adjusts her snug top, revealing a busty swell that more than makes up for a lack of guts. Amanda is my exact opposite: pretty, sweet, empty-headed, universally liked. Not the type of person I'd normally pick for a friend, but Karen sticks by Danny, and Danny's known Carlos since kindergarten, and dumbass Carlos has had a thing for Amanda for almost as long. *Stupid and Stupider,* Karen calls them when they're out of earshot, but even she doesn't seem to have the energy to find better friends.

"I totally think they should make a show about you, Callie," Amanda says. "They could call you the Queen of Dares. Or, like, the . . . Princess of Pranks."

"Hold up." Carlos squints like a thought is brewing somewhere in the boozy fug of his mind. "I got it. Callie is the—uh, whaddyou call it?—the *Patron Saint* of Pranks!"

He busts up laughing, beer sloshing onto the rug. It's a good one, for him.

"Idiot!" Amanda slaps Carlos. "You can be so freakin' insensitive!" Slap, slap.

"Ow! It was a joke! She knows that. Right? Callie?" Carlos makes his sad-puppy face, the same one he makes every time he says something stupid, which is often. The rest of them eye me like I'm made of porcelain, like I can't handle a joke.

"It's fine. It was funny." I stretch my mouth. "See? I'm laughing."

I'm about to suggest a new dare or grab another beer—anything to change the subject—when a child's face appears on the screen behind Danny. I punch his shoulder. "Hey. Turn it up."

Ana Langone's reappearance at a Bedford Street shrine is stirring up questions in New Avon. A police officer reaches for the mic. *We believe she was held at a nearby location. There are a number of details we're still trying to understand.*

This, for example, says the reporter. The camera cuts to a dress: It's a frilly thing, tiny white polka dots against a lemon background, layers of frothy lace. It's not normal, not something a normal person would put on a kid. It looks like something out of one of Tess's horror movies, something a demonic doll would wear. The left sleeve is gone, torn right from the shoulder.

The officer begins to say something about the ongoing search for the kidnapper, but the reporter stops him midsentence. *There's yet another twist to this story, folks.* I know right away where she's headed. She wants to talk miracles. The camera cuts to the church, where another smooth-haired reporter conducts a series of awkward interviews. Parishioners preen for the camera, talking about the power of prayer and their unshaken belief that Ana Langone would eventually be found. Liars, all of them.

The deacon's wife smiles breezily into the camera. *The police have been outstanding. The community too. But the person we need to thank above all is Teresa da—*

I reach past Danny and slam the off button. The room goes still.

"Dude, that dress was creepy," Carlos says after a long silence.

"You think he's still out there? Her killer?"

We all look at Amanda, who looks back at us, pink lips pouting in confusion.

Carlos: "The girl's alive, Mandy. He can't be her killer if she's alive."

Amanda taps her head. "Right. Duh." But then her face freezes. You can almost see the wheels working, smell the fumes. "So then a *kidnapper* is on the loose? What if . . . What if he—"

"Snatches another kid? Goes murder-spree apeshit?" Karen hops down from her perch. "That'd suck. This whole thing is loco, you ask me. Did you see how they cut that cop off? He was trying to give us some facts, and all they wanna talk about is some fairy-in-the-sky woo woo shit." She pauses. "No offense, Cal."

"None taken." I sit up taller. Karen's right. The last thing that kid needs is more people crowding her with their prayers. She needs rest, possibly a lifetime of therapy. A little justice might help. "These people don't care about that little girl. They never say anything real. It's a big joke to them, a fucking three-ring circus." Just like it was with Tess.

Four months she's been gone. My sister. I push a knot of curls from my face. My face is hot, my voice a little too loud. My friends pretend not to stare.

"What? You know I'm right."

Carlos and Amanda nod obediently. Danny too. Karen wraps her ponytail around her fingers, eyes on me. She doesn't say it, but I can see what she's thinking: Those reporters aren't the only ones who've gone a little loco.

Behind the curtains a machine sighs. The girl slows her breath to match its exhale.

K-shaaa.

K-shaaa-aaaa.

Her grandmother hasn't left her bedside all day and all night and now another morning. Each time the girl peeks over to double-check, the old woman smiles.

K-shaaa.

K-shaaa-aaaa.

The machine breathes, and the girl's eyelids droop.

"Ana." Her grandmother presses her uninjured arm. "No sleeping, remember?"

The old woman's eyes have dried behind their glasses, finally, but their rims are still tinged pink. "Only a few more hours, love. You just need to stay awake until the doctor can be sure. Should we do another movie?"

At the foot of the bed a table is piled high with flowers, beside them a photo of a teenage girl. She looks as if she wants to speak.

"Baby? Are you watching?"

The smaller girl lifts her gaze to the television, a bright squiggle of smiling, bouncing figures. Orange, lime, pink.

"Your favorite," her grandmother says, but the candy-colored motion makes the girl's stomach lurch. She lets her eyes fall closed.

"Ana." Her grandmother places a hand on hers, more firmly this time. "Just a few more hours, love. Everything will be okay soon. You'll see."

On the television, bright colors swirl. The girl holds her insides steady and watches, obedient.

4.

Cranston Street is quiet when I approach. Rows of duplexes and triple-decker apartments wedged tight as a box of crayons, thin strips of yard pressed up against the sidewalk. A streetlamp's burned out, and my building—three stories of palest green— nestles deep in shadow. I open the gate, smelling Rudy before I feel his fur against my legs or hear the low growl in his throat. "Shhhh, pup. Look. They're gone now." I point to the front porch, no sign of today's trespassers except for a scatter of candles they left flickering.

Rudy rumbles disapproval.

This shrine marks the spot where Tess sat each Sunday after church, smiling patiently as the believers approached, one by one, unloading all their hopes and heartache and pain. It's a tradition Ma invented, with full support from our very Catholic landlords, after reading about a healer in Albuquerque who held weekly office hours. Before the porch scheme, Tess got stopped on the street all the time by people asking her to lay hands or say a prayer. This new approach made other days more manageable; Sundays, meanwhile, became brutal.

She never complained, but we could see it in her face.

Anyone with eyes could see it was killing you, Tess.

Your chair sits empty now, but that doesn't stop them from opening the gate like I just did, climbing onto the steps, and leaving their odd little gifts and slips folded with prayers. Sprays of plastic lilies. Flags gone limp. Bowls of fruit left to rot. Rudy sniffs at one of the more heinous items—a stiff little bear, pink—and snarls. Smart pup. He knows: You hated pink. Teddy bears aren't supposed to have teeth.

I let my fingers stray over the funny little head. Technically, Rudy belongs to the Flahertys on the first floor, but if dogs could talk, he'd say he belongs to you. You're the one who gave him his name—Rudy, aka Rudster, aka Rodolfo, aka Stinky Pup. Everyone else calls him That Freakin' Dog. No longer a young dog, Rudy has all the bad habits of a puppy.

"He's just lonely," you explained whenever Ma said she couldn't open the front door without That Freakin' Dog jumping on her like a maniac. "Besides," you said, rubbing him all over his scruffy not-quite-brown-not-quite-gray body, "he's just too cute, yes he is, you're just so cute, aren't you, baby?"

Ma snorted. "Maybe if you hold your nose and squint."

(I tried that: the squinting and the pinching. It doesn't work, Tess.)

You loved Rudy despite his flaws. And let's face it, there are many: killer bad breath, patchy fur, odd body shape, torn ear, tendency to fart. Topping Ma's list: He leaps out into the street every time a car pulls up to the curb. (Someone always forgets to latch the gate.) "That Freakin' Dog is going to give me a heart attack one of these days," she'd say, back when she could joke about heart attacks.

You didn't say it, but that was your fear too—one day Rudy would jump out at the wrong moment, his manic energy met by the blunt force of metal. Of course, none of us ever imagined that the old dog would outlive his favorite girl.

Rudy presses against my bare calf, stinking to high heaven, and I'm overcome by it suddenly: the unfairness of it all. Seventeen is supposed to be the beginning. Sisters, you told me, are forever.

I snatch up the horrid little bear and, without thinking, chuck it as hard as I can out onto the street. Rudy's paws lift, falling back onto the porch with a soft click.

We stand there, watching as a truck barrels up the block, grinding the bear into oblivion.

Upstairs I slip off my sneakers and slide my key into the lock. I wait for my eyes to find a couch-shaped shadow, the television, the coffee table piled high with dried-out bouquets. On the stand where we used to throw the mail: another shrine.

I creep along the hallway to our room. If I'm lucky, Ma's fast asleep by now and we can have whatever conversation needs having tomorrow or, better yet, never. I tiptoe, feeling my way along the pitted plaster wall, hopping over the creaky floorboards you and I mapped out as kids. Late at night, after binge-watching the most terrifying horror flicks we could find, we'd retreat to our room, fingers laced, balancing each other on the leaps.

Tonight I brave the creaks on my own, managing to miss all but one. I pause for your applause and am met with . . . silence.

And then: the pad of slippers, a snap, and the hallway floods with light. Ma appears, hands on her hips, bathrobe splayed open over church clothes. She isn't happy.

"Carlinha Maria da Costa, where in God's name have you been?"

An apology would be the thing right now, or at least an explanation, if there were words to describe the bottleneck of feelings lodged at the top of my throat. Or if the sight of my mother standing there, lips pursed and hair unwound, didn't make me want to hurl heavy objects.

"Do you have any idea what time it is?"

I scan my bare wrist.

"It's half past eleven, Callie! I've been worrying myself sick. A girl your age can't be wandering the streets. Not with all these kidnappers and predators on the loose." Her eyes spit fire.

"Right. Predators." I step back just as Ma lunges forward, and maybe it's the time of night, but her outstretched hands look like claws.

She stops abruptly, nose wrinkled. "Have you been drinking?"

The front door is a thousand miles away and a hundred and thirty pounds of maternal rage block my path. She's saying something about the dangers of alcohol, the mistakes she made, how she wants better for me—the things mothers are supposed to say in situations like these. Somewhere between curfews and responsible cell phone use, my knees go slack.

"Callie, do you hear me?!" Her voice blasts me upright.

"Mmm-hmm," I say. "Keep phone charged, answer texts. Beer is bad, marijuana worse."

My mother never has to worry about being *heard*. Her lungs are practically world famous. She was voted "Most Likely to Make It Big" her senior year of high school. She was a knockout back then, a Portuguese beauty with a big, big voice. Everyone said she had Broadway, Vegas, or at the very least Foxwoods Casino written all over her. They knew that one day they'd see her name in sparkling letters. RAMONA DA COSTA: SOMETHING BIG. When they talk about it now, her friends' eyes still get starry. They don't seem at all disappointed by what really happened: Ramona da Costa, hospital receptionist, single mother of two.

Make that single mother of one.

"Are you going to tell me what you were thinking?"

"Well, I looked at the beer and I was feeling thirsty, so . . ."

"Callie! I'm talking about *church*. How you embarrassed me in front of everyone."

Right. This isn't about alcohol, or my safety, my future. We've moved on to the topic Ma really cares about: what her friends will think.

"Really, Callie. Sometimes I don't— What possessed you? Honestly!"

A smile tugs. Terrible timing. Can't help it. "You think maybe it was the Holy Spirit?"

I drop my eyes to the floor before the smile does more damage.

Tess would have cracked up at that one. A few years ago, Ma might have too. She had a wicked sense of humor once upon a time, didn't give a rat's ass what anyone thought about her or her kids. *As long as we're happy,* she always said.

And that's what we were back then: happy.

"Bishop Landry is just waiting for an excuse to shut down Tess's case, you know. All of the work we've done, all the sacrifices Tess made. And wouldn't all of his stuck-up pals love it if we came out looking like fools. Well, screw them. I'm proud of where we're from. Proud of what our girl means to this city. We're so close. And you—*how could you?*"

Ma's curls have broken free from their pins, framing her face in chestnut-brown confusion. For a second, I almost forget how it's her fault all this is happening—the vigils, the swarms of visitors, the deep hollow in my chest. I almost forget that Ma's the one who decided what we had wasn't enough, that Tess would be our salvation.

My finger slides along the wall, catching a crack. "Sorry I'm such a disappointment."

"I didn't say . . ." Ma huffs. "Christ, Callie. You're not the only one who misses her."

"I know." A bit of plaster crumbles beneath my nail. I do know. I'm just not sure that Ma's way of missing is the same as how I feel—scraped out, flayed, whole chunks of me gone AWOL.

"Forgive this child," Ma says to a blotch on the ceiling. It's large, kidney-shaped, probably something we should call the landlord about, but Ma's face is poised sweetly, like it's heaven she's looking at, not some rotted smear.

"She doesn't mean to hurt me," she tells the mold/God. "My daughter is lost, misguided."

"Ma, I'm not—" I take a breath. *Misguided.* Anyone in her right mind would see it isn't me who's lost track of reality. Right?

I can't do this. Not now. This will get ugly. I'm tired of ugly. What I need right now is my pillow. I edge along the wall, making a move toward my room.

"She saved that little girl, you know. Maxine put Tess's photo in her hands, and then—"

"Maxine?" I turn back to face Ma.

Ana's grandmother, Maxine Langone, is Ma's Archenemy #3. (Bishop Landry is #2, and Ma's sister Wendy holds the top spot—a mystery I've yet to crack.) Point is, Ma's been known to call Mrs. Langone a lot of things but never *Maxine*.

"She's come around, Callie. She may be the best witness we'll get. Her little girl is alive because of Tess." Ma jabs my chest. "And *you* should be happy about it. If you . . . If you—"

"If I what?" *Loved her as much as you do?* She doesn't say it, but it's what she means.

"Just think about all of the people who'll have a chance to love her now. Our girl: a saint."

It's one gut punch too many. "Ma, you . . . *this* . . . you've lost your mind."

Her head snaps back. Like I've hit her. Her hazel-gray eyes—same shape and color as yours—are practically glowing.

If you were here, Tess, this would be the moment when you'd put a hand on my shoulder and walk me to our room. *Let it alone, Cal,* you'd say. *Don't make this worse.* If you were here, you'd tell me afterward, quietly, that you were on my side.

But you're not. Here. And each day that passes, the gulf between Ma and me only grows wider.

"What's wrong with you?" Ma squints at me, her face all twisted, like she doesn't know who I am anymore. Like I'm some kind of monster. *Me.*

"What's wrong is *you*, Ma. *You* did this. *You* let them kill her. You—"

It happens quickly, without warning. Her hand. My cheek. A burst of heat. Outside, Rudy lets out a howl.

I hold my hand to my face for a long moment. Ma has never hit me before. Not once. It wasn't a very hard slap either—too clumsy, unpracticed—but somehow that little sting burrows beneath my flesh and into the muscles of my jaw. Ma stands before me, blouse unbuttoned and mouth propped open. She crossed a line. And she's sorry. It's written all over her face. But I don't care. That slap slides into the roots of my teeth, into the tiny vessels that carry tired blood back to my normal-sized heart, and all of me freezes up. Every bit of me turns flat and numb.

What's wrong with me? An unfair question. What's wrong with *us*? Tougher to say. All I know is that in this moment I'm done with all the pretending, done letting Ma call the shots.

I reach past her shoulder and slam the door between us.

5.

After the creaks and patter in Ma's room have quieted, I'm awake, thinking. I think about what comes next, what came before, and how we got to this place exactly. It's a circle that goes nowhere, swirling and bending and looping back, always, to another night, a memory I've gnawed on endlessly and can never manage to swallow.

Two years ago. Early June. I awoke to a rustling, your shadow moving in the dark. I let my eyes fall closed, waiting for you to return to bed, hoping you'd do it quickly. The closet door creaked. You cursed when it pinched your finger like it always did.

At the jingle of keys, I sat up. "Tess?"

You stood by the door in your white nightshirt with the little blue hearts. You were fifteen already, in high school, but a woman's size small still came past your knees. I was fourteen, still in eighth grade, and already taller by an inch.

"Go back to sleep," you whispered. "I won't be long."

A pair of sneakers dangled from one hand, a hoodie from the other.

"Tess?!"

You tiptoed across the room and sat on the edge of my bed, brushing my hair from my face with the same gentle touch you used whenever I had a nightmare. Except this time we were both wide awake.

"Shhh. I'll be back soon. I promise," you said.

"Is it the voice?"

You nodded. You'd been hearing odd things for several months. It was a woman's voice, you said, scratchy sometimes, other times crystal clear, like she was speaking to you and you alone. The words rarely made sense. None of it did.

"What did she say this time?"

"*Find the captain. The morning brings peril.* I have to go down to the docks."

"Tess, that's—" I caught myself before saying the word that had become off limits. *Crazy.* Tess hadn't lost her mind, I was almost sure. Her mind was just . . . different . . . right?

"That's a little dangerous, don't you think? Are you sure you have to go?"

"I'll be back before you even wake up." Your jaw locked stubbornly.

I threw off the covers, jaw set every bit as firm. "Then I'm coming with you."

A few minutes later, we floated down the hill on borrowed

bikes. Past bodegas, sub shops, and hair salons, their metal grilles locked tight. The cool predawn air sliced through the thin cotton of our pajamas, and we rode faster, faster, past rows and rows of darkened apartments. Abandoned lots appeared, then disappeared, like giant black holes, luring lost travelers into their depths. The last few blocks slipped past in a whoosh, until finally, with a jerk of the handlebars, we came to the cobblestoned heart of New Avon.

We bounced over the uneven surface, slowing our pace. The stink of diesel and yesterday's fish greeted us at the harbor's entrance. With the sun on the brink of appearing and a light fog hanging over the water, everything looked different from daytime. No noisy fish sellers. No delivery trucks with their plumes of exhaust and warning beeps. The stalls advertising whale watches were still closed up for the night. All that was left were the boats, huddled together, their colors indistinguishable in the mist, metal rigging crisscrossing black against the sky.

You pedaled straight for the third pier.

"Captain!" you cried.

I came up behind you, heart pounding. It was the first time you'd done this, taken the voice so seriously—done it so *publicly*—and I wasn't sure what to expect.

The boat in front of you, the *Avon Lady*, was smaller than its neighbors, a bit worse for wear. A handful of men ran to and fro, wheeling plastic crates and giant coolers, bellowing orders to those already aboard. Overhead, a seagull screamed.

"Captain?" you called, more hesitant this time.

A man emerged from the hold, his baseball cap tamping down tufts of white hair. *BAIT ME Tackle & Supply* read the hat. Gold letters across an image of a hook. The old man lifted the cap, squinting out at the pier to the spot where you stood, your pale nightshirt glowing in the boat's spotlights.

"Felicia?"

You looked around, confused.

"No, sir. I'm . . . My name's Tess. Some people call me Teresa. This is my sister, Callie."

The fisherman's eyes widened. The next moment, he registered me standing behind you in the early-morning shadows.

"Captain, you can't go out there. Not today." You pointed to the sea. "That's what the woman said."

"The woman?"

You glanced back at me, as if I'd know how to explain it better.

"Yes," you told the captain, wavering. "She wanted me to come out here and warn you. Find the *Avon Lady*. Find the captain. Tell him . . ." Your voice trailed off with a squeak.

I straightened my shoulders. "My sister heard a voice. It said there's *peril*." Even from my own mouth, the word didn't sound right.

"I think the voice is saying that you'll be in danger if you go out today," Tess attempted to explain.

I felt the crew's eyes on us and waited for the old man to laugh or turn away. I wanted to turn away too. This was ridiculous— telling a fisherman to give up a day's catch, talking about a *voice*. Like we were caught in some other century, not modern-day Massachusetts, the age of cell phones and the Internet.

But the captain didn't laugh. He surveyed the clear horizon and scratched his grizzled head. "It's a woman's voice told you that? You're sure she said *peril*?"

You nodded.

"Remind me who are you again?"

"I'm nobody, sir. My name's Tess and I hear things sometimes. This time it's about you."

It would become easier to explain yourself later on, once your reputation had spread, but this time you were working with nothing, a total stranger and a preposterous request. There's no reason he should've listened. Which was why it was such a shock when, after a long moment of staring at the dim sky above, the captain placed his cap back on his head and shouted to the men on deck, "Fellas, pack her in."

The crew stared at him blankly.

"That's right. We've had enough close calls lately. I ain't taking no more chances."

The men peered out at the clear horizon just as the captain had, then around at the other boats still prepping for the water. They lifted their own caps. It was their turn to scratch their heads. A couple of them cursed. One man climbed out onto the pier and pulled the captain aside.

By that point everyone was staring at us: two girls in their nightshirts on a pier before dawn. I wished right then that I'd knocked on Ma's bedroom door instead of tiptoeing past it. I wished I was curled up beside her right now, replaying the whole unbelievable story. But you'd made me promise, pinkie swear, not to tell her about the voice. Ma didn't need another thing to worry about, you said. More layoffs were coming, and it was already hard enough making ends meet, though she tried not to let it show. This voice thing would pass, you insisted. And if it didn't, we'd wait for it to make sense.

But it hadn't passed, Tess. It made less sense every day.

Now wasn't the time to argue. I pulled my bike up to the spot where you stood and threaded my free arm through yours. We were sisters. We stuck together. Whatever this was, whatever was happening, I'd be here by your side.

The captain and his crewman grunted in tones too low to hear. Finally, the second man spat something on the concrete and returned to the boat.

The captain approached us, hat in hand. "We'll stay put. For the morning anyway."

"Really?" Tess and I said at the same time. We looked at each other. *Jinx.*

"You got my word," the captain said.

And he meant it. Captain Barros kept the *Avon Lady* in that morning, the first good day he'd missed in nearly a decade. He had the vessel examined from bow to stern, found nothing wrong, had it checked a second and third time to be sure. Then, just after ten, the Coast Guard reported a violent, quick-moving squall in the captain's favorite area, his sweet spot. Two scallop boats nearby had nearly capsized. One met a wave so big it flooded the gear room and snapped one of its dredges free, dragging it out to sea.

When the other crews came back—wet, exhausted, swearing on their grandmothers' graves that the *Avon Lady* never woulda survived that one—Captain Barros got on his knees and prayed.

Right after that, he looked up our address.

"You saved our lives," he said, squeezing your hand with his sun-hardened paw, while Ma looked on, confused.

"I know it'll sound foolish, but when I first seen you this morning, I was sure you was my girl Felicia. And that word you said—*peril*—that's exactly what the doctors said about her. 'Course, I was too thickheaded to listen. My Felicia'd always been a healthy girl." The captain's eyes filled with tears. He pulled out a bandana and honked.

"Fact is, I doubt I'd have listened to you either if I wasn't so shook by the memory of my girl. My first mate says that voice of yours is no different from the way his arthritis tells a storm's coming—fifty percent of the time his old knee gets it right, and the other fifty, well." The captain chuckled. "I tell you, though, this is something else. This was a sign direct from God."

Your brave front was gone by then, your jaw turned wobbly and hands shaking. Ma was an even bigger mess once she caught on, hugging you to her one second, the next, threatening to ground us both for life.

"How could you keep this from me?" she whispered. At me.

It didn't seem like the right moment to point out that you had kept this secret too, so I kept my mouth shut and accepted the hugs that came my way. And they were many. Ma's a small woman, but her embrace is huge.

"I don't know what to think," she kept saying after the captain had left. "I just don't know what to think."

That was the thing: None of us did. In the end, it didn't matter. Before any of us could decide what we thought about what had happened, the story spread across our little city along with your name, and, one by one, the people of New Avon decided for themselves.

From the Journal
of
Tess da Costa

How did we get from <u>there</u> to here?

It's a question I ask myself a lot.

(I still have <u>sooooo</u> many questions, Dear Diary.)

Sometimes it feels like I'm stuck in someone else's time-warp dream. Two years of my life: gone. I keep wanting to reach for the pause button, or ask to read the script, but then another month whips by, and another, and I'm still stuck on the Crazytown Express, no clue where we're headed or how to find my way back home.

Callie and I spent a week at the library after the thing with the captain. It turns out I wasn't the first to hear voices—far from it. Callie took her time with the sciency stuff, fat books packed with ugly words like "hallucination" and "psychosis," while I read up on the more famous cases: the child saints of Fátima and Joan of Arc. (Joan and I might have the teen-who-hears-voices thing in common, but that is it. I mean: Leading an army? Telling kings what to do? And don't get me started on how things ended for poor Joanie: the names they called her, the betrayal, the gleam in their eyes as they watched the girl burn.)

47

The more I read, the more depressed I became. And frightened. None of those books described me. Not really. I wasn't angry, or troubled, or even very superstitious. There hadn't been any recent trauma in my life. (Unless you call starting high school traumatic, which, well.) I'd gone to church exactly twice per year for my entire life, so I hardly seemed like the type of girl God would choose for this sort of thing.

After a few days, I told Callie to put the books away. It was pointless.

Back at home we had another problem. Ma. She was handling things worse than anyone, holed up in her room, whispering on the phone at all hours of the night with our aunt Wendy. And the looks Ma gave me! She said she didn't know what to believe, but her lashes would twitch as she said it. I knew she was as afraid as me.

Then Rocío Porter came forward, saying she'd touched my hand at the Feast of the Benediction, and the next thing she knew: cancer cured. Stage four, they said it was, terminal. Her doctors were stunned. (No one seemed to care that I had no memory of meeting her.)

Next it was Tommy Tran, shot four times and back on his feet (after two surgeries and many prayers), and Yohaira Durán, whose missing brother reappeared as if sent by God. Then: Mrs. Khoury's sudden dip in arthritis pain, a happy end to a dockworkers' strike, a premature baby breathing on her own. The stories kept coming in. Some of the people I'd never even met, but they all claimed to know me. They'd prayed in my name, they said, and poof: Like magic, their wishes had come true.

Looking back, Callie says we could have stopped it at any point. But how? And when, exactly? When the mother with the car-wrecked kid came to me, heart breaking, begging for one measly prayer, was I supposed to tell her no? And what about the people who prayed to me in their own homes? Was I supposed to tell them which parts of their faith were and weren't true?

It was a whole lot easier to show up at church once a week, say prayers when asked, repeat messages when I heard them, and let everyone else decide what they wanted to believe.

Callie says Ma's the one who's really to blame. As soon as the voice-of-God option cropped up, Ma was there, leading the way as my number one fan. It was a little weird how fast it happened, seeing as she'd never been very religious before. But you could see that she really <u>wanted</u> to believe and that, pretty soon, she did.

Callie thinks Ma was attention-starved as a kid and says that's what this is really all about. Like, it makes her feel important or something. I don't know if it's quite that simple, but it's true that when the Church events committee put Ma in charge of decorations (printing her name right there in the bulletin), she turned a thousand shades of happy. And look, if being in charge of flower arrangements gives the woman who raised me so much joy, who am I to take that away?

As I look back at things now, it was probably a mistake for me to let anyone, even Ma, make such big decisions for me (hindsight, etc., etc.). At the time, though, I was pretty preoccupied. After the Avon Lady incident, the voice had gone spastic: little snatches of things, jumbled like a bad radio signal. Most of the time, it would be a person that would bring it on. Like, I'd be sitting on the bus, a woman would step on, and boom: MARK THE BEHOLDER. (Huh?) Other times, the voice came out of nowhere, linked to no person in particular but carrying with it a <u>feeling</u>, a tug, like the one that pulled me down to the docks.

In those early days, I wrote everything down in my journal.

FEAR NOT THE TEMPEST. BROKEN BONES TRAVEL. PEACE RESIDES IN TOMORROW'S FRUIT.

Are you sure she said <u>fruit</u>? Does she always sound like a wizard on crack? Callie asked.

Ha-ha. Callie likes to poke fun, but as soon as I say one of those things out loud, people light up. Yes, yes! The beholder! cried the woman on the bus, like it made perfect sense. To her, maybe it did.

Callie says they treat me like their own personal fortune cookie—taking words that could mean a thousand different things and making them into the one thing they want to hear. Fair point. But sometimes it gets eerie, okay? Like, who could have guessed that Wendelina Castro was walking around with two fractured ribs and a spleen set to rupture? The second she stepped into church, what do I hear? BROKEN BONES TRAVEL. Those words may have saved that girl's life.

And look, I'm not saying any of this makes me a <u>saint</u>. (I'm still me, still Tess. Not some conceited maniac.) I'm just saying I can't toss it aside as easily as Callie. Also? If I have to choose between having people look at me like I'm deranged and sick, or them thinking I have a gift that can help once in a while . . . Well, it's not really a tough choice, is it?

In any case, now's not the time for those big questions. A child's gone missing. If I hear anything that can lead us to her, then I'm going to use it. Except, so far, I haven't. It's been three days. A quiet I haven't felt in two years, a stillness so deep it makes my bones ache.

Luckily, there's enough going on to keep everyone around me busy. Since Saturday, we've been sticking posters to streetlights, knocking on every door in this city. It's abduction central on our block, police

cars coming and going, neighbors cooking up feasts and brewing big
vats of coffee for the search parties. Today is the biggest search yet.
Just after lunch we gather at the edge of the city, nothing but trees as
far as you can see. It's not far from where another kidnapped kid was
found a couple years back, someone tells us.

My heart lifts, then sinks immediately. Not alive, I whisper to
Callie. She nods. She knows.

We fan out along the road. The dogs go first, followed by the rest
of us, marching two by two into the woods. Soon the barking fades,
replaced by crunching underfoot. I hold tight to Callie's hand.

It's a squirrel, she says, when I look up toward a rustle in the trees.

A mouse, she says about a crackle in the brush.

Your foot, she says, at the snap of a twig.

A shrill cry cuts through the air, and we both come to a stop. It's
just a bird, she says, squeezing my hand tighter, pretending she's not
as freaked out as me.

We walk the length of a noisy stream, shine a flashlight across
a cluster of boulders, squint into the darkness between. The whole
time I'm thinking: I really hope Ana's not out here, because if I'm this
scared with my sister by my side and a hundred other people shouting
distance away, how would a little girl feel all alone out here?

Dusk comes early. Someone shouts that it's time to quit for today,
but I don't want to leave Ana. Not with all those crawling, scurrying,
skittering things—and God only knows what else.

Two more minutes, I tell Callie.

One. Just one more minute. That's all, I promise.

She has to drag me back to the road.

At home, Callie slips off her sneakers and sinks into bed, asleep before I've had a chance to turn out the light. I watch her for a few minutes, her face all scrunched and fierce even in sleep.

I pretend it doesn't bother me, the things people have begun whispering. Was it just a fluke, they're asking, that thing at the harbor? And all those things that happened since? If Tess da Costa is really so special, why didn't she get a sign before the child was taken?

I don't feel special, I want to tell them. I feel worried. I feel sad, confused. On a night like tonight, I even feel a little crazy. Because it's crazy, isn't it? These past two years. The person I've become?

6.

"m certain he'll say yes!"

I peel my eyelids open. Bright sunlight pours through the window, washing away the sludgy residue of a dream. I don't know when I fell asleep exactly, but from the sting of my eyeballs I can tell I wasn't out for long.

Ma's voice rattles through the wall: "He'll talk to the bishop's rep first. If all goes well, we'll get him on *Newsline* next." Laughter. "I know. National news. It's finally happening."

I squeeze my eyes shut, but it's too late. Reality rushes back, slamming me beneath the ribs. You: gone. Me: here alone. Ma: swimming off in the deep end.

"It's the strangest thing," she's telling whoever's on the phone. "Ana hasn't said a word. They're not sure if there's damage they just can't see or if it's what she's been through. The trauma."

Speaking of which, I test my cheek with my fingers—no sign

of bruising—then dare a glance at your bed, where you should be rolling over right now, a pillow smashed to your chest, ready to tell me about your latest dream. Instead, your bed sits empty, covers tucked, the pillow placed just as you left it. Beneath it, the scrap of blanket you slept with since you were a baby.

Your bureau is still arranged the way you left it too—lotions and hair clips pushed to one side, pens and pencils to the other, the center filled with cloudy glass bottles and funny figurines you rescued from yard sales. Treasures, you called them. Junk, I said. But who am I to talk? My side of the room looks like the place trash goes to die. Empty bottles, balled-up receipts, clumps of dust. So much dust. I don't understand where it comes from. Do bits of plaster fall from the walls while I'm sleeping? Do my sheets give up shreds of cotton with each touch? If I look closely, will I find flakes of my own skin? Will I find bits of you too?

The last thought flutters across my fingertips, and I flick it away.

Our cousin Eva couldn't believe we shared such a small room. We told her yes, there were squabbles sometimes, especially over the closet. But even when we were arguing about hangers (which I find mostly unnecessary), we knew we were lucky. How many girls have a built-in best friend, right there, ready to listen? The day that Minoska Torres decided I was uncool and turned my whole seventh-grade class against me, you were there with a big bag of Twizzlers and plans for a counterattack. (I never did find out what you said to Minoska on the bus the next day, but whatever it was worked. She steered clear of me for the rest of the year.) And it wasn't just bullies you helped me take down. You also had a way with the demons that lived inside me—those trash-talking bastards who rose up in the middle of the night, reciting all the things I'd done wrong that day, all the ways I'd never measure up.

You'd climb in bed beside me to listen. It was only in the darkness, with your arm around my waist, that I could bear to say those things out loud. And it was in the darkness that you scooped up each nasty lie and showed it for the piece of garbage it was.

"I think I have an anger problem," I told you.

"No," you said. "You're passionate. You really feel things, and that's good."

"I'm always pissing Ma off, saying the wrong thing."

"You keep her honest. Someone has to."

"Nobody likes a girl with so many opinions."

"I do. I love you so much, Cal. And, frankly, I need your opinions. I don't have nearly enough of my own."

"*That's* true." I cracked a smile. "Your opinions on books could definitely use some work."

"Hey!" You went in for a tickle, and soon we were rolling around, defending the merits of mystery novels (my favorite) versus bodice-rippers (yours).

That was how it was with us. Back and forth. You built me up one day, I did the same for you the next. We fell asleep talking, woke up talking, filled the moments between with laughter. We took each other seriously (to a point), and called each other on our bullshit when required. Any worry I ever had, any feeling too large to contain, you were there to help me wrestle it to size. And when the voice appeared and your life began to spin out of shape, I was there to help you restore order. Or I tried to anyway.

And now? Four months have gone by. This little room we

shared feels gigantic; the air that was once your exhale and my inhale is terribly still. Four months of thoughts litter my head, overgrown emotions pushing against my skin. They've grown gnarly without you, savage with neglect. I've considered reading your journals, just to drown out the clamor in my head, to hear your voice for a change. But it still feels wrong. Also, frightening. To see your thoughts spilled on the page? A record of all the ways Ma and I failed you? The three of us lived in careful balance for so long, but those last months sent us all teetering. I'm not sure I'm ready to relive all that.

"She'd be eighteen next month, you know. It's so hard to believe. My baby." Ma is still on the phone, but her volume has dropped. I wonder for a second if she feels a little of what I do. Then: "Wait'll you hear what we're planning for her birthday! The mayor's office is helping—a special Mass with a procession afterward! There could be thousands who come in to see it, a real boost to the local economy."

And there we have it, folks. My dead sister: New Avon's very own cash cow.

I throw off the blankets, plunk my feet on the ground. Ma's laughing now, something about finally sticking it to the bishop. I need to get out of here.

I remember, vaguely, something I'm supposed to do today—a take-home assignment, that teacher who keeps hounding me. I missed most of spring term and have serious make-up work to do. It's a whole thing. But not one I can deal with right now. I dig around on the floor, find a mostly clean tank top and the shorts

I wore Saturday—quick sniff, good enough. I scramble for my keys before Ma can say anything else, something that will turn me matricidal.

As the door shuts behind me, she chirps into the phone, "Good-bye! God bless!"

I don't know where I'm going until I see the pile of flowers and burned-out candles, the small white cross. It's not a surprise exactly. My feet knew where they were headed. The only real surprise is that someone else got here first. His back is to me, but I'd know that tousled head and sagging jeans anywhere. Danny.

What the hell is he doing here?

It's still early, barely eight o'clock, but the sun has risen high and fierce, crisping my shoulders. Bedford Street—one block, one-way, more of a shortcut than a destination—is quiet. It's the spot where they found Ana Langone yesterday morning. It had been one of Tess's smaller shrines, but from the looks of things, the memorial expanded overnight, now serving as a shrine to Ana too. Bouquets and gifts sprawl across the sidewalk, taking up three slabs of concrete.

Danny, who's surely spotted the unmarked cop car across the way, leans across the yellow tape, examining something. I scuff my sneaker gently into the sidewalk grit, and he shoots back up at the sound, cheeks flushing dark.

"Hey," I say, casual, like this isn't deeply weird and I haven't noticed what he was studying so intently (a photo of Tess). It's an old one, middle school, the Year of the Bangs, among several available for download on a site managed by the Sisters of Mercy. Tess smiles with closed lips, her eyes strained wide in a silent scream.

"You're up early," Danny says, scratching his ear.

"Yeah. Didn't sleep much," I say.

His arm drops to his side. "Me either. They kept talking about that little girl on the news."

"And you wanted to see for yourself."

He nods, embarrassed. I'm embarrassed for us too. Because we're idiots, aren't we? What did we expect, the truth spelled out on the sidewalk? A little scientific evidence scattered among the flowers, maybe. Or the girl herself here to explain that her injuries aren't as bad as they believed.

Tess watches us stiffly. It's a terrible photo. Cameras did that to her. One flash, and the real Tess fled the scene, leaving the face of a stranger.

I kick at a stray bunch of daisies. "Do you know they're planning a big procession? For her birthday. All of this is only going to get worse."

Danny mumbles something I don't hear.

"I just wish there was something we could *do*," I say. "It's a stupid idea, but you and I were both thinking it, right? That if people could see the truth about Ana, maybe they'd quit it with this crap once and for all. Maybe it'd stop all of the miracles."

I frown, realizing I sound like a grinch at best. At worst, a sociopath. Danny isn't laughing, though, or running away. His brown eyes are steady on me, listening.

"You get what I'm saying, don't you? I don't want to stop good things from happening. I just want them to leave Tess out of it. I want to rest in peace."

I hear the slip too late. Okay, fine, whatever. I guess I want some peace too. Is that so terrible? "I want *Tess* to rest in peace," I say, and Danny nods, his gaze dropping back to her face.

He gets it. Of course he does. These people caused her so much pain. They made her life miserable. All that pressure on her swollen heart. *They* caused her heart attack. *They* stole Tess from both of us. And it might sound selfish, but I won't let them keep her.

"My dad was a cop, you know." Danny flicks a glance at me. "Well, a detective, actually. He was always saying the city force had no capacity for this stuff. Wouldn't see a clue if it jumped up and bit them."

"Okay . . ." I'm not sure what he's getting at. "You think your dad could help us?"

"Nah." Danny's mouth twists. "My dad's gone, long gone. He was a real shitty dad but a good cop. He never took shortcuts like the other guys, and . . ." Danny's eyes meet mine, earnest, unsure. "What I mean is, what if there's a way to do what you were saying?"

"You want us to prove it wasn't a miracle."

"When you say it that way, I sound like an idiot."

"That makes two of us then." A pair of fools. "Okay. Yeah. Why not? What've we got to lose?" This could be it, the last chance we'll have to rescue Tess's memory from the abyss.

Danny checks my face to make sure I'm not kidding. I'm not. With a quick nod, we've sealed our pact. We—two teenagers with nothing but time on our hands and a whole lot of heartache—will take down a miracle and save my sister.

The only question is *how*.

I move toward the white cross instinctively. It's planted at the center of the shrine, wedged between a crooked slab of concrete and a smooth boulder that juts out from the unkept grass. It must mark the spot where Ana fell. I step closer, and Danny pulls out his phone to snap a photo. I follow his lead. Then we're both crouching, leaning, checking out every angle of the sidewalk, picking through the flowers and odd little gifts.

"Think this is something?" Danny picks up a tiny statue of a man cradling a child. His bald head is fringed like some sort of creepy clown.

"Nah. That's Saint Anthony. Finder of lost things."

"Damn." Danny makes a face. "No wonder they pray to Tess."

"You think he's bad, you should get a look at Saint Francis."

Danny doesn't laugh, not quite, but for a brief second, when his eyes turn to me, they become their true color, golden brown like they used to be.

We inch along, side by side, skipping past scowling saints and glitter-studded crucifixes. But there's nothing useful, nothing that offers a clue as to what happened to Ana. I'm about to give up when something catches my eye. Something yellow and partially hidden. A photo.

I reach for it. It's a little girl in a frilly dress, yellow, doll-like, identical to the one they showed on the news. Just as creepy. She's young with dark hair like Ana's. But I know Ana and this isn't her.

"How the hell did they miss *that*?"

Danny's at my elbow. We both glance back at the police car, but the tinted windows are still rolled up tight.

"Maybe someone put it here recently," I say. Judging by the size of the sprawl, I'd guess many gift-givers have come and gone since they found Ana yesterday.

I push the candles aside for a better shot, feel a new energy tingling at the base of my spine. Maybe this is it: Maybe *this* is how you disprove a miracle. On second thought, I snatch the original photo from its perch. "Finders keepers," I say to Danny's lifted brow.

They've taken plenty. It's my turn now.

Anyway, it's clear those cops don't give a damn what we do. We scour the rest of the shrine, stepping boldly over the tape, moving items to clear the pavement, and no one jumps out to stop us. We don't find anything else, nothing as interesting as the photo anyway.

By the time we stand to go, I've begun to lose hope again.

"Walnut Street next?" Danny makes a move toward his car, sees my blank look. "You didn't see the news? They found a piece of Ana's dress. They think she jumped from the apartment where he had her. Three fucking stories."

"Jesus." I picture my little neighbor, all tinkly giggles and fragile bones.

"I know, right? Pretty messed up for a miracle."

I cast a glance at the mountain of crap behind us, consider all that we've endured over the past couple years. "Messed up doesn't even begin to describe it."

7.

I catch up on the news as we make our way to Walnut Street. WBZ, WCVB, WHDH—the story aired on every channel this morning. We arrive at 55 Walnut as I finish the third clip. The building is a triple-decker the size of an ocean liner, edged with sagging porches and unkempt shrubbery. The broadcasts all focused on the spot where Ana landed: a small, half-dead bush out front.

The landlady told reporters that she discovered the scrap of cloth caught on a branch. "I wouldn't have even noticed, except it was the first time that the thing had a flower, so I had to come outside and give it a close look. I planted that bush after my daddy's funeral twelve years ago, and it's never bloomed. Not till this week."

"A message from above?" the reporter asked.

"Must be!" Mrs. Rogeiro cooed, not picking up on the

reporter's sly smile. "God likes to keep us on our toes, that's what I always say."

She didn't explain why God hadn't sent a sign sooner, before a child leaped three stories.

Danny waits at the gate while I creep up to the porch. The top floor is shuttered on all sides, vacant—or at least that's what Mrs. Rogeiro believed until yesterday. Two planks of wood have been nailed in a cross over a broken railing, caution tape draping end to end. I measure the distance to the ground with my eyes, imagine the impact on a small body.

"Inch or two in any direction, and she would've hit dirt."

I step back, startled. A woman's stout outline fills the screen door in front of me. "Don't worry, honey. Long as you're not another reporter, I don't mind you taking a look."

The door creaks on its hinges, and Mrs. Rogeiro shuffles onto the porch. Brown skin dotted with freckles, hair the color of rust. She's wearing one of those housedresses that went out of style long before I was born. She seems older, more faded, than she did in the videos.

"Police been in and out of here all night with their measuring tapes and cameras and what all. Got plenty of shots of my daddy's hydrangea." She points to the shrub in question. It's set apart from its neighbors, branches mostly bare, but at the end of one spindly branch, a cluster of blossoms has sprouted. I bend to get a closer look. Bushes like these grow all over New Avon. The blooms are usually a murky lavender, pale pink, or occasionally a pale powder blue. This blue is electric.

"So a bush saved her life," I murmur.

"That and some divine intervention, you ask me." Mrs. Rogeiro tips a glance heavenward. "The second-floor tenants say they heard scratching sometimes, thought it was a rat caught in the walls. Still can't believe it was a child up there."

Danny steps into the yard. "He's completely disappeared then?" He means the kidnapper.

Mrs. Rogeiro nods. "Mmm-hmm. That's my fault too. I locked him out on accident. Got a locksmith out here soon as I seen that broken railing. Figured it was some kids messing around up there. Police say he likely woulda cleared out quick no matter, but if that's true, why'd he leave all his things inside?"

"His things?" Danny's voice is cautious.

"Old mattress, hairbrush, few more of those baby-doll dresses. They say he painted a big picture of wings on the ceiling too. The detective was saying it was the strangest thing he's seen in a long while."

"You didn't go up and see it yourself?" I ask.

"With these knees?" Mrs. Rogeiro chuckles sadly. "Still can't get over it. That man had been squatting—*living*—right here in my building. Who knows how long." She pulls a rag from her dress and wipes at her eyes.

"Sorry we bothered you," Danny says. "I'm sure you've had enough trouble without more people getting in the way."

"Trouble knows my address, that's for sure." Mrs. Rogeiro slides her glasses back onto her nose, looking first at Danny, and then at me. "You know my son was killed overseas not more than a year ago?"

"No. I, uh . . . didn't . . . know," I say.

"His wife moved my grandkids down to Florida. They was all I had left."

"Wow, that, um . . . sucks?"

She blinks at me, expecting something more, but whatever it is, I don't have it.

After a long pause, she sniffs. "Well, we all have our trials, don't we? Take as much time out here as you need, kids." She waves the wadded-up hankie and retreats inside.

"You have a way with people, you know that?"

I cross back to meet Danny, who's studying the balcony, one hand shielding his smirk from the sun.

"What did you want me to say? *I'm so sorry for your loss? I bet your grandkids miss you too?*" That sort of thing always sounds so cheesy and insincere—words people say but never mean.

"Either of those would have been great, actually." Danny's brows lift. He finds my lack of people skills amusing. I scowl to make it clear that I don't.

"So what do you think?" He points his chin back toward the yard. "Saved by a miracle or a shrub?"

I turn to face the balcony, the hard-packed earth below, one lone shrub so oddly out of alignment. "Bad landscaping is hardly a miracle."

"Definitely not around here."

I have a sudden urge to say something witty, something that will make up for my failings, but a gravelly voice interjects: "Was goddamn magic saved that child. No doubt about it."

We turn to find a woman perched on the neighboring stoop.

Bleached-out hair, gray-toned skin, limbs ropy as a feral cat's. She's probably not much older than my mother, but the years have been less kind. She flicks ash from her cigarette into the grass below.

"Seemed a harmless fella to me. A little shy, maybe. Flinched whenever you said hello."

"Wait. You *saw* him?" Danny and I walk over to her stoop.

"I got a pretty bad case of insomnia. Spend a lot of time out here, looking at people coming and going. Thought he was one of those guys who just don't know how to be social, you know the type. My brother Lew says I'm being too nice, though. Says that guy gave him the creeps. Ain't that right you said that, Lew?"

A large nose emerges from the window above, followed by a small, ratlike chin.

"Sure, I did." Lew's voice is even more wrecked than his sister's. "Guy was a goon, you ask me. He'd be coming home all type of hours. No car. Never saw him with another person. Not once."

"He had glasses," the woman says. "Always wearing short sleeves, even in winter. Black hair."

"I'd say it was more brownish," Lew says.

"A big guy."

"Well, not so much big as compact. Muscles, you know?" Lew demonstrates.

"But soft around the middle."

Lew and his sister look at each other.

"That what you told the police? There was nothing soft about him, Myrna."

"Not except for his pudgy middle." Myrna knocks a column

of ash into the dry grass, daring her brother to contradict her again.

Danny coughs politely. "So you never saw the girl then?"

Lew and Myrna break their glare to look at Danny.

"Nope."

"Uh-uh."

"Not ever."

Lew scratches his stubbled chin. "If she ever shouted, we didn't hear that neither. So many kids running wild around here, not sure we'd know the difference even if she had."

Myrna takes a long drag on her cigarette, exhales a cloud of smoke. "Police think she might've hushed up early on. To survive." She squashes the finished butt and drops it into the brush. "They don't think she was raped, though. Least there's that."

We're all quiet as the thought sinks in.

"Question is, if he wasn't some kinda pedophile rapist, what was he doing with a little girl?" Lew raises a brow at me and Danny, like we'll have an answer.

The window next door scratches open, and a neighbor sticks out her head, offering her theory: kiddie porn. "What other explanation is there for those dresses?" The police found several more yellow dresses in a bureau.

Another neighbor appears on the next stoop over with another idea: child sweatshop. They were making those dresses, shipping them to China.

"Sending them *to* China?" someone else says. "That makes no sense."

His point is drowned out in the din. More neighbors have gathered, offering additional theories and questions too. Danny jumps into the fray with his own questions. No, none of them saw Ana jump that night. From what they hear, she twisted her arm pretty good, though. Someone heard she broke a few ribs. According to the news, the poor kid got mashed up real bad.

"It's a miracle she survived," Myrna says.

There are a bunch of *amens* to that. Then someone says it's nothing to do with God—"It's luck is what it is"—but I can't focus on who's saying what. Something's wrong with my head. My stomach too. Black spots sprout in front of my eyes.

"Callie?" Danny latches on to my elbow.

I place my hand over my belly, too late to block a liquid growl.

I unhook my arm from Danny's, avoiding his eye. "I'm fine. I just forgot to eat."

It's true. I didn't *mean* to skip breakfast. Or dinner last night . . . or . . . when was the last time I had a real meal?

The neighbors are still jabbering about miracles versus luck, how you tell one from the other, but Danny's eyes, color of warm caramel, are on me. My belly grumbles again.

"Where to next?" I ask.

He doesn't hesitate. "Next stop's McDonald's."

From the Journal
of
Tess da Costa

This morning after church I'm a celebrity stepping down from her limo. My fans line up to greet me at the front gate: Tess! Tess! Have you heard from God yet? Has he told you what happened to Ana Langone?

It's been four days since that little girl went missing, and their attention is turning. To me.

Ma guides me to my spot on our porch, whispers to stay calm. I'm a pro at this, she says, it's no different from any other Sunday.

I smile as the believers approach, one at a time.

Do you hear anything now, Tess?

Have you asked God for his mercy?

Have you prayed for the poor child?

Rudy woofs at each question, and Callie stands stiff at my side, flicking her fingers, looking ready punch the next person who asks about Ana. I wipe moisture from my lip. It's a warm day, a burst of springtime in February, no sign left of last week's snowstorm aside from a few crusty mounds on the curb.

After a while, someone gets the idea to invite Ana's grandmother to speak with me. They'll even let her cut the line, this once. They knock on Mrs. Langone's door gently, then louder. Maybe it's my imagination, but her shades seem to pull tighter the more they knock.

Are you sure you've said the right prayers, Tess?

Their questions grow louder, and I see a flash of poor Joanie strapped to her pyre. Callie mutters something, and I grab her wrist. I appreciate her trying to protect me, but the last thing we need is a scene. I tell her to go inside and bring the dog too.

To the others, I say in my cheeriest voice: I pray every morning, noon, and night.

They're good people after all. Not bloodlusty witch roasters. They're mamas and grandmas and brothers and neighbors. They just want to help.

What have you heard, Tess? they ask me.

This is the part where I fudge the truth. Nothing, I tell them. Nothing yet.

But the truth is, I have heard the voice. It returned late last night, a crackle in the darkness. At first I felt relief, but then fear set in as I tried to figure out what the words meant. And couldn't.

I'm tempted to toss them out into the gathered crowd now and let them figure out the rest. But it's too risky. I'm not sure even who the words are intended for. What if these people hear it all wrong? That's the thing: There've been just as many misses as hits with these messages I hear, but no one ever pays attention to the fumbles.

This time is different, way more important. A child is missing, the city is watching. This time there's no room for mistakes.

I make my way upstairs after the believers have gone home and the final candle is lit. Ma makes the popcorn, Callie finds the Advil, and we snuggle up to watch one of her detective shows. For a while the world seems a little less horrible: an obvious criminal, smart cops, clear clues, a tidy resolution within reach.

It's only after Ma's in bed and we've crawled under the covers that I tell Callie what the voice has been saying.

INTO DARKNESS COMES THE LIGHT, is the first thing. Then: SHE RESTS ON A PILLOW OF STONE. There's something else too. HOME IS NEAR, the voice says, over and over. THE SAVIOR CANNOT PROTECT.

Callie is quiet. She wants to say the right thing, the one that will make me feel better, but we both know it doesn't exist.

You're sure this is all about Ana? she asks.

I shrug. I'm never sure about anything.

Listen, she says after another pause, I found this book. By a new group of scientists? They say everyone used to have another level of consciousness, like a sixth sense. But then our brains changed, so now it's only some people who have it, and the rest of us can't access it—or understand it—anymore, so we call it hallucinations. But it's really more like . . . an evolutionary glitch.

She starts to hand me the book but stops when she sees my face.

A glitch? My breath catches. You think that's what I am? I know I'm not as smart as you, Callie, but Jesus.

She shoves the book under her pillow, out of sight. That's not how I meant it, she says. I was only trying to help.

I know, I say. I do.

Callie would never hurt me on purpose. She just has this idea that life is like one of her TV shows, that there's an answer to everything if you look at all the evidence, read the right books. It's endearing, most of the time. And then sometimes it leads to moments like this, to words like glitch.

Here are some more words: <u>broken</u>, <u>crazy</u>, <u>schizo</u>, <u>freak</u>. Not much of a jump from one to the other, is it?

We're quiet as I turn out the light. I hear Callie rustle, flip to one side, then the other, and finally land on her back with a loud sigh.

Yes? I say with just a touch of a laugh. (I can't help it. My little sister's so <u>dramatic</u> sometimes.)

Tess, if it's not your brain that's causing this, what is it? I mean, do you really think it's . . . God?

We haven't touched this question in a long time, and I still don't have a good answer. There's Ma on one side, Callie on the other; believer and skeptic, equal but opposite forces. Do I believe it's God speaking to me? Am I sure God exists? I guess I don't see how one girl can answer a question people have battled for centuries.

Does it even matter what I believe? I whisper into the darkness.

Tess! Of course it matters! Come on, I won't be mad. You can tell me if you do. Is that really what you think? That it's God talking to you?

It sounds so ridiculous when she says it that way. I drop my head on the pillow with a moan. I don't know, I say.

Idon'tknowIdon'tknowIdon'tknow.

Callie is quiet, digesting this new tidbit. (The last time this question came up, my answer was a firm no.).

Okay, here's what we do know, she says after a bit. We know you've put a lot of energy into looking for Ana, and we know we could both use a good night's sleep. We also know the police are on top of this, so maybe it's not the best time to make any big decisions. Like, maybe just let the voice say whatever it's going to say and don't be so stubborn about figuring out what it means.

I roll my eyes so hard they creak. At the idea of it. Callie telling me not to be stubborn. Callie, who's sworn off haircuts since the day we found a lock of mine on eBay. They won't get another da Costa curl from me! she says, beating her fist against her chest like some kind of snarly-headed ape. It's been a year and a half now. She's beginning to look like a cavewoman. Or a pirate.

It's not your fault Ana's still gone, Callie whispers. Cavegirl wisps poke up over the blankets, and worry—real worry—shines in her eye.

I know, I sigh. It's the sane thing to say, the smart thing to believe. It's what everyone keeps telling me, even Ma.

A girl's gone missing. I'd be nuts to think it was on me to save her. Even so, after Callie rolls toward the window and lets out a cavewoman snore, I stay propped up against my pillows, listening.

8.

The breakfast rush at McDonald's is over, lunch more than an hour away. Behind the counter, the cashiers and cooks cackle and hoot like they have the place to themselves. Danny and I grab seats by the window. My belly's now rumbling like a tractor trailer on an empty road. The first two McNuggets disappear in a single bite.

"You think he's still in the city?" Danny says, chewing his thumb.

"Who's that now?" I dig into the oily sleeve of fries with one hand, the chicken with the other. My brain can only process one problem at a time, and right now it's how I can get as much food into my stomach as possible.

I take a sip from my soda. "If you're talking about Mr. Brown-Hair-Black-Hair-Compact-but-Soft-in-the-Middle, the answer is no. I'm guessing he's long gone. Wouldn't you be?"

Danny makes a face, spits out a bit of fingernail. "He may not be thinking logically, this guy. Why keep her so close to home, right where anyone could find them? And what about that painting they found? *Wings?* What kind of freak goes around painting giant wings on the wall?"

"The ceiling."

"What?"

"She said the wings were on the ceiling."

Danny drops his thumb, looking squeamish. "Like I said: *not* normal."

I lower nugget number five back into the box. My stomach is already shrinking, and talking about that pervy creep isn't helping.

It *is* strange that he kept her so close. *Home is near.* The phrase Tess heard pops into my head. I wonder if Danny's thinking the same thing. Did Tess tell him those lines too?

Into darkness comes the light.

The savior cannot protect.

She rests on a pillow of stone.

I picture the rough-edged sidewalk we examined this morning, the smooth boulder beside it where we found a photo of another little girl. Would you call that a *pillow of stone?*

Ugh. I sit back in my chair. I can't start thinking like this. Like I told Tess, those phrases she heard could have meant anything. Or nothing at all.

Danny's phone buzzes and he shoves it aside.

"Who is it?"

"No one. Karen." His food's still untouched.

I lean across and unpeel the wrapper from his burger. "C'mon, eat," I command.

He picks up the burger reluctantly, and I wipe my fingertips on a napkin, reach into my back pocket for the photo we found. I lay it flat on the table. It's one of those cheesy studio shots. The girl—she can't be more than six or seven—smiles nervously, one hand on her chin, the other on a stack of blocks. Her frilly dress foams about her knees.

"You think he kidnapped her too?"

Danny shakes his head, straining from the size of the bite he just took.

"You sure?"

"Certain." Danny swipes his mouth along his arm and pauses to swallow. "We'd have heard about another missing girl. And besides, look"—he swallows again, points to the background, bright turquoise in one corner, fading to green—"this isn't a recent photo. It looks like something from the eighties."

He's right. "The hair too. The bangs are all poofy." It reminds me of my mother, those pictures of her and Aunt Wendy that hung in my grandparents' house. The two of them were inseparable as kids, until whatever it was that happened.

Who is this girl, I wonder. Where is she now? I trace her rounded leg down to her ruffed sock. Why did this photo show up at a shrine for my sister?

Danny polishes off what I swear was a Quarter Pounder moments ago. "Put it away, Cal."

"Why? It's the only interesting thing we found. Walnut Street was kind of a bust, don't you think? A miracle shrub? A guy no one can identify?" I reach for the fries, folding one into my mouth. There was, of course, that other detail: the wings.

"It's not the kidnapper we should be thinking about. It's Ana. These cases are like quicksand. If you start digging, you'll wind up obsessed. Trust me."

Is that what happened to Danny's father? A case turned to quicksand? "You're the one who asked if I thought the guy was still in town," I remind him.

"Yeah. My bad." Danny crumples the hamburger wrapper and tosses it on his tray. "Look, we're not going to catch a criminal. And he's not going to get us to the real issue anyway: the miracle. Isn't that the point of this? Ana's recovery. That's what we gotta focus on. That's how we'll help Tess."

"Right. Tess." Of course Tess is the whole point, but the sound of her name—appearing so suddenly—does something to me, like someone's looped a cord around my air passage.

I push the photo away reluctantly, my fingers straying over the girl's tiny saddle shoe. She must be a woman now. If she's alive. And Danny's right, of course. We're not going to be the ones to catch a kidnapper who eluded the police for months. Still, it's hard to pinpoint where one crime ends and the other begins—the theft of a six-year-old, the theft of my sister.

"Callie . . ." Danny eases the photo out from my fingers, like I'm a toddler who needs help giving up her toy. "You sure you're okay talking about all this?"

"I'm great," I say, sitting back in my chair. "Just perfect. Why don't you tell me your big idea? The one where we bust up a miracle."

Danny hesitates, then leans in, hands flat on the table. He seems different suddenly, more awake or more confident or something. It's weird. "I was thinking we should focus on what happened between the time Ana fell and the time she woke up. If what those people were saying is true, her injuries weren't all that bad. I mean, she got up and walked all the way to that shrine, right? It's been a long time since I went to church, but broken bones and a concussion don't seem like miracle material to me. Didn't people use to rise from the dead and stuff?"

"If you believe that crap." I reach for a fry. "It was a lot easier to impress people in the old days. Modern science changed things. Cure for bronchitis? Not such a big deal anymore. Premature baby survives?" I pop another fry in my mouth.

"Little girl survives a bad concussion? Happens all the time." Danny grins, like he's already solved the whole thing.

"It happens *sometimes*," I say.

"Makes you think about the saints from way back, doesn't it? I wonder how many of those old miracles would make the cut today."

Danny's grinning bigger now, a smile just like the one he wore on that hot day last summer when he figured out how to jam the slushy machine at Tedeschi's. *Free refills for everyone!* I find myself starting to smile too—until I remember. It's not as simple as it sounds.

"Didn't the doctors on TV say she was in a coma for a while? If it was that serious, it might be hard to prove it's not a miracle."

"Waking up from a coma's a miracle?"

"Not necessarily, but if the doctors didn't expect it . . . Look, there's stuff that stumps them even now. Like, there was a kid out in Seattle a few years back whose face was being eaten by some kind of bacteria. None of the treatments were working, so people started praying to this Native American woman who died hundreds of years ago. She became Catholic as a teen and was like this Church hero, but no one had been able to make the case for sainthood. This time, the prayers to her went viral, the kid got better, and no one could explain it. The doctors didn't say it was a miracle, not in so many words, but they had no other explanation. The Church canonized Saint Kateri a year later."

I look Danny in the eye to make sure he's getting what I'm saying. "That's all the Church needed. Not proof of a miracle, but *lack of proof* that it was anything else."

His smile has faded, and I feel bad about that for a second, but then he pauses and a new grin alights. "Doesn't your mom work at the hospital?"

"What does my mom have to do with this?" I pull back from the table.

"I don't know about you, but I'd really like to know what medical experts are saying about Ana. You know, in the place where they treated her."

"My mother's only a receptionist. Even if she knew something, she wouldn't tell us."

"But she'd have access to the records, right? Couldn't you get to them somehow? Like drop by for a visit and . . . ?"

"Steal the file?"

Danny nods, oblivious to how insane that sounds. Or how impossible it would be for me to talk to Ma right now.

"Even if that wasn't completely illegal—like a class-A felony—it's the wrong part of the hospital. My mom works in general medicine, and Ana's probably in intensive care."

"I doubt it's a felony, Cal." Danny slides my fries closer to his side of the table, tilting his head in a way I'd swear was flirty if I didn't know better, if it wasn't Danny. "Doctors share files all the time. When I got a concussion from football, they sent me to the ER first, but my pediatrician did the follow-up. We just get you on your mother's computer, tell her you need to look something up, and . . . *bam*."

"Bam?"

Another grin threatens to crack open Danny's face. I inch the fries back to my side of the table. I'm pretty sure this much optimism is bad for the health.

"I didn't know you played football." It's a lame attempt at changing the subject. But a valid question too. Danny Delgado is the opposite of an athlete—right size, wrong mind-set—a kid who won't even run when chased.

"Seventh grade. Hardly counts." He brushes the question aside and, eyes twinkling, stretches a hand toward the last of my fries. "C'mon, Cal. I dare you."

They ask the girl questions, so many questions.

Was he young? Old?

Brown eyed?

Violent?

She wants to make them happy, tell them all they want to know. Even more, she wants them to stop talking, to leave her in peace. So she nods her head, shakes it—and when that doesn't work, she opens her mouth, searching for the best word to describe him, but her tongue remains still in her mouth.

She tries using her eyes instead, props them open wide for *No, keep guessing,* blinks rapidly for *You're getting close.*

Does she need sleep? they wonder. *Should the doctor check out her eyes?*

Why is she staring at that door?

The girl gives up, exhausted. They don't understand her. Not like he did.

They don't understand him either. They don't know how he held her in the night, arms like shields to hold back her fear. It's true he got angry sometimes.

Desperate. Violent: just the once. (The night she finally flew.) She knows if they push him hard enough, make him sad enough, he'll turn violent again.

Another thing they don't know is how her monster cries too.

9.

The hospital elevator is packed. A cluster of women part reluctantly, allowing Danny and me to board before sliding back together and encircling us in their knot.

"Marks on her hands, I heard . . ."

". . . a mysterious perfume . . . *roses*."

"No, it was something else. *Hydrangeas*, they think."

"Oh, Blessed Father!"

Danny and I exchange a look. This. *This* is the type of insanity that will only get worse if no one puts a stop to it. (Really? The stigmata? Could they get any more clichéd?) I take a deep breath. Just give us a few hours, let us get at the truth of what happened to Ana Langone. We'll knock the legs out from under these rumors so fast the old geese won't have time to honk in protest.

On the third floor, the ladies waddle off onto a crowded hallway. The usual suspects have arrived: the blue-haired busybodies, the camera-clutching rubberneckers, and, of course, a few nuns. A nurse is trying to get everyone to hush, but no one is listening.

I jab at the buttons, and the elevator doors glide shut. The air cools as the elevator rises. A pair of doctors exit on the next floor, and then it's just me and Danny. We slip past floors five and six in silence. I smooth back my hair, tell my heart to slow its beat.

"You'll be fine." Danny squeezes my shoulder. He's right. I've done plenty of dares more dangerous than this one and I've never once been caught. Why should I be nervous now? And why oh why did I eat so many McNuggets?

The doors open, and we step out into a wide hallway, all bright whites and shining linoleum. A group of nurses scuttle by, heads bowed in conversation. Our sneakers squeak as we turn onto another, narrower hallway. Machines wheeze and whir behind rows of closed doors, holding their secrets close.

We veer left toward the Ellison wing, and at the end of the next corridor, I see her: familiar chestnut curls bent low over a computer. I step up to the counter, tap it gently.

"Callie! What's wrong?"

Ma's on her feet in an instant, hurrying out from behind the desk. She's petite and almost as skinny as me, way more put together. When she sees Danny, she stops short and her eyes go sharp. According to Ma, teenage boys are the devil's own minions. It's a lesson she learned the hard way, courtesy of my father.

I step between them. "I'm okay, Ma. I just lost my cell phone. I mean, I forgot my keys. I mean, I forgot to bring my bag with my cell phone and my keys, and so I couldn't get into the apartment or call you or . . ." The story I prepared scrambles in my head, and Ma's forehead puckers. Not my best work.

Last night's words still hang heavy between us, not to mention the slap.

"Were the Flahertys out?" she says.

"Either that or they turned off their hearing aids again."

I straighten a bit. Much better. Lies work best when they're bold, specific. I just have to hope Ma doesn't verify my story with our landlords downstairs.

"You got some work done today, I hope?" she says. "That teacher's been calling me. If you don't turn something in soon, she says they'll have no choice but to hold you back."

I dip my head to avoid Danny's curious look. I haven't told my friends how bad things got, especially with all the school I missed after Tess died.

"It's fine," I tell Ma. "I've got it under control. I swear." Another lie.

She studies me for a long moment before turning back to her station, unlocking the bottom drawer of her desk. "No boys in the apartment when I'm gone. And make sure you're there when I get home. Put the keys in the basket right away so you don't forget. I'm too tired to wait up for you while you're out goofing off with—"

"Ma." I place a hand on her shoulder. "I'll stay home. Alone. You don't have to worry."

Her muscles twitch beneath my touch. "Make sure to keep the shades down so it doesn't get too hot."

"I will," I assure her. "I'll water your plants too."

Sometimes I think my mother has forgotten how to communicate like a human, that the church has stolen her brain and strings of commands are all she has left.

She turns toward me, keys outstretched. She looks exhausted, her color drained and lines in places I've never noticed before. A spot of mascara has migrated to the hollow below one eye. Without thinking, I reach out to rub it away. She closes her eyes like an obedient child.

Danny coughs.

"Listen, Ma. Why don't you go get some tea or something? You seem tired. I can watch the phone for a bit. Looks like things are slow around here anyway."

Her eyes narrow suspiciously.

"I know I've been a jerk lately." I look down at my ratty old Chucks, put on my sorriest of faces, and for a moment, I really do feel sorry. "I know things have been rough for you, and I haven't helped."

When I look up, Ma's eyes have gone swimmy. I hesitate. There's still time to walk away, to just take the keys and go. I consider doing it—getting right back on the elevator before I make matters worse—but then my gaze drops to Ma's throat, to the tiny gold cross glinting under fluorescent lights.

"You should take a break, Ma. Go. I'll stay here."

She brushes the moisture from her eyes, nodding. "Lena should be back any minute. Can I get you anything?"

"Nah." I shake my head.

She turns to Danny. "You?" (One thing you have to give my mother: She's always polite.)

Danny straightens to attention. "Oh. No, thank you, Mrs. da Costa," he says in an octave I've never heard before.

It takes an effort not to laugh. Danny is always well behaved around adults, like he's afraid to let them down or something, but this takes it a new level. I'll have to remind him later that my mother isn't a *Mrs.* The Sperm Donor didn't stick around long enough for any of us to bother adopting his name.

As soon as Ma rounds the corner, Danny and I assess the scene: The reception area sits in the crook of two hallways. No one's around. Even the phones are dead. But that could change any minute.

Danny stands guard and I wait for his signal before slipping into Ma's cushioned chair. I scroll to the top of the computer screen, trying to figure out which tab is which. The phone begins to ring. I collapse the Web browser and study the items on the desktop: *Trash, H:drive, E:drive,* something called *Gateway.* Looks promising. I click.

The phone rings a second and third time, then stops. Out in the hallway a woman laughs. I scoot the chair closer to the desk and peer over the counter, find Danny flashing someone a broad smile, like he's auditioning for the role of boy next door. It's too much cheese. Any sane person would see right through it. But then I hear a titter. I crane my head out farther and glimpse Mrs. Reynoso touching her coppery hair, giggling.

There's no mistaking her posture: Mrs. Reynoso—my mother's middle-aged supervisor—is flirting. With Danny. Or thinks Danny is flirting with her? Either way. Ugh. I touch my queasy belly—definitely didn't need those fries—but there's no time to be sick.

I sit back down and focus on my task. A pop-up box offers a space for a user name and password. Danny is saying something in Spanish. I type my mother's name in the first space, then try a few of her favorite passwords: her childhood address, Tess's birthday, mine.

Three strikes. I'm out.

"Callie? What are you doing here?"

I close the window and roll away from the computer.

"Oh, hey, Mrs. Reynoso. Long time no—"

She's frowning at the computer, and I turn to look too. The screen saver has loaded, covering my tracks. I release a breath.

"It *has* been a long time, m'ija, too long." She brushes a loose curl from my shoulder, points her lips across the hall. "Why don't you take a seat over in reception? Those chairs are more comfortable, better for the back too." She touches her own back with a wink.

By the time Ma returns, Danny and I have been seated in the waiting area for a good ten minutes. He's been keeping Mrs. Reynoso entertained with stories about his family's last visit to Puerto Rico (his *tía's mofongo*! these *tiempos tan duros*!). Each cheesy smile sends Ma's boss into a fresh fit of giggles.

Meanwhile, I've lost a battle against a massive scowl.

"That was just what I needed," Ma says when she sees me. Her face is several shades brighter, and the skin around her eyes has lifted.

She latches on to my shoulders, pulling me into a hug. I'm taller than her these days, but she smells the way she always has: like cocoa butter and fresh-baked bread. "Thanks, Cal," she whispers.

The hug lasts too long. I wriggle out of her grasp, but before I can pry away completely, she has my tank top between two fingers. "What happened here?"

My belly lurches. Something gave me away.

Ma tugs on my shirt. "Soak this in water soon as you get home, eh? I'll put some lemon juice on it tonight."

I glance down to where she's looking . . . Is that *barbecue sauce*? Ugh. I cover the splotch with my palm.

"Thanks for the keys, Ma."

I step back, right into Danny, and then we're tripping over each other, practically running for the elevators.

"Don't forget about the shades!" Ma calls as we round the bend.

I slam a thumb into the down button, scowling for real now. I failed. Completely. I found nothing about Ana, made things even more confusing with my mother, and to top it all off, messed up my shirt. No wonder Ma's always telling me what to do. I'm a disaster.

As the elevator doors close, Danny places a hand on my shoulder. "Don't worry, Cal. I got us covered." His chest puffs and he flashes another Crest-commercial grin. "Dr. Gillis in Neurology. He's the guy who knows the truth about Ana."

10.

Dr. Gillis? The same Dr. Gillis who goes to my church? He treated Ana Langone?"

Danny nudges me out of the elevator and into the crowded lobby. "Take it you don't like him much."

"*Like* him? Like the guy who—" I'm sucked into the revolving door, forced to hold on to the thought and let it ripen to its full bitter flavor. The door lurches, spitting us onto the sidewalk.

"Dr. Gillis is a complete asshat," I say, "for starters."

"Is that the technical term?" Danny's still grinning. I stab him with one of my darkest looks.

The pavement burns through my sneakers, and the air is pure soup. I'm really not in the mood for teasing, if that's what he's doing. Or gloating, which is what it sounds like. And that smile: God. So aggravating.

We make our way to Danny's car, which he, speaking of

asshats, decided to park on the far side of the lot. (Less chance of it getting scratched that way.) (Because a scratch on a 1998 Hyundai would be a disaster.)

"Dr. Gillis is the one who went on TV a couple years back," I tell him. "He told the reporter Tess needed a neurological evaluation. He said, and I quote, *No responsible parent would let her child struggle with auditory hallucinations and not seek medical attention.*"

Danny whistles. "Bet that pissed your mother off."

"Uh. Yeah. That's putting it mildly."

Dr. Gillis—or That Stuck-Up Bastard, as Ma prefers to call him—is number two on Ma's list of archenemies. The pain he caused Tess earned him a spot on my list too.

"It *is* interesting that your mother never brought her to a doctor. She never considered it?" Danny gives me a careful glance, but I'm not about to argue on that point. He's right.

"She has a whole thing about doctors, which is weird considering where she works. It's partly 'cause she's seen what goes on in hospitals." Tess—who never fought Ma on this, or anything—suspected the other part traced back to our grandma. "We hardly even went to the doctor as kids, not unless it was a broken bone or something," I tell Danny. "And . . . I don't know. Tess didn't *seem* sick is the thing. Not in the beginning."

Danny is quiet, and I can guess what he's thinking: Would Tess still be here if we'd gotten her to a doctor sooner? I wonder that too. Frequently.

But right now we're talking about Dr. Gillis. "He lost a son last year," I tell Danny. "Hung himself, I think. Or maybe it was pills. The doctor and his wife have been coming to church a lot since. They look terrible, like they died too." Not that I'm judging. I know how that story goes.

According to my mother, Gillis grew up in one of the roughest parts of town, big Irish family with more than its share of problems, and he shed all of it—including the drug-addicted mother—when he went off to college, then medical school. Came back years later talking like a newscaster—all hard *r*'s and clean grammar—acting better than everyone around here.

Ma hates people like that. I do too. Which is dumb, I know, and unfair. Especially seeing as I was supposed to follow that path myself—college, career, never look back. It's what I used to dream about, what Tess never stopped wanting for me. She kept at it, pestering me long after my grades began dropping and it became clear it'd never happen.

Danny pauses at the car, looking across the roof, hopeful. "You think the doctor would talk to us? If he was such a skeptic back then, maybe—"

"No way. Not gonna happen." I duck inside before Danny can push the point.

I understand his reasoning—of course I do—but why would I want to talk to the guy who made Tess feel like a total head case? Why would he agree to talk to us?

The Hyundai is spotless inside, ironic considering the state of Danny. The air's so hot it makes my skin itch. Danny doesn't start the engine right away. He's busy scribbling something on a slip of paper. I, meanwhile, study the splotch on my chest. Why didn't Danny tell me I'd dropped half my lunch on myself?

And what kind of idiot can't guess her own mother's password?

"That lady in there was really nice. Said I reminded her of her nephew. She knew a lot about Ana."

I lick my thumb and scrub at the stain. "That lady was Mrs. Reynoso. I wouldn't take anything she said too seriously. She's not exactly the brightest bulb, if you know what I mean."

Danny raises a brow.

"I'm only saying you could have been less obvious. With your tactics."

Danny puts the cap back on the pen. "My what now?"

"If you flirt with everyone we try to talk to, people are going to catch on."

Danny starts to laugh but stops when he realizes I'm not joking. "Callie, she's older than my mom! I wasn't flirting. I was being *nice*." He punches my arm. "You might want to look into it sometime."

I cover my wounded arm with one hand, my spitty chest with the other, a move that requires far too many elbows.

Danny's face shifts. "Are you pissed at me? You really think I was flirting? Do you think Mrs. Reynoso did too?" He shoots a look back at the hospital, alarmed, and I feel like an asshole for being so harsh, killing his buzz. A *sour puss* is what Ma calls me. *You're honest,* Tess said. *You tell it like you see it. The world needs people like you.* Only she would see it that way. Only my sister could hold a mirror to my ugliest features and find their light.

"You were fine," I tell Danny. "It was no big deal. I was just being . . . me."

"Okay, good. 'Cause wait till you see this." Danny leans over, grinning once more, and I tighten my arms around my middle.

What's he about to do? Teach me to flirt? He drops something onto my lap, and the glove compartment clicks open, then bangs shut as Danny retreats to his side of the car.

The car starts with a blast of air, and I flatten the page across my knees. Danny scribbled down a bunch of medical terms and symptoms—spelled wrong, no doubt—followed by a list of tests the doctors ran. "She told you all this?"

"Couldn't shut up about it. Not sure I remembered everything, but I think I got the main stuff."

As we pull out into traffic, I read through Danny's notes again. *Signs of subdurill hema (something??). Nothing on X-ray. Unresponsive 5 hrs. No seizures. No vomit. No damage to skull.*

Jesus. All this in under ten minutes? I make a mental note to learn how to flirt.

"She could get fired for talking about patients, you know."

"Which is why we won't tell." Danny presses a button and liquid shoots across the windshield. Wipers wick it away, leaving a crisp view of the lumbering mills that line this end of Main Street. Their smokestacks are quiet, windows boarded up and smeared in graffiti. In the distance, the church spire rises watchful against a sun-drenched sky.

Just the sight of it reminds me what we're up against. Every day that passes, their case grows stronger, bringing Tess closer to sainthood. "We should go to the library. Now," I say. "So we can look this stuff up."

"Aye aye, Cap'n." Danny hits the blinker, looking a little too smug.

"Of course, if this is a dead end, we'll need to come up with a backup plan."

"Huh?" The wipers go quiet. "Dead end? Callie, did you see what I wrote down?"

Like I said: smug. "There are other ways we could prove them wrong, you know. It's not all about the miracles."

Danny looks confused.

"A saint has to be good, right? Virtuous. She has to follow the teachings of the Church. If it came to it, all we'd have to do is show them that Tess was never perfect, never close."

Danny fumbles with a switch. The vents blast louder, hotter, before settling to a hiss.

"I don't know how you'd prove that," he says quietly.

I turn, knees knocking against the gearshift. "Really? Nothing occurs to you?"

"Callie . . . you said . . ."

"I know. I know." I sigh. "I won't share your secret. Don't worry." And I mean that: I won't—I'm not a *total* asshole—but, still, I can't help seeing how easy it would be if Danny loosened up about it, just a little.

"Imagine what would happen if we did tell. Hypothetically. If you told them that you and she . . . what you . . . I mean, if you . . ." I scratch my nose. *Sex, Callie. Just say it. Did they have sex?* My face has grown uncomfortably warm, and whatever Danny did to the AC isn't helping. I hold down a button until the passenger window drops away and a breeze licks at my temples.

"I'm just saying they'd change their tune real fast if they thought she wasn't a virgin."

Danny's gripping the steering wheel.

"Was she?" I ask. "Did you?"

You'd think a sister-slash-best friend would have the facts on this, but Tess and I found it easier to talk around certain subjects. I knew the basics about her and Danny, but she kept a lot of the details vague. Maybe she thought I was too immature or that it would put a gulf between us, her on one side of love, me left behind on the other. But now she's gone and facts are facts, and we all know how the Church feels about sex.

"Callie, please. Can we not talk about this?" Danny's elbows have locked, tendons switching beneath his skin. A bit of an over-reaction, if you ask me. It occurs to me that he may be carrying bigger secrets than I realize.

I let the subject drop (for now), but the tension remains thick. If Tess were here, she'd make a corny joke, and the air would thin back to its natural state. But she's not—here—and my mind is still stuck on an idea.

I angle toward Danny. "Did you know Tess was into horror flicks?"

His brow furrows. "So?"

"So horror movies happen to be full of witchcraft and other unchristian behavior."

"They're movies." Danny's arms slacken a touch. "It's made-up."

"*I* know that, but the hard-core church people don't see the difference. One time some guy stopped Tess at the theater and started lecturing her about Christian values. It was Saturday night, total nightmare. Someone else stood up for her, pointing out that the movie we'd just seen was only PG-13. And then a fight broke out and it was total chaos and everyone forgot all about Tess. But she was so humiliated by the whole thing that she swore off anything R-rated after that, plus everything with ax murderers."

"But ax murderers were her favorite."

"I know! We still watched them at home sometimes after our mom was asleep." Couch cushions pulled to the floor, candy stashed in our slippers, limbs entwined under blankets. You said the scary parts made your toes tingle, made you feel more alive.

"I would've punched that guy. The dude who yelled at her?" Danny demonstrates on the steering wheel, and I smile. I've dreamed about pounding that guy to a pulp.

"She liked romance novels too, you know."

Sideways glance.

"Did you know *romance* is basically code for girl porn?"

Danny takes his eyes from the road for longer than he should.

"I'm serious. It's not just trembling loins these days. Even the white knights don't keep their armor on for very long. You should take a peek next time you're at CVS."

Danny coughs. There's definitely a smile on his face now. A laugh might be within reach.

"So the question is, do we think a girl who hid lady porn under her bed and watched *The Exorcist* more than thirty times would be considered holy?"

Danny grins. "Probably not."

"Definitely not."

We edge into the city center, quiet. After a long pause, Danny says, "You know we could never tell them that stuff, right?"

My shoulders sink. "Yeah. I know."

Tess's biggest fear was that people would turn on her, like that guy at the cinema but a thousand times worse. Even now, I couldn't do that to her. And truthfully? A big part of me is too selfish. They've already taken so much. I don't want them to have the girl she really was.

Danny clips the blinker, and we're here: downtown New Avon, six blocks of brick storefronts wedged together like mismatched toys. Blink, and you could miss the whole thing. At the end of the strip, the city library rises, four stories of concrete and glass.

I reach for the slip of paper in my lap—every fact we have about Ana, one of them a possible key to her miracle. "Let's go see what all this means."

From the Journal
of
Tess da Costa

February 6

Wednesday's vigil starts with a question that's been on everyone's mind: How does a six-year-old girl disappear without a trace? A week she's been gone, still no sign.

Then: You think there's a chance she's alive?

Then: Is anyone even listening to our prayers?

They look at me, and I bow my head, quiet.

On Monday, I went down to the police station, figuring I should tell someone what I've heard, but before I could even get out the phrases, the cop at the desk told me to save my Magic 8 Ball tricks for idiots who believe that crap, he had real work to do. I ran out, cheeks on fire, while he and his buddy laughed, calling me a crank, a nutcase, a loon.

(Not the first time I've been called names. But still. By a cop?)

And that leaves me where? Who can I tell? Maybe if Mrs. Langone would come out of her house, I could try talking to her. But she's been holed up inside for a week now. When I think of the pain she must be feeling, I can't bring myself to pester her. What if I'm wrong? What if it's all nonsense and I really am a nutcase like those cops said? What if I only cause her more pain?

No, I'm better off sorting this one out myself.

Ma tells my fans to cool it with the questions, says they don't understand how miracles work. If That Woman can't look to God on behalf of her own family, none of us can help.

That Woman = Maxine Langone. None of us knows her too well. She's mostly kept to herself since moving here a year ago and isn't part of any church we know of, which no one seemed to care about before, but now Ma won't even say her name, says if That Woman thinks she's too good to pray with her neighbors, then maybe they should focus their charity elsewhere. On someone who wants to be saved.

It's harsh, but the others nod as she says it. They've been hurt by That Woman's silence too. Their questions grow more shrill: Is she even a Christian? Where did she come from anyway? Is Attlebury an actual place? And isn't it strange how the girl's mother has never been in the picture? What about the father? What else is That Woman hiding?

As the evening drags on, a knot forms in my skull, pulsing in time with their shouts.

They aren't bad people. They're just frightened, confused. I know this, and yet at the end of the vigil, when we form a circle and the candles are lit, all I see are the flames reflected in their eyes.

Today, I wake up with a plan: Forget about it. All of it. I'm going to have a normal day for a change, as normal as I can manage. I put on my good jeans and send D a text.

D is the one person who doesn't care how many prayers I said today, or my thoughts on Jesus. He says he doesn't deserve me, but that's just ridiculous. He might not be Mr. Varsity or whatever it is he thinks girls like. He's something better: a good guy. He doesn't swagger around like the other boys, or pretend to be something he's not. He's the type of boy who will help a teacher out when her papers spill everywhere, even if it's a teacher everyone hates, even if the other kids snicker. Because he's polite. And kind. I noticed it the first time he smiled at me and then again later the same day when he saw me carrying a heavy stack of books and hurried ahead to hold open the door and I almost fell over from the shock.

D insists he's nothing special, that it's all me—I make him want to be a better person—which makes me laugh. 'Cause when I'm with D, I become wicked. I become free.

Today I skip out of school a little early—cramps! doctor's orders! (Perk of being a so-called saint: Teachers believe anything you tell them.)—and catch a bus headed downtown. I set up shop on the library's front steps and decide to sneak in a prayer for little Ana while I wait. Hands folded, I send one out to Jesus, Allah, Buddha, and all the angels and prophets. (I'm keeping my bases covered.)

When I open my eyes, a man stands on the sidewalk in front of me, staring. I let out a startled cough.

Miss Teresa. He steps closer. He's wearing short sleeves despite the chill, and thick, old-timey glasses. His eyes are pale brown, his face soft, like a slab of dough that hasn't been properly cooked. Miss Teresa. His clammy hand latches on to mine and my heart scrabbles up to my throat.

I search the street for D—where is that boy? It's not like him to be late. I try to ease my hand back slowly, but the dough-faced man clutches tighter. His knuckles are chapped, raw, and his voice is strangely flat. Miss, I been looking for you. I need to tell you. I need to thank you for my sister.

I tell my rabbit heart to chill. This is the price of being a local celebrity. When they find me like this, out in the open, the best thing to do is nod politely and listen.

So that's what I do—nod, smile, listen—listen, nod, smile—my mouth stretching uncomfortably while the man's thick fingers bite into my wrist.

Thank you, miss, he's saying. My sister, she come home.

That's great, I say, working to hide the tremble from my voice. I'm so glad, I tell him, though I have no idea what he's talking about or if he's even speaking in present tense.

Still, poor fella, now that I look more closely at the directness of his gaze, the smooth expanse of his face, no twitch to acknowledge how awkward this is, I realize he's maybe a few marbles short of a set. And he does seem awfully happy about his sister. That's sweet, right?

I wiggle my fingers, hoping he'll take the hint.

And then—out of nowhere, like a knight responding (awfully late) to a cry for help—D appears at my side. He uses his extra inches to wedge himself between me and my new friend, and I'm torn between wanting to swoon over my gentleman protector and wanting to pinch him like a naughty child. I'm not <u>that</u> helpless, thankyouverymuch.

The dough-faced guy falls back, mumbling. He's harmless, I tell D, shaking feeling back into my fingers. He just wanted to say hi.

At least, I think that's what he wanted. The man—yes, definitely a screw or two missing from this one—is speaking more softly now, saying, Thankyouthankyou. My sister too, she say thank you.

Uh, you're welcome? I say, still not sure what we're talking about.

D is all brown-eyed concern. Really, the boy is every bit as sizzly as the farmer-turned-nobleman in that novel I read last week. Callie makes fun of my taste in books—predictable, she calls them, clichéd—but is there something wrong with being able to count on a happy ending? That sudden twist, doom: averted, last stop: happy ever after. If that's a cliché, well, I'll take it. In fact, if we weren't on a public sidewalk, I'd suggest D and I reenact one of those tumbly barn scenes this very minute.

My new pal is still here, though, muttering something so soft I barely catch it—did he just call me an <u>angel</u>?

D flexes muscles I didn't know he had, which is cute & hot. Also: unnecessary. I grab him by the biceps, pushing him toward the library entrance. As I turn, I catch sight of a dark car parked across the street, its tinted window sliding shut. Has someone been watching? Mr. Dough Face is still muttering—thankyouthankyou and some other stuff I can't make out. Ugh. I reach in my bag and pull out one of the prayer cards Ma makes me carry, the one with Mass times and food pantry hours printed on the back. He seems like he might need it.

So glad I could help! I tell him in my most cheerful voice. Say hi to your sister for me!

He stares at the image on the card (me, gold-framed, mortifying), and for a second, I consider snatching it back. But no. I'm being silly. It's fine. He's harmless.

The car across the street is gone now. See? Everything's fine.

Before I can overthink any of what's happened, I grab on to D and yank him up the steps. He holds the door open for me, which only makes me more eager to get him inside.

Who was that guy? Were you waiting long? Why are you looking at me like that?

D is full of questions, and I am full of something else. I drag him past the magazine racks, through a metal door, and down a long aisle, into a corner of the stacks that I happen to know no one else ever visits. D looks around at all the dusty books.

What's this? Lives of the Saints? Catholicism in Contemporary Life? Where are we? His forehead has folded into a million sexy crinkles, and I feel a surge of something. Wicked, delicious. My backpack hits the floor, jacket right after. I tug at the zipper on his sweatshirt.

My nobleman laughs. Miss me much? The crinkles melt away, and D's hands find the crook of my waist. I tip back to find the rest of him.

Rawrrr!

11.

I leave the library at closing, alone. Danny stayed with me until just after six, when his mom texted, needing a ride to the store. There was really no reason for me to stay either. We'd already looked up every detail on Danny's list, run down every rabbit hole that mattered, smiles passing between us as we hit on hopeful bits. *No vomiting* and *no seizure* were both good signs. The fact that Ana woke up after only five hours: even better.

But there were contradictions too. If the first scan really showed blood on her brain (correct spelling: *subdural hematoma*), why didn't the MRIs find anything in the days that followed? Was she badly injured or not? Was this really a situation requiring divine intervention?

And why hasn't Ana spoken since? Is there some lingering damage the doctors still can't see? If she's not fully recovered, can they claim this was a miracle?

After two hours of searching, the best we could say was that Ana's head injuries may have been life-threatening, or not. Fully healed, or not. Was her recovery explainable by medicine? Still hard to say.

"We can't know for sure unless we talk to Dr. Gillis," Danny said. He wanted to try calling the doctor at home, tonight, but I told him we'd need a better plan than that.

A plan that doesn't involve Dr. Gillis would be even better. I keep seeing Tess's face when she came home from school, freshman year, after a troop of boys got the bright idea to follow her around enacting their version of a *psychiatric disturbance*. Dr. Gillis had given them those words. Ma isn't the only one who hates him for what he did.

After Danny left, I spent another hour digging through the stacks, hoping to find some obscure fact we'd missed. Some detail that would prove with 100 percent certainty that what happened to Ana Langone puts this safely in the realm of science. I came up with: nada.

And now, dusk is falling fast and my belly is grumbling (again). I hurry along Front Street, notes clutched to my chest. A group of teens have gathered in the plaza by Domino's. They laugh and shove playfully. I cross the street to avoid dealing with all that or seeing their side-eyed pity. A sixteen-year-old girl, summer evening, all by her lonely.

God, I was an idiot to bring up the sex thing with Danny. He probably thinks I'm a pervert. Or worse, jealous. But I'm not. I swear. I'll admit, it was nice spending the day with someone who gets it. There was even a moment—brief—this afternoon when I forgot to be sad. A second when I didn't feel so alone. But I don't have it twisted: Danny is my *friend*. He still belongs to Tess. It's clear every time he says her name, the way his whole face softens, and his voice.

The same thing happened to her. Just one mention of Danny and her shadows filled with light. He's the one person who managed to make my sister happy in those last months. If I feel anything toward him, it's gratitude.

Cars rush by in a hurry to get wherever, and a guy shouts something from the corner. I give him a look that shuts him up quick.

I lean into the hill, heart picking up speed. Fast but not too fast. They ran tests on me after Tess's heart attack. Ma—in an about-face on the whole doctor thing—insisted we both needed to get looked at. My heart, lungs, and other organs are perfectly healthy. I can expect to live a long life. Every day, my heart will keep beating, my blood pulsing, energy coursing, trapped beneath my skin.

The sun slants low, glinting off cars and painting the buildings in golden warmth. Radios sit in open windows: a thump of hip-hop, brassy blast of merengue. From one window, I catch the tearful trills of fado, those old-world songs of longing that made my grandfather stand up and sing.

Doçura e sal, he called Tess and me. Sweetness and salt. One without the other will ruin a dish, but in the right balance: divino.

On the next corner, she appears. Little bowls and burned-out candles. Silk flowers and a stuffed rabbit that must have been on clearance from Easter. I don't know what miraculous event this shrine is meant to commemorate. Her fans have gone overboard lately, erecting little memorials in every place she supposedly touched. In the center of this one Tess stares wide-eyed from a silver frame, her smile crooked, uncertain.

If you pick apart our features—the curls, the hazel eyes, the dusting of freckles—we are identical. But somehow, together, our features don't add up to the same face. Hers was always a tiny bit rounder, softer. A face you'd do anything to protect.

It surges up suddenly. Sadness, rage; sticky, hot. I do it without thinking, lift the cheap frame from the post where it's tethered, yank until the wire snaps free.

It's not enough. Anger pounds in my temples, zings down to my feet. One kick sends a bouquet flying. A swipe, and the candles cascade off the makeshift table, shattering on the sidewalk. A siren wails in the distance, and I freeze, shoving the frame under my shirt. Quick check: No one has seen me. Heart pounding, I turn and run, leaving the rest of it behind—the crushed flowers and horrid gifts—letting them sit there, offering themselves up to a great big nothing.

Rudy enters the shed ahead of me, growling a warning into the pitchy blackness. There's a soft thump and I go still. Is something back there in the shadows? There's a rustle and the sound of footsteps. On pavement. Outside. Not in here. I flick on the ship-in-a-bottle lamp, whispering a calming word to Rudy. But he's one step ahead of me, his edginess melted by the flush of light. He rushes around to greet old friends: a sack of dirt, a pair of old beach chairs, the giant glazed seagull Tess couldn't believe anyone would sell for a dollar. A lopsided bookshelf is stacked full of her trashy romances and my thrillers.

We spent a lot of hours out here, talking, reading. Hiding

from chores. Like Rudy, the shed technically belongs to our land-lord, but old Mr. Flaherty ceded it to us years ago.

I pull the items I'm carrying out from under my shirt, laying them carefully on your old trunk. "A real antique," you said as you dragged it from the curb on trash day. You fancied yourself a col-lector. I wonder what you'd make of my new collection. Three pho-tos. Three different shrines. I made another quick stop on the way home, not sure why. No one was looking, it was so tempting, and anyway what I did isn't stealing, not exactly. You never belonged to them, Tess. You know that, right?

You stare back at me, silent and stiff.

I consider the best spot to hide you. Behind the lawn mower? Under that rickety chair? Outside, a car door slams and Rudy jumps. I shove the frames behind a bag of grass seed and follow Rudy out into the driveway.

My pulse steadies as I take in the scene. Yard: empty. Ma: nowhere in sight. A car has pulled up to the curb in front of the Langones', lights on and engine running.

From the shed's doorway, I have a clear view of the two-story duplex across the way. It's set back farther from the street than the apartments on either side, with a slightly bigger yard. Its windows are completely dark.

Rudy yips softly as a pair of shadows emerge from the car, and I move with him toward the fence. Up and down the street, porch lights snap on, neighbors appearing as silhouettes.

The two shadows glide toward the stoop, and when the second one turns to reach into a bag, we all see her: a child huddled in the old woman's arms.

Screen doors creak open. "Is it *her*?" someone whispers. "Why'd they send her home so soon?"

Ma's always complaining about this: how the hospital sends people home the moment they can stand on two feet. It's not even two days since Ana was found. Maybe this means her injuries weren't as bad as they said. Could this be a point for Team Skeptic?

Mrs. Langone digs something out of her purse and hands it to the other figure, who I now realize is a cabdriver.

"Can she talk yet?" a neighbor asks, a little too loudly.

Mrs. Langone's head jerks up at the sound. She squints toward the street, clutching Ana to her shoulder. "We'll both be fine when they find that bastard. You hear me?" Her glasses glint in the darkness.

Ana lifts her head, seems to follow her grandmother's gaze. I can't make out her face in the gloom, at such a distance, but there's something strange about the angle of her neck, the intensity of her stare.

More than six months she's been missing. I can't even imagine what she's been through. Or how she'll recover.

"Did you all hear me?" Mrs. Langone's voice is craggy and shrill.

The neighbors nod. Yes. They've heard. But from the way they look at the child and then back at one another, I can tell no one believes her for a second.

12.

They think he's still in town," is the first thing Danny says when he answers the phone. "They think the fucker's still in New Avon."

I went upstairs to find an empty apartment and an angry note from Ma, who rushed off to a church event after getting Mr. Flaherty to let her inside. I felt a pang of guilt when I checked my phone and saw the missed texts, remembering that I still had her keys. I considered texting her back but decided to call Danny instead.

I expected him to laugh off my worry—the bad feeling that took hold when I saw Ana, a sudden understanding that no miracle could fix what happened to her—but it turns out Mr. Let's Leave the Kidnapper to the Cops was feeling some of the same things himself. Danny had been listening to his dad's old police scanner since he got home. The chatter started just after dinnertime, he said, when a guy was spotted hanging around Cranston Street, muttering. He was gone before the police got there.

"That's my street," I say. "Ana's street."

"Which is why one of your neighbors freaked out."

"You think it was him?"

"Hard to say. The person who called it in sounded pretty unreliable. Still, I wouldn't bet a kid's life on it."

I tell Danny about the scene I just witnessed: Mrs. Langone staring down the neighbors. Ana hunched in her arms, so quiet, so still.

"What if we went back over there? To Walnut Street, I mean. Tonight. We could slip inside, take a quick look around. Just to be sure they didn't miss something obvious."

Danny is quiet.

"I know we said focus on the miracle. I know we're not cops. But Tess isn't the only one getting hurt by all this. What if Ana needs help too?"

"Callie—"

"We'll be careful, Danny, so careful. No one will know we were there."

I haven't lost it completely. I know exactly how out-there I sound, but the thought of spending another night cooped up in this apartment? My head feels too hectic and energy crackles beneath my skin, like something has awoken and won't be put back to sleep.

"How about this?" I say because I have to make Danny say yes. "If you come with me tonight, we can call Dr. Gillis first thing tomorrow. I'll do it myself. This is just one little detour, Danny. No sand traps or whatever."

"Quicksand," he says.

"Right, none of that either. We'll be back on course tomorrow, I promise."

I can hear him hesitating.

"C'mon, Danny. I da—"

"Don't," he says. "Don't say *I dare you*." But I already have, and I've already won.

I half expect Danny to bail after we hang up, to call back with some lame excuse, but when I creep downstairs at a quarter past crazy, the old Hyundai is purring by the curb.

We pull up to Walnut Street and Danny cuts the engine. I place my hand on the door, waiting for the blood to stop fizzing in my ears. We've parked a few doors down, within sight of Mrs. Rogeiro's white whale of a building, which is now swaddled in darkness. From the look of things, even her insomniac neighbors, Myrna and Lew, have fallen victim to sleep.

"Remind me why we're doing this?"

I give Danny a hard look. "Because of Ana. She deserves justice, answers." Because maybe *I* want justice too.

"If you're going to wuss out on me, go ahead and get it over with," I say sharply. "I'm going in either way."

I open the car door and step out onto the curb. A moment later, I hear the creak of the driver's-side door and Danny joins me on the sidewalk.

It's that strange, in-between hour before late becomes early. Cars hunker low along the curbs, and the buildings squat in the loamy blackness, their front doors secured and upper windows gaping. The only sign of life is a convenience store on the far end of the street, its windows a jumble of neon light, like a stranded spaceship sending its signal out into the void.

"What's the plan if the door's locked?" Danny says, too loudly.

"Shhhhh." I put a finger to my lips. "That's what this is for." I unzip my messenger bag, giving Danny a peek at the tools I collected after Ma went to bed: a screwdriver, a barbecue skewer, and an unwound clothes hanger. My plan, I'll admit, is pretty bare-bones: Find a back entrance, get in somehow, don't get caught.

"Is that your library card?"

"Jesus! Didn't anyone teach you how to whisper?" I zip up the bag as soundlessly as I can. "It's to shimmy the door. I didn't have a credit card. Don't look at me like that. I have more experience with these things than you."

Danny's eyes glint in the dark. "If you're talking about the time Karen got you to break into the yearbook office—"

"Shut it, Danny." I yank him out from under the streetlight, slinging the bag over my head. We have to move quickly, before someone wakes up. I take the lead, clinging to the sidewalk's shadowed edge, and Danny trails close, his sneakers scritching in the grit.

We pause at Mrs. Rogeiro's gate. The building seems even bigger at night, ghostlike, the porches hanging like bones. To the left, the driveway forms a moonless canyon. It's impossible to tell how far it stretches, or what lies at the opposite end.

We feel our way along the building's lip, hunting for a side door. The first one we come to is locked. I curse softly, shine my flashlight up ahead, then down toward our ankles, where a small window provides access to the basement. Thin spiders of light pierce the inky gloom, revealing bulky furnaces and crisscrossing vents. I probe the panes with my toe, but the window doesn't budge. It's the type that doesn't open. Fuck.

"That's the smallest flashlight I've ever seen." Danny's voice is so soft that I can feel it as much as hear it.

"It's a reading light." I click it off and scrub his breath from my scalp. "Stop talking and help me look."

"Yes, ma'am." He places a hand on my waist, and I straighten with surprise before he slips around me, edging deeper into the shadows.

We move forward more quickly now, pausing at the sound of something rattling behind the fence to our left. Danny reaches for my hand, and we stumble ahead, pace quickening as the noise intensifies, the clatter of metal joined by animal grunts.

At the end of the driveway, we're greeted by a burst of moonlight. Stillness. Shadows shape-shift into recognizable things: a dumpster, a pile of old tires, and balancing atop the fence: an overweight raccoon. Its eyes glow yellow, and it lets out an angry hiss before hurtling back to the other side.

We split up, circling the back of the building. Danny studies the balconies while I hunt down below for another entrance. I find one tucked under a fire escape. Locked.

I try the knob a second time, pushing gently in the opposite direction and saying a quick prayer to the patron saint of breaking and entering, whoever that may be. The door opens inward with a quiet click. Sticky latch. I smile.

I wave Danny over, and we slip into the pitch-black hallway. "Shit," he whispers.

"What?"

"I forgot my phone in the car."

"So?"

"So it's got a light brighter than that." He points to my flashlight, which, it's true, barely makes a dent in the darkness. But it's better than nothing.

"Too late now." I move forward, probing the walls with my fingers, until my foot finds a staircase.

We climb together, elbow to elbow, backs hugging the wall. Moonlight trickles from a window somewhere above, and I turn out my light to save the battery, pushing my toe into each step and using my hand to feel a few inches ahead. The plaster is cool. And moist. I try not to think about that. I try not to breathe.

On the second floor a television blares from behind a closed door. Danny hangs back. What a wuss. I grab his t-shirt and tug him across the landing. We creep up the next flight.

Another corner, and the stairs end abruptly. Danny grabs my hip to steady me, and I stretch a hand out into the blackness. There's nothing before us, just space.

Danny breathes. "Fuck."

"What?" My shoulder bumps against his chest. I don't even bother to push him back or rub away the sensations zinging through me. There are so many. I can't see a damn thing.

"Where's a tiny flashlight when you need one?" Danny whispers.

I jab him gently and fumble with the switch. The thin glow is devoured immediately. I thump it against my palm, willing the bulb to grow brighter. No luck. And of course extra batteries are the one thing I forgot to pack.

I reach my arm blindly ahead, helping the flashlight pick out a jagged crack along one wall, a locked door, and then something shiny. Something . . . yellow. Is it . . . ? Yes. Police tape.

Danny squeezes my elbow. Victory.

The door to 3C is open. I fold sideways, climbing through the crisscrossed tape, and Danny follows.

The air in the apartment is stale, coffinlike. Danny reaches for the wall. I hear a light switch snap and grab for his arm too late.

Nothing happens, though. No light. Not even a buzz in the wall. The electricity's probably been cut. Speaking of which, my flashlight's fading fast. I move to the wall, shine what light is left in small arcs. It's like a creepy kaleidoscope—tiny snatches of things, all chopped up and out of order—a doorknob, a faucet, a corner of tile. Now you see me, now you don't.

I sort the fragments in my mind as best I can, fitting them together into an image of the whole. The apartment is tiny—a single room, small kitchenette tucked along one side, a bathroom that's no more than a toilet and showerhead. The window to the outside has been boarded over. The only furniture is a small, bow-legged bureau and a mattress. Danny reaches for my hand, guiding the flashlight toward the ceiling, where it catches on something. The light sputters in my hand.

Holy Mother.

Thick black lines curve and swoop above us, reaching as wide as my own arms could stretch. The strokes are sloppy, thick, confused. Still, there's no mistaking what they're meant to be: a giant pair of wings.

"Jesus," Danny whispers.

Wide across the top, tapering to pointed tips. It's a crude rendition, but I've seen that shape enough times to know these aren't just any wings. Those same curves repeat over and over—hundreds of times, thousands—in the arches of the church.

"It's supposed to be an angel," I whisper.

"It's creepy as hell, whatever it is."

I bring the light back to the floor, feeling unsteady and slightly ill. I get it now—why the neighbors were so disturbed. As if the dresses weren't weird enough. Who *does* this?

I turn off the flashlight and press my fingers to my forehead to think. We came here for a reason, and so far we haven't seen anything that others don't already know. What are we not seeing? What might the cops have missed or misunderstood? In my detective shows, they often skip over a key detail the first time. It's always something obvious, hidden in plain sight.

I click on the light and do another careful scan of the window, the mattress, the matchbook-sized closet. I make my way back to the bureau.

First drawer: empty. Second: empty. Third: . . . empty too. But it sticks when I slide it closed. I jiggle the frame and hear something thunk to the bottom. I reach inside, feel around, until my hand brushes against something.

"What is it?" Danny curls around to see.

"An envelope?" I shine my flashlight on the packet I've extracted. It's manila, marked with a grid, like the ones you see sometimes in offices. I unwind a string from the top, and the first thing my fingers pull out is a photo. *Hello.* It's the same little girl, the one from the eighties, but she's seated with her arms around a boy, younger than her. There's a business card in there too, and a couple of other scraps, but it's something else that stops me cold. The paper has been folded, tattered, like someone had carried it close. Despite the creases, her face is unmistakable. Dark hair, nervous smile, eyes wide like she has an itch she's afraid to scratch.

Tess.

Danny's hand stacks above mine, grabbing for a better look. I focus on breathing. It's one of the prayer cards Ma had printed. A picture of Tess on the front, her face snaked in gold, a bunch of church info on the back.

My hands are trembling. My knees are too. Did he go to our church, the kidnapper? Was he one of her followers? Did he ask my sister's forgiveness for stealing a child?

Danny takes the packet from my hand, which is quaking visibly now. I rub my palm across my shorts to get rid of the kidnapper's touch. I have a sudden urge to leave, to get as far from this place as possible and never, ever come back.

I make a move for the door, and my foot hits a creak. The wooden moan is followed by another sound—hollow and vaguely human.

My flashlight tumbles to the ground, goes dark.

"Holy—"

"What the—"

A second cry, more shrill, cuts through the air.

I drop to my knees, heart pounding now, hands fumbling across the floor. My fingers close on the flashlight, and I click the button on and off, off and on, shaking frantically. It's no use. The battery's dead. I rise, wavering, no longer sure which way is up and which is forward, my eyes filled with blackness.

"Callie?"

I step closer to Danny's whisper but can't find his shape in the dark. It's a moment from one of Tess's movies, the second right before the ax murderer jumps out from the closet, a script so predictable I'd laugh if my face weren't rigid with fear.

Another cry breaks. It rises high-pitched and mournful, up, up, up to an unearthly note before descending into a moan.

I spin for the door—or at least the direction I hope is the door—and my foot snags on something else. I topple, reaching out, grabbing for a wall, or Danny's arm, and instead getting . . . a handful of chest?

Danny catches my hand in his and holds me steady, palm over palm over heart. We cling to each other, listening as the silence deepens, until it's nothing but our breath, the gurgle of fear in my throat.

Danny's chest is warm, thick, more muscled than I would have expected. *Does he exercise in secret?*

Ack. No, Callie. Weird thought, weirder timing. I try to pull away, but Danny grips my hand tight. "Wait." His voice is barely a scrape.

Something crashes below, and Danny's heart bucks, a caged animal stuttering into my open palm. The next second, all hell breaks loose. The air fills with screeching, scuffling, thumping. There's a throaty yowl, then a violent bang as something slams shut.

The building goes quiet. Danny has both my hands now. My feet are wedged between his, knees alternating, bodies touching in too many places to count. Warm, soap-scented Danny. *Thump, tha-dump, thump, thump.* At first, I think it's my heart, or his. But then I realize the sound's coming from below. A soft, rhythmic patter. It's a sound I know . . . from childhood, from weekends with my grandparents—paws retreating across a wooden floor.

A laugh ripples through me. Danny's head tips in confusion.

"A cat." I pull one hand free from his grasp, wipe a tear from my eye. "It's a cat."

Not a ghost. Not an ax murderer. A *cat.*

Danny still has my other wrist tight against his shoulder. Our feet are interlinked, and our knees, our thighs, our . . . We both take stock at the same moment, and the sudden release sends us both stumbling. Danny crashes into the bureau, and I flop onto the mattress, laughing audibly now. Danny's laughing too.

"Shh-h-h-h!" I try to hush us both, but it's no use. More laughter erupts, and the cat—yes, it's definitely a cat—lets out an angry howl.

I howl too. It must be hysteria, some weird side effect of panic. Because this situation is disturbing, not funny. Those wings. Tess's face. This coffinlike apartment.

"Shhhh. Let's go. Before someone hears us." Danny's shadow stoops low, and I let him pull me to my feet.

The instant I'm upright, my laughter goes still. The darkness has begun to lift. Fingers of gray light creep through the boarded-up windows, sliding across the ceiling toward those strange black lines—arcing, swooping, ready for flight.

Danny tugs me toward the door, and maybe it's the motion or a funny trick of the light, but I swear I see those wings move.

When the girl closes her eyes, he's there. Wisps of dark hair, pale moon face, hands fat like overfed rodents. He opens his mouth to speak—to shout—but before the words cross his lips, the girl's eyes fly open.

The room is quiet, no machines. Only an old woman's soft snore, the gentle whine of crickets, the raspy bark of a neighborhood dog.

The girl rolls to her side and reaches for the water, whimpering without meaning to. Her grandmother startles upright in the chair.

"Baby? What is it?"

Her grandmother sees something in the girl's face. Her arthritic hands reach. Gingerly, at first. Then, sliding onto the bed, the old woman pulls the girl into her arms, cradling her.

"It was just a dream, love. A dream."

The girl presses her ear against her grandmother's chest, listening to its irregular beat. Her grandma strokes her hair, sings a few notes. A lullaby, shaky and off-key.

The girl can see that her grandmother is trying to stay calm, but her heartbeat betrays her, and her right hand coils tense on the pillow, ready to fight.

From the Journal
of
Tess da Costa

February 9

When I pick up the phone before breakfast, there's a voice on the other end.

—can't keep pretending you can control this, Mona. It's like with Mãe. Remember how—

I know the voice right away. My Aunt Wendy always talks like this, like she's late for something and she told you a hundred times anyway, so it's your fault if you haven't caught on.

Not everything has to do with our mother! a second voice interrupts, so quiet I don't realize it's Ma right away. Past is past, she says. You need to let that shit go.

What shit? What past? I wonder. I press the phone to my ear, and that's when I hear it: my name.

Tess is a healthy seventeen-year-old girl, Ma tells Wendy. This is a different situation.

Wendy: You admit it's a situation then?

Ma [grunting]: I really don't need this from you.

Wendy [snorting]: If you ask my advice, I'm not gonna just give you the parts you want to hear.

Callie thumps into the kitchen right then and bangs open the cabinets. I clamp my hand on the receiver. Not fast enough.

Callie! Tess?

Ma shouts from the other room, and I slip the phone back into its cradle.

Were you listening to Ma's call? Callie asks.

No, I grumble, busying myself with coffee making and orange juice pouring so Callie won't see the lie all over my face. Or the questions. A situation? Advice? Is this what they do: have secret conversations about me when they think I'm not listening?

Well, you shouldn't spy without me, Callie says and snatches my cup of OJ. She never pours her own—a whole glass is too much, she says—but the way she's slurping at mine, I wonder what she'd do without me. Die of scurvy?

It's early afternoon before I finally have the apartment to myself. I don't know what I should be looking for, exactly, but there's clearly something Ma's been keeping from me.

I start in her room. In the bottom drawer of the bureau, I find a few photo albums—the old, sticky-page kind—and bundles of letters. The first set is from someone named Nick. (My _father_?!) I knew Ma lied about not missing him. The letters must have been from when they first fell in love, before two little kids came along and made them scream about everything. I make a mental note to show them to Callie.

The next bundle is tied with a bit of black lace. Even before undoing the knot, I know I've found something. I take a seat and a packet of old Polaroids tumbles loose: My grandparents when they were married. Vovô in his shoe factory days. My mother as a girl, arm in arm with Wendy, surrounded by cousins.

I pause on a photo of Grandma. My memories of her are scattered & blurry, but I remember those eyes, rich like molasses, hands like birds, always moving even when the rest of her was still. She loved to sing while cooking and sip brandy while watching TV. She called me minha querida, her little love.

I fold the lace carefully at my feet. Each envelope is addressed to the state mental hospital in a bold cursive I'd know anywhere. The first letter begins, I miss you, Mãe . . .

There are a couple dozen letters, all starting the same way: I love you, I miss you. Everything is good at home, don't worry. We're doing great.

Ma tells Grandma she's finished high school, postponed college, found love. She worries that Grandma will be disappointed by the news, mentions some argument they had, says not to worry—she's doing fine. They're all fine.

Ma was a terrible liar, even back then.

Not one letter says what was wrong, why Grandma was in the hospital in the first place. (Why has Ma never mentioned any of this? Did Grandma get cured? She wasn't sick when I knew her—at least, I don't think she was.) There's just this one little clue in one of the last letters, dated a few months after I was born: We both know they got it wrong, Mãe. I believe you, always did, always will. The doctors can't see what you see. They don't know you like I do.

A photo falls from the final envelope. It's Ma as a teenager, not much older than I am now, big hair and earrings, a small, pointed face. In her arms sits a tiny baby, wrapped in a striped blanket. Me.

I flip back to the first letter. I miss you, Mãe . . .

Callie stumbles in then, giggling about something her friend Karen did. She stops when she sees my face. Tess?

It's too late to hide what I've found. I hold out the letters, and Callie takes a seat on the floor beside me.

There's no other explanation, right? I say. Letters to the loony bin?

Callie doesn't answer right away. She goes through the pages one by one, studying each like it's an ancient artifact. When she's done, she folds them back in their envelopes.

We'd know if Grandma was mentally ill, she says. Ma would've told us.

What else could it be? The doctors can't see what you see. I repeat the line that's still troubling me most.

It was a different time, Callie says. They probably put women away for lots of things back then.

You mean back in the nineties?

Callie sets her chin. It doesn't say anything about a voice, Tess. There's nothing here that says she was like you.

That's when I tell her what I heard on the phone earlier, and even though Callie tries to play it off like it's not a big deal, I know her face too well. I can see from the way she bites the inside of her lip that she gets it now. This is why Ma flies off the handle when people use words like "schizo" or "crazy." Or when they ask why she hasn't brought me to a doctor.

Callie, do you think I'm—

No! Of course not!!! She slaps down my question with more exclamation points than are strictly necessary. It's the rest of this city that's gone off its rocker, she says. There's another explanation. We just don't know what it is yet.

I want to believe my little sister—I really, really do—but even as she's playing calm and working to keep my fears in check, her eyes jerk a little too fast in their sockets. She wondering the same thing as me: Could this be the answer? Am I going crazy?

13.

Dr. Gillis has a last-minute cancellation this morning at his downtown office.

"I'll be there!" I tell the receptionist. "Nine fifteen."

I slide into Danny's car a few minutes later, and he hands me a cup of coffee. I stare at it, confused for a moment (I don't drink coffee), but one look at my disheveled pal in the driver's seat and the whole thing feels exactly, comically, right: a scene ripped straight from a detective show.

"What, no doughnuts?"

Danny slurps from his cup. "Next time," he says. "Next time."

His chin has more stubble than usual, and his eyes are smudgy shadows. Probably because we only got home a couple hours ago. Our adrenaline was pumping hard as we scurried down Walnut Street, away from that creepy-ass apartment. Neither of us could think about sleep. Danny moved his car up a few blocks, out of sight of Mrs. Rogeiro's building, and we turned on a light to examine the contents of the package I'd found.

The envelope itself was like the kind you'd see in the front office at school. Did the kidnapper have a day job?

We looked at the business card next. *Julie Donnelly, LCSW, South Shore Community Health Center.* I called the number and got a disconnected message. A quick Google search told us the center had closed last fall. No current listings for a social worker by that name.

The other items in the envelope were equally puzzling: a blank lined sheet pulled from a notebook, another with what looked like the beginnings of a letter, all crossed out, and then one torn out of some sort of pamphlet. Both sides of the last page were printed with tiny alphabetical names: Beth Santos through Adam Zuleski. The light on Danny's phone caught a faint mark next to one name: *Lara Tilsbury.* My fingers fumbled as I did a quick Google search. The only match that came up was an old lady in Arizona selling handcrafted gnomes.

"Maybe the last kids he abducted lived in Arizona?"

"Arizona in the eighties?"

"Making him the slowest serial kidnapper in history. No." I sighed. "There's something we're not getting."

Was it possible that the envelope belonged to someone who'd lived there earlier? I recently found a pair of underwear that had been wedged in my own bureau circa kindergarten. But no. Danny and I tossed out that theory right away. There was that photo, after all: two children, the girl roughly Ana's age and the boy in a matching bow tie—her brother, we decided.

We sat in Danny's car as the night faded to dawn, talking through the possibilities, each more far-fetched than the last—he was running a kidnapping ring with a band of renegade social workers; they sent each other trophies via interdepartmental mail; our perp wasn't a man at all, but an old lady who memorialized her victims in the faces of gnomes. We were no better than Mrs. Rogeiro's neighbors with their silly theories. None of what we knew added up.

"Should we bring this to the police?" I finally asked.

"And tell them we found it when we broke into a crime scene? On private property?"

I sighed. Yeah, that wouldn't work.

After some debate, we decided we'd hang on to the envelope for a day or two. By then, maybe we'd come up with a plan—a way to get the information to the police without getting ourselves arrested. In the meantime, we'd keep thinking.

Top of our list: figure out what a pervy kidnapper was doing with one of my sister's prayer cards. Ma had thousands of them printed, I explained to Danny, which would make it tough. They were mainly handed out at church events or on Sundays when people visited Tess. Was it possible the kidnapper had been to our house? Did he know Tess?

Not a comforting thought.

The conversation began to turn then. Pretty soon we weren't talking about the kidnapper anymore. We were talking about Tess. And then, just talking. About my mom and what must be driving her inane quest, and Danny's mom, who's always been a hard one to read. He told me that he worries he disappoints her.

We talked about how neither of us ever thought we'd be here, him with a crisp new diploma and no clue what comes next, me with no plans beyond this very moment. Just the thought of going back to school in a few weeks—and all of the work from last year that I still haven't done—makes my head hurt. The idea of a great big future without Tess is still inconceivable.

The longer Danny and I sat there, the faster the words tumbled out. It'd been four months since I'd talked—really *talked*—to someone. No. Longer than that. Because those last months were different. Tess was different. For a moment, I saw her pinched face, heard those terrible words I'd hurled—*You're selfish, Tess. Weak!*—before slamming the door. I quickly pushed it all back down, burying it under layers of sediment where it belonged.

Danny listened to me quietly, his cheek pressed against the headrest, eyes dark in morning shadows. It wasn't the same as talking to Tess. But it was something. It was . . . *nice.* We talked until the sun crept onto the horizon and we both realized what time it was. We sped back to beat Ma's alarm, talking the whole way. Like two old friends who did this all the time. It felt totally natural, nothing weird about it at all until that moment when we pulled up to my house and I placed my hand on the door, and then Danny leaned over, and I thought for a second—

No. It doesn't matter what I thought.

He unlocked the door for me, and as I stepped out onto the walk, I told him, "I'll call Dr. Gillis first thing, okay?"

I hadn't forgotten the deal we'd struck. Our trip to Walnut Street was just a detour, a wild idea—one that turned out to be pretty eventful—but it provided no clear next steps. We'd keep thinking about the envelope. In the meantime, we had an obvious move before us, one that might lead straight to the question of miracles. We had the name of the doctor who treated Ana Langone.

And that's how, barely three hours later, I find myself back in Danny's car, holding a hot cup of joe.

The truth: I don't actually *like* coffee (too bitter, hurts my stomach), but I'm not going to tell Danny that. It's the thought, right? As we make our way toward Main Street, I take a tentative sip, scalding my tongue. It's sweeter than I expected.

"French vanilla," Danny says. "Her favorite."

I rub my roughened tongue against my teeth. "It's good," I say, which isn't a total lie. I take deeper sips as it cools.

Danny, meanwhile, sets in with the questions. Did I give the receptionist my real name? Will I pretend to have a neurological disorder? Won't Dr. Gillis recognize me? How will I get him to talk about Ana?

Great questions, but the drive is short—there isn't time to talk through it all. We've arrived at the clinic before he's even touched on the bigger issue: how I'll figure out where the doctor stands on the miracle question—and what I'll say if Ma already has him on her side.

At the reception desk, I fill out the forms quickly, hand over my insurance card before I'm asked, and do my best to act like a normal, trustworthy person, despite the jitter in my hands. (Caffeine: terrible idea.) I sign a waiver that says a referral is being processed. The receptionist seems uncertain.

"My mom will be here any minute," I tell her. "She's finding parking." I give her my best smile.

I'm perched on the exam table when Dr. Gillis enters the room, head bent over a folder. Lines crisscross his forehead, and thinning gray hair flies up in a hundred directions.

"Miss da Costa, how can I help you?" The doctor squints, like he's only just making the connection. "You say you've been having headaches?" He checks his folder.

His voice is smooth, hard around the edges, not like someone from around here, even though he grew up right in the city.

"Really bad ones," I say, touching fingers to temples. A cool bead of sweat rolls down my side. The coffee was definitely not a good move.

My quivering fingers must be a convincing touch. The lines in the doctor's brow deepen. "Given your recent loss, that doesn't surprise me. Headaches are a common expression of emotional distress. Have you consulted your primary care physician?"

"I don't—" *Have a regular doctor,* I almost say. But there's no need to set off the alarm bells. My mother and her thing about doctors: It's too messy to explain.

"I wanted to talk to a specialist. I'm worried that I may have high blood pressure like my sister, and . . . uh . . . doesn't that put me at risk for an aneurysm?" Ugh. Really, Callie? An *aneurysm?*

"Who referred you here exactly?" Dr. Gillis consults his folder. "Let's see, the nurse who took your blood pressure just now found it to be normal. I don't think you have anything to worry about there. Miss da Costa, I'm not sure—"

"That's what killed my sister, though, isn't it? High blood pressure? Stress?"

The caffeine is zinging through me, and I can feel myself veering off course. But it's a question that's been eating at me. After Tess died, the doctors explained her heart condition—something called *hypertrophic cardiomyopathy*. (Unrelated to any hallucinations she may have experienced, they said. Tess was extremely unlucky, biologically speaking.) The doctors made it sound like there was nothing we could have done, which is exactly what you say when everyone's dumbstruck with grief. But I've spent time on WebMD. I know stress is a trigger for heart attacks and anyone paying attention would have seen Tess had more than her share of that.

Dr. Gillis closes the folder. "I didn't treat your sister, Miss da Costa, but I do know a bit about her condition. Sudden death is not uncommon. Any number of factors can bring on cardiac arrest. Something as minor as a steep set of stairs can be a trigger. Maybe if a doctor had caught it sooner, but even then . . . these things aren't always treatable. Your sister's heart was, in effect, doing double duty." He lowers his glasses and meets my eye. "I realize it's difficult to hear this, but it was truly only a matter of time. In a case like this, there's nothing anyone could have done."

Nothing? In the corner of the room, a machine lets out a soft bleat. For a second, I think the sound has come from me.

"Miss da Costa. It's hard enough to lose a loved one. Sometimes there is no explanation other than terrible, terrible luck."

The doctor removes his glasses and sighs into his fingers. When he looks at me again, the skin around his eyes has been bruised and stretched out of shape, irises the color of blue jeans washed into submission. In this moment I know that Dr. Gillis isn't the hard-hearted man Ma says he is. This is a man who knows grief from the inside.

I blink, break his gaze. It takes me a second to remember why I'm here. Speaking of kids with terrible luck . . . "Is it true that you treated Ana Langone? Have you heard what they're saying now? That it was my sister . . . that she . . ."

"They're saying she saved the child's life." Dr. Gillis replaces his glasses, and I stiffen.

"That's your medical opinion?"

"Oh. Well. Now. I wouldn't . . ." He clears his throat. "The child had a terrible fall. I can't go into details—doctor-patient confidentiality, you understand. Suffice it to say, we went to great lengths for her."

"Did you pray to my sister, Doctor?"

The pager at his waist beeps.

"Your sister was a very special young woman."

"Special? A couple years ago you told people she needed meds, that she was crazy."

The doctor's brows pull together. "I'm a physician. I have never used that term. The brain is a complex organ. Trauma, chemical imbalance, and genetics can all provoke unusual experiences, like your sister's. I made the mistake of offering medical background to the press, and my words were misconstrued."

"Misconstrued? Kids called Tess a *schizo* for months."

"I am truly sorry for that."

Maybe it's his expression as he says it, or those faded eyes, but somehow I believe him.

I shift forward, and the paper on the exam table crunches. "What if Tess wasn't the only one? What if she wasn't the only one in my family with what you call *unusual* experiences?"

I hadn't planned to ask this either, but the words are out now, too late to take back. It's a question that plagued Tess ever since she found those letters.

Dr. Gillis stoops, peering at me more closely. "Are you experiencing something unusual?"

I flatten my palms against the exam table. "No. No. Not me. I was just asking, uh, hypothetically."

"I'm not sure what you're trying to tell me, Miss da Costa. If there's something more than headaches troubling you, maybe we should take a look. I may want to run some tests." He pulls a pointed tool from a rack and I edge back against the wall.

"Really, the headaches aren't that serious. I'm sure you're right. I'm being paranoid."

Christ Almighty. I need to wrap this thing up before I blow it completely. The *miracle*. That's why I'm here.

"My mother's been telling people you're going to talk to reporters about Ana Langone, that you'll talk to the bishop's rep too. Is that true?"

Just this morning I awoke to another of her loud phone calls, Ma crowing the news to a friend: The doctor had confirmed, and *Newsline* bumped up its schedule. The Gillis interview clinched the story. He'd tell them Ana's recovery defied medical explanation. They'd take it from there to the Vatican.

Dr. Gillis replaces the tool on its hook. "She said *what* now?" His face has hardened, and the out-of-town veneer has slipped from his voice.

"I was surprised too," I say, sitting taller, thinking about what Danny learned from Mrs. Reynoso. "Because from what I hear,

Ana was only in a coma for a few hours, and the scans were incon-clusive. The reporters will probably ask about that, don't you think? Wouldn't you be putting your reputation on the line?"

Dr. Gillis's eyes narrow, like he's seeing me for the first time, seeing a different Callie. "I don't know where you heard any of this, but I'm not at liberty to speak on this subject."

"But you'll talk to *Newsline*? What'll you tell them? That you've never seen a patient make a surprise recovery?"

It's little convenient, if you ask me. Two years ago he's all about science. Now he's the grieving father come back into the Church's fold, using his degrees to certify a work of God.

If Ma is right about his intentions, that is. Judging by the look he's giving me right now, I'm not sure she is.

"I've seen many surprising things over the years and many ter-rible things as well. What happened the other night . . ." He runs a hand over his head, pressing his hair into place. He doesn't finish his sentence.

"Was it *miraculous*, Doctor?" Sarcasm clings to the word. I can't help it. "Is that what you'll tell the reporters? Don't you think people will be suspicious when they hear the details?"

The doctor's blue eyes have gone brittle. "If by details you mean privileged information you acquired from this hospital, you would be arrested. Your mother, or whoever shared that informa-tion, would be fired."

His *r*'s have fallen away completely. No more Mr. Fancy-Pants doctor. There's a quick throb in my skull, a sharp taste in my mouth. I hop down from the table, wiping my palms across my shorts.

"Okay, well. Thanks for your time, Doc. My headache doesn't feel half as bad as it did."

"So glad to hear it," he says drily. "Why don't I write you a prescription anyway? It's a treatment I'm sure your physician would approve."

I twitch, glance up. "You're, um, not going to tell my mother about this, are you?"

His blue eyes are unreadable. "I don't see any reason to involve her at this stage." He tears a page from the pad, smooth doctor voice returned. "So glad I could be of help."

I wait until he's gone before reading the prescription: *Drink plenty of fluids, get a good night's rest, and stay out of trouble.*

14.

It might not be bad advice," Danny says.

I ball Dr. Gillis's prescription up in my fist. My head hurts for real now, and my stomach isn't doing so great either. And now Danny's agreeing with the doctor? I follow him through the narrow passage to the parking garage, glaring daggers at his back. "Did you hear what he said he'd do to my mother? That he'd get her *fired*?"

"You did kind of threaten him—that thing about if he went on TV? And did you have to mention the X-rays and stuff? If Mrs. Reynoso gets in trouble over this, I'll feel like such an asshole."

"Maybe that's 'cause you're being an—" Danny holds the outer door open, and I stumble over an unmarked step. I turn to look up at him, glaring even harder. "I can't believe *she's* the one you're concerned about right now."

"Oh, believe me, I'm concerned about you too."

"You think I fucked up."

"I think when you let things get you too heated, you don't always make the best calls." He bites his lip. "What I mean is—"

My eyes narrow dangerously. "No, don't stop now. Go on. Tell me what you mean."

Danny's shoulder lifts, uncertain. "You do seem a little stressed?"

"Stressed? You think I seem *stressed*?" I step up until my chin is level with his chest. "If the only person who ever loved you was dead and being pimped out by your mother and the entire medical establishment was lining up to support her, DON'T YOU THINK YOU'D BE STRESSED TOO?"

My voice echoes across the low-ceilinged garage. Danny inches back, eyeing me the way you'd monitor an uncaged zoo animal, the kind that may bite. The parking attendants glance over at us, chuckling.

Lions and tigers and pissed-off girls, oh my.

I fumble with a loose bra strap, embarrassed at my sudden heat. Yes, I get worked up sometimes. Especially lately. There are worse flaws to have. But that thing I just said about the medical establishment didn't even make sense. God, what's wrong with me? After all that trouble, I still have no idea where Dr. Gillis stands on the miracle question. But that gauzy look on his face when he described Ana's recovery? Not a good sign. Not to mention the one he gave me as he tore off the prescription? Knowing my luck, I drove him straight into the arms of the miracle mongers.

And now here's Danny giving the play by play.

"You said we should be brave," I tell him in my best attempt at calm.

It's true. Last night, after the adrenaline subsided, Danny said he admired my courage. He said he always let so many things stop him—school, teachers, his family. He told me how after his dad left, his mother told Danny her marriage was the biggest mistake she ever made, a complete fracaso. Danny told me that ever since then he wanted to be the opposite of his old man. He wasn't doing too great at it, terrible grades and more weed than homework, but then he got put in Tess's homeroom last September and found himself going to school every day just to see her. Things started to change.

"I don't know why she was so nice to me," he told me. "It was like she saw something in me that nobody else did. I just—I don't know—the way she looked at me made me think I *could* be better. Like, if I tried hard enough, I could be the type of guy a girl like her could be proud to call her boyfriend."

Danny got a little hoarse on the last part and I couldn't be sure in the darkened car, but I thought I saw a shiny thread glistening down his cheek. "It's all I've wanted since," he told me. "To make Tess proud. To be that guy. The one she believed I could be."

I really felt for him too. I knew exactly what he was talking about: that superpower my sister had, her ability to see the best in everyone she loved. I understood, too, why that feeling would make him want to do right by her now, to stand up for her memory. Which is why I'm so confused to see him giving up just a few hours later.

"You said we needed to stand up for her, that we shouldn't let anything stop us," I remind him.

Danny sighs. "And I meant it, Cal. But we gotta be smart how we approach things. There's bravery and then there's . . ." He pauses, looking for a safe way to put it.

"Being stupid," I say. "Reckless."

He lifts his brows. A gentle, almost imperceptible yes.

When we finally open the car doors, we're hit with the reek of sweat and stale coffee. Danny tosses the cups and opens the windows, muttering something about the AC being busted. We head south along Main Street, away from the water. The sky is overcast. Empty warehouses loom large, menacing, against the darkening clouds. My hands have stopped shaking, but my stomach's gone sour and my head hurts more with each second.

Danny spins the radio dial past droning newscasters and discount-furniture ads, landing on one of those bland pop stations no one would ever choose on purpose. The singer wants to start over, do things right this time. I pinch my achy forehead, thinking he should start with a different career.

I hate that Danny can just sit there, tapping his chewed-up thumbs, when I feel like we're caught in a trap: Every path ends in a brick wall. More than that, I hate that Danny's probably right. If I hadn't let myself get so worked up—if I hadn't gone in there alone, reckless, without a real plan—maybe we could have squeezed more information out of Dr. Gillis. Instead, he sent me packing, like a naughty little girl. *Stay out of trouble.* As if trouble asks permission before shoving its way into your life.

"Our grandmother heard things too. Did Tess tell you?"

(Speaking of topics I completely bungled in there.)

Danny turns down the radio, a crease in his brow. "She heard voices?"

"Not sure if it was exactly like Tess, just that she ended up in a psych ward."

I didn't tell Tess at the time, but the letters she found didn't really surprise me. I'd always sensed there was something different about Grandma. Or maybe there was something different about how others spoke about her, how Ma and Wendy always hushed up whenever her name was mentioned, like saying it aloud would cause too much pain.

Danny listens as I tell him about the letters.

"This was in February? As in, a few months ago February?"

I nod. "I remember because she ate a whole bag of Valentine's candy that night and made herself sick."

Danny's lashes flutter strangely. "Have you told anyone else?"

"Of course not."

Although I'm starting to wonder if maybe we should. Tess would hate it, of course. She was supersensitive about the mental illness question. (Not surprising, considering what people said about her at school. And really, who wants to think their mind is broken?) As for Ma, she'd—well, I don't know what she'd do if I told. That would pass any line we've crossed before. Even the slap.

I press my thumbs into my temples to quiet their pulse. *What's wrong with you,* she asked the other night, like she no longer knew me. I massage my head, wishing I had an answer.

Danny's giving me that look again, the zoo animal one. "You don't hear . . . I mean, you aren't—"

I drop my hands. "Jesus, Danny. No! I'm not *mentally ill.* I'm just having a crappy day." A terrible year. Also, my mouth tastes foul, like a French vanilla rat died in the back of my throat. "I do not and have not ever heard the voice of God. Or the voice of anyone who was not right in front of me. I'm not anything like Tess, if you haven't noticed. I'm not nice like her, or pretty like her, and I don't give a fuck about other people's problems."

Danny's quiet for a long moment. The radio whines softly. "You don't really think all that, do you?"

I scrape the bitter coating from my teeth, feel his eyes flick toward me.

"You're not a bad person, Callie." His voice is gentle, and I snort.

"Sure, okay." I don't know what he wants me to say. I didn't ask him to blow smoke up my ass. I just miss her is all. Miss her so much it feels like my chest's cleaved in two.

"I mean it, Cal. I'm not bullshitting you. You have a lot going for you. You're smart and funny and not exactly bad looking either."

"Wait. What?" I turn to look at Danny.

His focus snaps back to the road. "I just mean . . . I don't know . . . just maybe you don't have to be so down on yourself. Maybe if you look around, you'll find . . ."

"What? What will I find, Danny? A nice boy to love and protect me?"

I stare at my friend—that broad nose and sensitive mouth, puckered with worry, two solid arms gripping the wheel—and a thought knocks against my ribs. A picture, really: of a future Danny with a future wife, a boxy little house and a family all his own. He'll be the devoted dad his own father wasn't. It doesn't take a special gift to see it. A boy like Danny will find love again, no question.

And no matter how many months or years go by, I'll never have another sister.

Danny is still blathering, trying to make me feel better, but it's only getting weirder the harder he tries, and then it takes an extra-uncomfortable turn as he wonders why in all the time he's known me I've never once had a boyfriend or even shown interest in any of the guys we know, how my life might be better if I just—

It's too much. *I've never shown interest?* What an idiot. What a total, clueless prick.

"You think I need a boyfriend, Danny? Is that what you're trying to say? You think I'm a sad, broken girl and all I need is some guy to come along and fix me?"

"No, that's not at all what I—" His chin wavers. "I just meant you might be happier if . . . You might not feel so . . ." He dares a glance. "Forget it. I don't know what I'm saying."

"No," I say. "You don't."

This would be a perfect moment to turn up the radio, tell a joke. That's what Tess would do. But it's too late. The heat is already building, clouds of steam gathering in my veins. *Stay out of trouble, Callie. It's not your fault, Callie. What's wrong with you, Callie.* Outside, the sky has gone almost black.

"Is that how it was with you and my sister? You were feeling bad about yourself and there she was? She made you feel like less of a loser?"

Danny's hand fumbles on the wheel. "No. What—"

I turn to face him. "I'm right, though, aren't I? You were just like the rest of them. Using my sister to feel better about their shitty little lives."

The car slows. Danny's eyes are darker than I've ever seen them, practically opaque. "You think I used Tess?"

I stare back—at his messy jeans and terrible haircut, at this precious little shitbox of a car—and the truth lands like a brick. I don't have to say anything else. He reads it in my eyes.

We pull up to his house in silence. Thunder rumbles in the distance, and the air is a blanket of moist heat. Danny peers through the windshield at the gathering clouds. My head's a swirl of sharp, pointy feelings. Anger, shame, regret. Part of me wants to take it back—the thing I didn't quite say—but the rest wants Danny to feel exactly as terrible as I do. Just as alone. Just as unloved.

Our friends pounce as soon as we open the car doors, hitting us with questions about where we've been and why Danny hasn't answered his cousin's five hundred texts.

Danny mutters something about a doctor's appointment, errands. His face is a map of hurt. I realize I never told him what Dr. Gillis said about Tess's heart, not that it matters now.

The sky threatens. Karen sidles over as we move toward the house. (Today's t-shirt reads: *I see dumb people*.)

"So?" she says.

"So what?"

"Is this the gran secreto?"

"What?" I look at my friend: With her thick black hair and toasted brown skin, she's a smaller, sleeker version of Danny, his opposite in personality. Are we really still stuck on the secret thing? In addition to being persistent as fuck, Karen has the worst timing of anyone I know.

"C'mon, Cal. It's time to spill the habichuelas."

"What are you even talking about?" Pain pierces my skull.

"The beans, Callie. The beans." She slings a skinny arm through mine and lowers her voice to a whisper. "So you and the D Man, eh? Hot little fling? Or is it somethin' more?"

"Oh my God. *No*." I pull my arm back. If she had any idea, at all, what she was saying . . .

"Always knew there was a reason he didn't show much interest in girls. I figured either he was the dirtiest-looking gay boy I'd ever seen or he had a girl on the sly. Well, now we know." She looks me up and down, assessing. "I guess ol' Danny boy coulda done worse."

She says the last part at full volume, and I feel the others turn. Amanda with her glossy pout, Carlos already looking halfway hammered, and Danny with those eyes. God, those eyes! Two bottomless wells. Really, Karen couldn't have picked a more awful moment for this crap.

Carlos reaches for Danny, gripping him in a headlock. "Cabrón, how could you keep that shit from me?"

Amanda giggles, all trembling blond highlights.

"He didn't," I say. "It's not what you . . ."

I wait for Danny to speak up, defend himself, but he's too busy staring at the ground, the fight knocked out of him.

Karen bumps me with a boney elbow. "You gotta go easy on my primo, Callie. He's a Taurus, you know. Superloyal, muy sensitive. Perfect for a—"

"Karen, you have no idea. Don't—"

"—prickly little Scorpio like you."

Thunder cracks, and I step back from all of them. I have a sudden urge to vomit.

"What the hell, Karen? Why are you like this? Why can't you learn when to shut up?"

My voice has gone into a special register, one that Tess called *hysterical cavewoman*. My blood churns hot against my skin. I see it from their eyes: how wild I must look, fists pumping, hair sprung wild by the coming storm. But it's too late. The valve has come off.

"God, you're all idiots. I don't even know why I come over here anymore. What's the point? We never do anything. It's always the same bullshit. Don't you have lives? Don't you have anything better to do?"

It's low. Mean. (Of course they don't have anything better. I don't either.) But low and mean is what I feel right now. Low and mean is what I am as I spin away from my sorry-ass "friends" and head toward the street.

None of them tries to make me stay.

A car honks as I step off the sidewalk. I move out of the way as a second one comes whipping down the street, tires squealing. It disappears down the hill as the first few raindrops splatter the ground.

I hurry toward the main road and, on a corner by the supermarket, another shrine appears. Fresh bowls of candy, cheerful daisies, a pair of tiny shoes. Fat drops splash into hissing candles, and light and shadow play across her uneven smile. The girl everyone loves and none of them really knows.

I grab her and smash the rest to pieces.

From the Journal
of
Tess da Costa

February 14

Thirteen days since Ana disappeared, and the same four messages rotate on repeat, like a sad song my head just can't shake.

INTO DARKNESS COMES THE LIGHT.

SHE RESTS ON A PILLOW OF STONE.

HOME IS NEAR.

THE SAVIOR CANNOT PROTECT.

I take the lines apart, juice each word for meaning. I even swap them around to see what happens: INTO LIGHT COMES DARKNESS. THE PROTECTOR CANNOT REST.

Ack. Even more depressing.

Rudy licks my face, tells me not to worry. But, silly pup, how can I not worry? A child is missing, and I may be the only one with a clue where she's gone. Either that or—

I spin the words round and round, trying to hear them in a way that doesn't mean (a) I'm crazy like Grandma or (b) Ana Langone is dead.

Because that's what it sounds like, right? A pillow of stone? The light?

And yet . . . somehow . . . there's something else—not words, exactly—telling me that Ana is still out there, waiting to be found.

Where is the question.

I keep listening, scanning my body for some other sign, for one of those feelings I sometimes get, and give up in frustration. This sense I've been blessed with—or cursed with? (still can't decide)—came with terrible GPS. If I'm really God's instrument, then I must be the knockoff clearance-bin version. In other words: useless.

More and more, I'm wondering if the answer is more straightforward, five simple letters spelled out right before my eyes: C-R-A-Z-Y.

I wish I was braver, stronger, and could look those letters in the face. But it's scary, all right? I don't want to be put in a hospital or become an old lady who mumbles to pigeons in the park. I don't want Ma to be sad when she sees me, or D to turn from me in disgust.

Because that's what will happen, I know it. They'll say they still love me, but I'll know the truth. They'll see me differently. In their eyes, I'll no longer be Tess.

On Thursday D brings a bright red rose to school and a box of Milk Duds, sneaking them to me by my locker. He's hoping for a smile, and I do what I can, but my teeth feel too square, my face creaky and stiff. He touches my shoulder, worried, but I stop him 'cause it's school. People will see.

Later, we sit alone in his basement, popping candies until caramel glues our jaws shut. This is where Callie spends most afternoons, coming and going as she pleases, hanging out with whatever people she chooses. I'm not angry about it, or jealous. I mean, Callie should have choices. I'm glad my little sister can have a mostly normal life, and I'm grateful for days like today when she offers cover so I can spend time with D.

I pick candy from my teeth and think about how grateful I am. How really, truly grateful.

Tess, are you okay?

D strokes my hair. Can I do anything? he asks, his forehead smooshed up like a teddy bear's. He is literally the sweetest boy that ever was, sweeter, even, than a jumbo box of candy. Too sweet, sometimes. But I can't blame him for that. Can't blame him for days like today when even my favorite candy turns sour the second it hits my tongue.

I unlock my jaws from the last bit of goo and answer his question with a kiss. It's a big kiss. A tackle, almost. D laughs and tackles me back.

And then we're kissing, and it's almost as good as the first time last fall. No, it's better. Because I'm not shy anymore. It doesn't mortify me when my body arcs up, pushing against his. Or when I let out a strange sound, like a small animal's cry.

When I accidentally bite him, on purpose.

D speaks low in my ear, asks me do I want to stop.

No, I never want it to stop, I tell him. I want it to go on and on and on. I want it to be like this every single second. I want his lips right there, his hands just like that, his shoulders caught in my grip. My head: blinked-out bliss. I know how selfish I am, how completely, totally greedy. Savage. I know I should be worried about something right now—what was that thing?—but then my shirt slips off my body, and his follows it to the floor. There is more kissing, more tackling, more warm breath in my ear.

And more besides.

After, he touches my hair. You didn't answer my question, he says.
Which one was that? I turn my face to his so our noses touch.
Are you okay?

I look away from those velvet eyes, let my fingers walk down his chin, throat, collarbone, that silky chest, landing on his tickle spot. He responds with a blast of laughter.

I'm terrific, I tell him.

He looks at me, the devil in his eyes. You are. You're magnificent.

Yup.

A true master.

I giggle.

He lifts himself up on his elbow, wicked grin. I wonder how many saints have done what you just did?

I sit up too, and the carpet rubs raw at my elbows. It's a good question. A great question. I reach for my sweater.

You can't tell anyone, I say. About this, us.

His gaze falls to the carpet.

Did you hear me? I say. Not one person. Ever.

He nods. I heard.

You have to promise me, I say, collecting my things from the floor, untangling straps and underwire. They'd hate you if they knew. They'd hate me.

I wouldn't be their little saint anymore. I'd be the butt of their jokes, the end point of their fears. I don't say that last part out loud, though, or mention the other thought that's rattling around. About other girls who heard voices. One minute a savior; the next, burned at the stake.

No one can know, I tell Danny. <u>Promise me.</u>

My long-limbed boy curls on the rug, quiet, like a used-up rag that's been wrung out and flattened.

I promise, he tells me. No one will ever know.

15.

Back at home, cooking smells drift from the surrounding apartments. The streetlamps have come on early, fighting off the gathering darkness. One light is still out, a white utility van tucked in its shadow. Someone must have finally called in the repair.

Rudy appears, snapping at the raindrops. He noses the frames in my hand, the tiny cut on my wrist. From the corner of my eye, I think I see a shadow, moving in the darkness at the far end of the driveway. I stiffen, clutching the frames tighter. But there's no other motion, no sound except for Rudy's happy snuffle. I edge forward cautiously and, when I reach the base of the driveway, kick the shed door open with one foot.

Silence. Darkness.

Raindrops splat gently on my face.

I slip inside the dry shelter, Rudy at my heel, and flick on the lamp. Rudy lifts his tail, inspecting as I place the newest photos on the ridge beside the others. Seven in all. Our collection is growing.

I lean down to scrub his head, finding that place Tess showed me where his scruff turns to silk. *It's not stealing,* I consider telling him, *she belongs to you and me,* but the way Rudy gazes up at me, with those enormous brown eyes, I realize I don't need to say a thing.

This dog already understands. Everything.

Ma's on the phone when I get upstairs, her voice pitched with worry. "He won't do it? Why not?"

She glimpses me in the kitchen doorway, hair soaked from the rain, and pulls the phone away from her ear for half a beat. She points to a covered dish on the table.

"Yes, I understand that part," she says into the phone. "But we weren't even asking him to do that." She pinches the bridge of her nose and sighs.

Ever so casually, like I'm not even listening, I scoot over to the table and lift the plate covering my dish. The scent rushes up before I can prepare myself. Feijoada. Heaven in a bowl.

I sink into the nearest chair. The stew is loaded with tender bits of meat and red beans, the way my grandfather made it. "Food for the heart," he'd say, smacking his lips. "Whatever ails you, take one bite and you'll be healed."

Vovô was a wise man. Too wise, maybe. (*A wiseass,* some said.) Always concerned with discovering the truth of things: the Church, the government, our nation's history. He put facts first, consequences later, asked questions that made people squirm. I used to want to be just like him when I grew up, before I realized that most people, including Ma, found him irritating.

If Vovô were alive to hear about this sainthood mess, I can only imagine the stink he'd raise. Four years, he's been gone. But a presence like his doesn't just disappear. When I close my eyes, I can still hear him railing. When I place a spoonful of feijoada on my tongue, the ache in my chest dissolves almost immediately.

I peek across the table to the counter and, sure enough, Ma bought pastéis de nata too, the creamy little desserts I loved as a kid. That I still love, if we're being honest. If marrying pastries were legal, that's the one I'd choose.

Ma is making an effort, I realize. She's trying to patch up the last couple days with an age-old ploy: food. Can a rift as big as ours be fixed so easily? I decide I don't care. I'm exhausted, rage supply down to zero. Right now I'll take every bit of comfort I can get.

Ma hangs up the phone. "It's good?"

She comes to my side and places a hand on my head. I'm tempted to lean back against her hip. I want her to pull me close, tell me it's all been a bad dream—these past four months, these past two years—that I'm still the girl she loves to pieces, that she's still the unshakable mama who'd do anything to keep her girls safe, that Tess will be home any minute.

Ma's fingers tug gently at my hair. It feels good and for a moment, I let myself forget all that's passed between us.

Then, "You've got to let me take you to the salon, Cal. You're starting to look like something a boat dragged up from the harbor."

Sigh. So much for that. I pull my chair forward and glance up to see Ma bite her lip. She sees her misstep. Too late. (It cuts both ways, disappointment. Back and forth, over and over again.)

She takes the chair opposite mine, watching as I eat. The pit at my center feels bottomless.

Ma's cleared a space for Tess. She hasn't gone so far as to set out a plate, but she might as well have. Tess is just as present as Vovô. A different feeling, not as comforting. Hers is more like a giant void, a wind tunnel that sucks the words from the air around us.

A minute goes by, then two. No sounds but the canned laughter from a TV on the second floor and rain pattering above. The scrape of my spoon hitting bottom. One of Ma's hands slowly rubs the other.

"Ma? What is it?"

She sighs. "Dr. Gillis canceled his meeting with the bishop's rep and with *Newsline* too. He won't tell anyone why."

Beneath the table, my feet bounce up in surprise.

"He *did*?" I hope she doesn't hear the squeak or catch the smile that cuts quick before I can stop it. *Dr. Gillis is backing down. Because of me.*

Ma kneads her knuckles. "It doesn't make sense. Just yesterday he said he'd be glad to talk. He told me himself that Ana Langone was brain-dead when he first examined her, that he had no hope for recovery. A cut-and-dried case. That's what he planned to tell the bishop. Now he has his interns pulling her charts and won't say a thing."

I should do a victory dance. I should run to call Danny. (Would he even pick up? Would he forgive me if he knew?) I want to feel the wash of relief. We did it! We took down a miracle! But as I watch Ma rub harder at her own hands, I realize once again that things are never as simple as they seem.

"It must be the other doctors who got to him," Ma says. "They've been saying things, acting like they're above God with their fancy degrees."

She's a reverse snob, Ma. Educated people have always made her suspicious. I wonder sometimes if that's a part of our struggle. She was proud of me when I was little, reading a year ahead (thanks to Tess) and doing long division as a party trick. But a twelve-year-old who joins the city math league, a fourteen-year-old who's begun talking about out-of-state colleges—I guess that's not as cute. It was like, in Ma's eyes, I'd become some sort of alien.

It looks like neither of us has to worry about that anymore, not with the grades I got last year. I can't blame Tess's death for it either. My grades were already slipping before the end-of-year plummet. I'd been cutting classes with Karen for months, skipping homework, forgetting to study for tests. I can't explain what caused the change in me exactly. It was like all of the effort Tess put into being this saintly role model caused an equal and opposite reaction in me. Stupid, I know.

"The truth is, I feel sorry for the man." Ma's still talking about Gillis. "He's felt so helpless since his boy died. He told me he'd stopped believing in God. People don't get what a big deal it is, what it means to people like us when something good happens for a change."

"So you and Dr. Gillis are friends now?"

"We talk occasionally. He angered me in the past, but I realized that if Jesus could forgive Judas . . ."

I lay my spoon flat. I didn't know Ma had reached the *What would Jesus do* stage of things. I didn't know Catholics even had that stage.

And if she's forgiven two archenemies, I have to wonder: "Does this mean you forgive Aunt Wendy too?"

A vein pops on Ma's temple. "That's really none of your business, Callie."

She unfolds a napkin to announce end of discussion. But I want to know more. What could have been so bad to split apart two siblings? Best friends since childhood? I have my guesses. Aunt Wendy slipped out of our lives right around the time things really got going with Tess. There are still hushed phone calls sometimes—Tess intercepted at least one. But we haven't seen her, or had a holiday together, in almost two years.

"Did you two fight because of Tess? Because she heard voices like Grandma? That's why they put Grandma in a psych ward, isn't it?"

Ma nearly knocks over her glass.

"Don't ask how I know. I just do. It's my family too, Ma. I deserve to know."

Ma studies my face for a long moment. Then, as if making a big decision, she slides over to Tess's chair. "This is only for your ears, de acordo?"

I nod.

"All they'd need is a hint." She pinches her fingers to show how tiny the hint. "If we thought those reporters were nasty before, it's only going to get worse from here on out. Now that there's a miracle in the mix, Father M says they'll be asking all types of questions."

"Ma, I get it. I won't tell."

She sits back, studies me another second before releasing a breath. "It was different with your grandmother. She sensed things sometimes. *Saw* them is the way she described it."

"Like, the future?"

Ma raises one palm. "Who really knows? She was embarrassed is all I know. People were very narrow-minded where she came from. They used to say things."

"Did they say she was crazy?" Suddenly Ma's aversion to the word makes sense.

"That. Yes. And some of the old-time folks said she was a bruxa. Can you imagine being a young girl and everyone in town thinks you're a witch?"

"Or a saint," I say quietly, but Ma isn't listening.

"It was her own decision to go to the hospital. She could be very strong willed. Your vovô always said he loved her the way she was, but he wanted her to be happy too. She was never happy, not before and certainly not after. We told people she was going back to Portugal to care for a sick relative. Even her closest friends never knew the truth. Your grandfather always regretted letting her go, I think."

"Why? What happened?"

Ma rubs her nose. Her chest rises. "She was different when she came home. The meds sucked the life right out of her. I never thought I'd miss all the ways she used to get on my case, but . . ." Ma's voice catches.

"That's why you didn't want Tess to see a doctor."

A hundred emotions flit across Ma's face. Pain, sorrow, maybe a tinge of guilt. Does she blame herself for what happened? Does she think Tess might be here now if a doctor had seen her sooner? Even though Dr. Gillis said the heart attack was inevitable, I have to wonder what might have happened if we'd caught on sooner and gotten Tess help.

"And that's why you and Wendy fought? Because she wanted to bring Tess to a doctor and you didn't."

Ma nods. "Wendy saw everything that happened to your grandmother differently. She can be such a pill when she thinks she's right. But you have to understand: Our mother wasn't sick. She just wasn't like us. Doctors made her problems so much worse." Ma bites her lip. "You understand why I did what I did, don't you? I couldn't let the same thing happen to Tess. I had to protect her."

For the first time, yes, I understand. Maybe not everything, maybe not entirely, but it's a start. And even though it has nothing to do with anything, I like knowing that Grandma got on Ma's case sometimes too. It seems important, somehow.

"No one else knows? Just you and Wendy?"

"And Lena Reynoso. I went to her for advice early on. She worked the psych floor and knows what they do to people up there. We can trust her to stay quiet."

I raise a brow. Can we?

"Anyway." Ma moves back to her chair and begins to eat. "Thank God the Langone girl isn't the only claim we've got."

A sip of water sticks in my throat. "There are more?"

"Mmm. Hundreds, probably." Ma licks her spoon, like this isn't a huge revelation. "We'll keep trying with Ana, of course. Who knows, Dr. Gillis may still come around. But if he doesn't, well, we need to have some others in the pipeline. That's what Father

Macedo says. It'll happen. He's only beginning to get through the mail. More letters and emails come in every day—word's really spreading now. It'll take some time to sort out what's what."

I push the last bits of food around my bowl, digesting this new information. Emails? Letters? Ma's never mentioned any of this before, but now as I listen to her, the enormity of the situation hits me: Ana Langone is only the beginning. These people will keep trying until they find a miracle that sticks.

Or until someone does something to stop it.

Ma checks the clock. "Mind if I turn on the news?"

She points the clicker toward the counter, and a young-ish reporter appears, yammering brightly about violence and vandalism on the rise, blahdy blah. She stands on a corner near Stop & Shop, eyeing the boys in their hoodies and the girls in bright-colored tops, beaming because she doesn't have to live here. To her, New Avon is exotic, practically the third world—the stuff news is made of.

It makes no sense—I hate this place too—but when someone like her casts a snooty eye, it makes my skin itch.

I lift my glass to my lips and, as I do, Reporter Barbie says something I'm not expecting. Water shoots back into my lungs. *They've dubbed the perpetrator the Shrine Smasher,* she says, point-ing cheerfully to a pile of mangled flowers.

I cough, liquid burning in my chest.

Ma turns up the volume.

It's at least the fourth attack in two days, and the damage appears to be escalating. Many are wondering what it all means. The attacks have been too targeted to fit the profile of typical vandalism, police say.

Some wonder if the Shrine Smasher is trying to send a coded threat to the followers of the recently deceased Teresa da Costa.

I cough more forcefully, gasping for air. Ma stares at the screen in shock.

New Avon police have asked us to remind everyone that destruction of public property is a crime, one that carries a stiff fine, if not ja—

A burst of rain slams against the open window, drowning out the rest.

Ma and I jump up as a wet gust blows through the kitchen. I reach across the sink and slam the window shut while Ma runs for the bedrooms. The TV blares loud, gone to commercials. *Do you struggle with depression? Lack of energy? Ask your doctor if—*

I press the power button, and the apartment goes quiet, no sound but the rain beating against the glass. In the other room, a window slams shut, then another, one more, and the two of us are sealed inside. A wanted criminal and her miracle-peddling mother.

What would Jesus do with this, I wonder.

The girl's grandmother is different lately. Quieter. Always watching: the news, the door, her child. She seldom laughs and never sings. Instead she trembles, checks the locks.

The girl knows a lot about locks. She's studied them, understands their principles. On this door, they're set on the inside. Much easier that way. When her grandmother's in the kitchen, the girl tests them. Right, left. Click, clunk. Satisfying plunk of metal on metal. On the street outside, children scream with laughter.

Her grandmother returns to the living room, wilted and slow. "What're you doing, love?" She pulls the girl to her lap, taps her small toes.

The girl is quiet.

This time, she's ready. Her escape: prepared. When the moment comes—that sharp stab of panic foretelling worse to come—she knows what she'll do. Last time, she flew. Next time, she'll run. Until then, she'll sit calmly in her grandmother's lap while together, they watch the front door.

16.

It's still raining when I go to bed. My head swirls with a thousand uncooked thoughts. I want to sort it all out before I let my eyes close, lift each question from the pot, brush it off, and find its solution. The photos we found (Who were those kids?), the kidnapper (Did he know Tess?), the shrines (What in God's name was I thinking? Are they really talking jail time?), not to mention that thing I said to Danny . . .

Each time I reach for an answer, it skitters away, slipping through my fingers. My mind tries again, clamoring to hold on to a single lucid thought.

In the end, exhaustion wins.

A dream I know well: I'm sitting at a desk, sophomore history, classroom full of idiots, teacher up at the board droning on about something. Occupation. Annexation. Manifest Destiny. The clock has stopped moving.

On the other side of the smudgy windows, pavement stretches cracked and pitted, dark zigzags of black tar struggling to hold it all together. Two birds hop across the uneven surface, beaks bobbing at a puddle, testing its thin shell of ice. They are ordinary brown things, bursting with fragile energy. They peck at the cracks in the asphalt, seeking green in the still-frozen ground. They're determined, focused. They don't look up even as an ambulance pulls quietly into the lot.

At the back of my mind, a warning bell pings. But my eyes stay on the birds. An ambulance? Just another fight gone nasty, I think. Just another doped-up freshman scraped off the girls' bathroom floor. Just another Tuesday at New Avon High.

The yellow lights whirl.

The teacher is going on about somebody's doctrine. Time passes. So slowly, it passes. Then, someone—the nurse, or maybe it's the guidance counselor—is at the classroom door.

"Your sister," he says.

He has to say it several times before I understand. When the words finally click into place, I'm out of my seat, running. The bell rings and students pour into the hallway. I search for an opening, a small break that'll allow me to join their current, but the bodies whip past. Mrs. Reynoso in hospital scrubs, giggling. Captain Barros appears next, lifting his cap. Then Dr. Gillis, his right hand making the sign of the cross. I watch an entire city drift by. Old, young, short, weeping, a hundred shades of flesh. For a second, I think I see Vovô, his clear eyes set on the horizon, and beside him, a small, birdlike woman, but they're gone as quickly as they arrive. Ma appears, her head turned upstream. She doesn't see me. I call out, but she can't hear me either.

Then, a pair of familiar eyes: dark brown with hints of caramel. He beckons. I step out into the current, fighting against the pressure, trying to get upstream, toward Danny—and Tess—but the river pulls in the wrong direction. The bodies begin to congeal, a wall of bone and muscle and grit. I push and kick, but they only tighten their grip. Crushing. Squeezing. Taking my breath—

Rrrrup! The crowd breaks in a great burst.

I'm left with feet planted on pavement. No strangers. No Danny. Just a flash of color and a faint wail in the distance. The parking lot is an ocean, water stretching as far as the eye can see. If I try to cross it, I'll drown. And if I don't—

My sneakers are off before the thought's complete. My fingers hit the icy water and I gasp.

The next moment I'm sitting—on my bed—eyes wide in the dark. Ocean: gone. No birds, no more whirling lights. There is real sweat on my body, though, a real ache in my legs, a wild energy in my chest. My heart pounds so loud I can hear it.

No, that's the rain, coming down heavy now, beating against my window. I shiver, pull the damp sheet up to my shoulders. It was just a nightmare, I tell myself. A dream.

"It was just a dream," I say, aloud, in case you were worried. In case I whimpered in my sleep, as I sometimes do.

I turn, and your empty pillow stares back at me.

For a long moment, the dots fail to connect. One nightmare

enmeshed with another. But no. One of them's real. Reality hits then: blankets heavy as concrete, the sea rushing up to my throat. Grief rips through me, as fresh as the first time, leaving me flat on the bed, heaving.

After the worst has passed, I pull myself upright, wait for my insides to settle before placing my feet on the floor. I shuffle over to your bureau, find my reflection in the shadowy glass. I look less like you than ever. Cheeks pinched, nose too sharp, eyes scooped out and hollow. Hair like something dragged up from the sewer.

The girl in the mirror barely even looks like *me*, I realize. She's so small standing there, her shoulders narrow and breastbone fragile. One push and you could topple her. If I didn't know any better, I'd think she was the kind of girl who is easily undone.

Before I can think, my hand grabs for your pencil jar, fumbling through plastic pens and rulers until my hand closes on metal. The scissors open with a scrape. One slice, and the first snarl drops to the floor.

From the Journal
of
Tess da Costa

February 16

D's been acting funny since Valentine's Day. Not ignoring me, exactly, but the fizz has gone out of his smile, the pep from his step. Yesterday as he passed me in the hall, even his jeans looked depressed. I had an urge to leap into his arms, declare my love with trumpets, bonk him on the head with bucketsful of roses—use every gesture ever invented to bring my boy back to life.

Except, of course, I couldn't do any of those things. Because: school. Because: gossip. Because: if people knew . . .

What he . . . What we . . .

How many saints have done what we do?

D meant it as a joke, obviously. He didn't think I'd go home and look up the sex lives of saints (surprise! the ones with steamy backstories were born with man parts). He didn't think I'd make a list of every public shaming in recent memory either—every idol dragged through the muck as soon as their sins emerged. And look, I'm not saying I'm like Lindsay Lohan or that sext-happy congressman, but there are plenty of others closer to home. For example: Marcela Brandao, Portuguese Princess two years running and everyone's favorite girl till she had too many sips of poncha at the parade after-party and was found dancing topless on the autoworkers' float. People heckled Marcela so badly afterward she had to quit cheerleading and eventually left school completely. These days, she can be found down by the bus depot, one of the dead-eyed girls everyone pretends don't exist.

How's that for terrifying.

The thing is, I'd probably still be the good little virgin they all wish I was if no one had messed around with the homerooms this year. It started out so innocently. Girl sits in her alphabetically assigned seat, turns around expecting Valerie Dionne, discovers a cute boy instead. See? Not my fault.

I knew a little about D from Callie, but she never told me how, up close, his brown eyes are shot through with amber. She definitely never warned me how they'd light up when I said a flustered hello. How I'd feel a pair of bright spots burning in me for hours afterward.

It still happens. Every time D looks at me that way, I lose a piece of my mind and, lately, articles of clothing. (I really feel for Marcela now!) The worst part is, I can't talk to anyone about it. I don't trust any of the girls at school, even the semi-nice ones. And forget Callie: She gets squirmy whenever I mention D. She's good for many things but boy talk isn't one of them. As for Ma? Can you imagine?!

Even if I could talk to Ma about D, she's got enough on her mind lately. This week it's a possible coup at church. A new group of ladies has arrived on the scene, wanting to run the vigil for Ana. They call themselves the Mothers of the Lost Children, and they told Ma that if she had ever lost a child, she would understand: Tulips are definitely the way to go.

Either they missed the memo about Ma being boss of all things floral, or they don't care. Ma gave in on the tulips—how can you argue with a bunch of grieving mothers?—but last night, while I helped her with dinner, she pointed out that none of these women had <u>lost</u> a child either, so what do they know? Their children were not missing, like Maxine Langone's. Theirs were dead and, in the case of Marisol Jenkins, in prison.

Not the most solid argument. Even she could see.

Of course, the real thing that has her in a tizzy is that the MOLC didn't pick me as their patron. I tried pointing out the logic: Saint Anthony is an actual saint who has been successfully finding lost things for a <u>very</u> long time, whereas my track record is rather spotty.

Details! Ma said, waving the carrot peeler.

But what if it's more than that, I said. What if I'm not really . . . I couldn't say it.

Ma looked at me for a long second. I'd never come that close to asking. It caught us both by surprise. My opening was there to ask the next question, the one that must be on her mind too: Ma, do you think I'm crazy? But I couldn't bring the words to my lips, and she was waving it off moments later, reaching for the lettuce, telling me not to let those ladies—those <u>traitors</u>—get into my head. She'd make them see: Saint Anthony is for those lacking conviction! Lilies are far more poignant!

This morning Ma's up early, bustling around in the other room before her Saturday shift, while I lie in bed considering what I still think was a fair question. The phone rings, and I know right away that it's Father M, because Ma's voice rises to a pitch she saves for priests and police officers. Oh, really. Uh-huh. Oh, my. Today?

Callie shoves her head under her pillow, groaning, and a minute later, Ma knocks on our door. The bishop's rep wants to meet with you, she says.

With me? Right now?

Speaking of doubters, Bishop Landry has been on the offensive for two years now, dashing off weekly missives about the sanctitude of sanctity and other babble that boils down to this: He thinks sainthood is a serious business that should be judged by serious men. A teenage girl, in his view, will never make the cut. Father M, meanwhile, thinks saints are meant to be chosen by the people and that they come in surprising forms. He's done his best to keep me out of the fray—Let me handle the theological bullies, he's said—but I guess you can only hold off an irate bishop for so long.

My hands jitter as I get ready. Ma makes it worse, suggesting a different shirt, nixing the lip gloss, tugging on my hair. Callie grumbles from beneath her pillow. Men of the cloth do not care about the height of a ponytail, she notes, and if this one does, we have another type of problem on our hands.

Ma ignores her and puts a finishing touch on my hair (two clips, no ponytail). Our eyes meet briefly in the mirror. It's just a sliver of a second, a look like thousands we've exchanged before, but this one makes my rabbit heart skid to a stop, makes me want to drop it all, spill everything, all of my questions, fears. I want to ask her, How did we get this far? Is this what being a saint is meant to feel like? Am I supposed to be so confused?

Ma fixes my collar, plants a kiss on my head. I wish I could go with you, she says.

I put on my brave face. Go to work, Ma. I'm sure it's nothing. Father M will be with me. I'll be fine.

At the church, everyone's gone full-on bonkers. Father M's shirt is buttoned all wrong, and Mrs. Driscoll, the secretary, is wringing her hands, spluttering something about Dunkaccinos and cappuccinos and soy. A man I've never seen before—tall, thin, colorless—peers suspiciously into a Styrofoam cup.

Brother Andrew handles public relations for the archdiocese, Father M tells me. He has a few questions for us.

The younger priest's face is a beach in winter: hair sparse like dune grass, eyes watery as eels'. As soon as we're seated his fishy jaws snap: How well did I know Ana Langone? Who told the parish to direct their prayers to me? It's been two years since these saint rumors began. Why hasn't that nonsense stopped?

Father M tries to say something, but Brother Andrew hushes him, his pale gaze fixed on me.

I'm trying to explain the gifts people bring me sometimes (I don't ask for them! No, no one has ever given me money), when there's a knock on the door. It's the florist, arrived early, toting armloads of lilies (?!).

As soon as Father M is gone, Brother Andrew wraps his pale fingers around my chair. If you really want to be a savior, you'll put a stop to this, he says. And you'll do it soon, before you the entire Church is in jeopardy.

He must see the confusion on my face. (The whole Church is in trouble? Because of me?) The archdiocese has weathered many trials, he says. The last thing we can afford is another scandal. Our numbers are too low as it is.

But—my brow squinches—aren't the numbers way <u>up</u>?

Brother Andrew waves a hand. Only this parish. It's temporary, an aberration. Superstitious fools who will go back to their fortune tellers & psychics the moment they learn the truth.

I flatten my feet so he won't see my knees shaking. The truth?

Brother Andrew peers down his reedy nose at me. I've been following you closely, and I believe the people of this city have been gravely misled.

You do? I squeak.

I don't expect you to understand the complexity of these matters, he says, and you cannot be held responsible for the poor decisions of your elders, but you do have the power to put a stop to this foolishness before things get even more out of hand.

Callie would punch this guy—What a condescending prick, I hear her say—but now's not the time to make enemies. What do you want me to do? I ask.

I want you to tell the truth. (Fishy smile.) Or I will.

My leg pops up, bouncing like a jackhammer.

Brother Andrew leans close. We know all about you, Miss da Costa. While it is currently in our common interest to keep certain matters quiet, should things go too far, our interests may diverge.

By the time Father M returns, my whole body is quaking. Our interests? Certain matters?

Back at home, I head straight for the shed. I can't bear to face Ma just yet. That horrible man said he'd been following me closely. (Like, literally?) I think of the dark car I spotted at the library last week, the one I swear I've seen a couple times since. Did he see me with D? Is that it? Have my fears come true?

Rudy's ears wiggle. He agrees that it's all horribly sexist and unfair.

Why should I be expected to live like a nun? I mean, look at Saint Augustine. You don't hear anyone complaining about that philanderer.

And D is the best, isn't he? I'm lucky to have him, right?

Rudy pants. It's a yes.

Suddenly I'm mad, really truly deeply mad. It's <u>so</u> unfair! How dare they treat me like this! I whip out my phone and send D a text loaded with hearts and insinuation. Because I want to. Because I can. Because maybe I'm a saint and maybe I'm not, but one thing I won't take is being told what I can and cannot do with my body by a celibate old man.

My phone buzzes a few seconds later, lit up with an emoji grin. D misses me too.

17.

I ring the doorbell and wait. The Hyundai is parked out front, so I know Danny's home, though he hasn't answered my texts. I feel strangely off balance without all that hair, the base of my neck exposed to the elements for the first time in years. I cut off more than I meant to, right above the shoulders, shorter even than how Tess wore hers yet close enough that I spooked myself in the bathroom mirror earlier.

I push a pair of her sunglasses onto the crown of my head to keep my curls at bay and press the doorbell again.

After the fourth or fifth ring, Danny appears. He's wearing the same clothes as yesterday, his face puffy with sleep. He doesn't say anything when he sees me, doesn't even open the outer door.

"Dr. Gillis caved," I say through the screen.

Danny yawns, staring past me to the trickle of cars on the street.

"The Langone claim is dead without him—for now, anyway. My mother's pretty upset."

"Congratulations. You must feel great."

"Yeah," I say, "great." But I don't feel great. Not at all. I feel miserable. Lonely.

Be a big girl, Cal. Just say it. Tell him you're sorry. I feel Tess nudging me forward.

I pull air into my chest and lift my head. "Look, I didn't really mean what I said about you and my sister yesterday. I was being an asshole."

"Yup." Danny's eyes are still too dark, still a little bit stabby, but at least they're on me now. I don't flinch or look away. I want him to know that I mean it: I'm really, *truly* sorry.

"Why did you say it?" he says. "Why do you get like that?"

I thump the stoop with my toe. "I don't know."

That's the truth. I've always been a little too quick to react. *A live wire like your grandfather,* Ma used to say. (*Maybe just more alive,* said Tess.) But lately it's a thousand times worse. Feelings surge up so fast, a riptide that yanks me under without warning. And now here I am, shipwrecked, reaching for the one person stranded out here with me.

"I'm not like them, Callie. I never cared about the saint stuff."

"I know that." My finger hooks a hole in the screen. "Tess knew it too."

It wasn't sainthood that drew them together. It was something else. Something in Tess that isn't in me. Sometimes I wish I knew what that missing ingredient was, the thing that made people love my sister so intensely. Then again, maybe I'm better off not knowing. Maybe it's not just one thing. Maybe it's everything.

Danny moves his hand to the door handle, but he doesn't open it. Not yet. He wants more. What? I push my sneaker into the door frame. "I thought we could go see Father Macedo. He's getting more claims."

"Like, miracles?"

I lift a shoulder. "My mom thinks maybe. She says Ana's just the beginning."

A fresh wave of nausea washes over me. Four months ago I watched, helpless, as those whirling lights carried her away. And now? Maybe I'm overreacting—what's the chance of another miracle-grade event happening so soon?—but I need to see those letters for myself. I need to know we have Tess covered.

Danny's squinched-up brow gives me courage. I know he feels the same way, even if he's too angry to admit it. "You can't give up because I act like a jerk sometimes. You'd never forgive yourself. Remember what you said about being brave?"

I search Danny's face for a sign of softening, some small something that I can grab on to. God knows I can't do this by myself. Good sleuths come in pairs. Anyone who's ever watched TV knows that. They balance each other out, have each other's back, make sure the one with the chip on her shoulder doesn't go too far off the handle. I think we both know that one is me.

Danny's hand falls from the door. "I'm not giving up. It's just more complicated than I thought it'd be. You and me, this. People are already saying stuff."

"People? You mean Karen? You can't take what she says seriously."

"She's my cousin, Callie. Family. And she's real pissed at you, by the way."

"Yeah." I don't know how to begin fixing that, or even if I want to. I'm ashamed of how I acted, but honestly? I'm still a little pissed at her too. After all this time, Karen should know better than to push me like that. "I don't know how you put up with her," I say.

"Same way I put up with you." The words are sharp, but the edge is gone from his eyes. "It takes practice is all. Patience. Her heart's in the right place, Cal. Yours is too. At least I think it is."

He's dangling a rope. I latch on before he can change his mind. "It is. I promise it is. But I can't do all this by myself. You've seen what a mess I can be. And you're so good with people." I open my lashes as wide as they'll go, channeling a bit of Rudy. "It's like you were made for this, Danny."

A startled laugh blasts from his mouth. He swats at me through the screen. "Cut it out, or I'll think you're flirting."

(Mental note: I was. And it worked.)

"So you'll come to church with me?"

"I don't know. Is that priest even going to let us see the letters?"

"If we offer to help him he might. Ma says he's getting more mail than he can keep up with on his own. So we'll ask if we can help. Father Macedo is all about service. *Every one of us has something to offer,* he says in like every single sermon. He's been pestering me to volunteer at Sunday School forever."

"So you'll tell him you changed your mind and now you're down with Jesus?"

"I won't go *that* far. Baby steps. I'll let him think he's helping me with my . . . you know . . . *grief.*"

The word leaves a sour taste. It's probably the worst word ever invented—one tiny syllable meant to capture a feeling so enormous it could flatten whole cities.

The door creaks on its hinge, and Danny steps onto the stoop. "Talk me through this a little more. Won't Father Macedo think it's weird that I'm there t—" He stops, looking at me more closely. "Did you . . . cut your hair?"

I've pulled the sunglasses from my skull, letting my curls float free, and from the sudden stiffness in his shoulders I know Danny saw it too: a flash of Tess.

I inch back to the edge of the stoop.

"All Father Macedo has to know is that Tess mattered to you too. You don't have to lie. Just tell him she left a mark on your life. That's true, right?"

Danny nods, but he's still looking at me strangely, eyes flickering from the crown of my head to my bare collarbone. For a second, I think he's going to hug me, or do something even weirder. But then his posture shifts and he reaches for the door.

"You might as well wait inside. I should shower if I'm going to church."

18.

Danny's car strains up the hill toward the church. At the steepest part it hovers for a moment, wheezing, threatening to roll back toward the harbor. A pair of gulls watches as Danny cranks hard on the shift. Gears grind, tires grab, and with a jolt of speed, we lurch over the crest.

St. Thomas's sits atop of the tallest hill in the city, filling an entire block. It was built in another era, a time of rich whaling ships and mills, when building a cathedral-sized church seemed like the thing to do. (You can't grow up around here without having *that* history shoved down your throat.) Anyone who looks at the church today might say it's too much, all those tiny arched windows and black pointed spires, angels and saints carved into every crevice. And they'd be right. Because it is. Too much. It's completely, absurdly over the top. Still, there are moments like this one, when the morning sun hits the rose-colored granite, setting it alight, and you could be tricked into calling the old church beautiful.

Danny pulls around the back, where a brick annex building squats in the shadow of its more impressive sibling. It takes a moment to adjust to the office's darkened interior, to pick out each awful detail: the warped bookshelves, mismatched chairs, piss-colored linoleum that's come loose in spots, revealing crumbling mortar beneath. If the church represents a time of wealth and hope, the annex is a reminder of its opposite.

Mrs. Driscoll, the church secretary, asks us to take a seat while Father Macedo finishes up on the phone. "It's just terrible what they're doing to your sister," she says to me. "I'm so very sorry."

I pause to look at her more closely. Pearl-buttoned blouse, pale cloud of hair, pink nails to match her pink lips. Could this manicured old lady really be on our side?

"Whoever's stealing from those shrines is a sicko," she says. "It's such a shock to all of us who loved your sister. Don't worry, though, dear. I'm sure they'll find whoever did it soon."

I turn away. "Right. The sicko." I feel Danny watching me, but I pretend to be interested in the view before us. Across the foyer, a door has been propped open. It looks like a category-three hurricane has torn through the room inside, leaving drifts of paper in its wake.

Mrs. Driscoll sees where my gaze has landed and clucks. "Too much work for one man, I tell you. Did you know when I was a girl this parish had three priests?"

Danny jumps in. "And now it's just him? You both must work really hard." He flashes one of his neighbor-boy smiles, and I start to roll my eyes—this lady's too smart to fall for that crap—but then I stop. Because it's working. My God, does it work. Mrs. Driscoll, a woman I once considered dignified, rubs her rosey lips together, matching Danny's cheese with a bright flash of dentures.

"I do what I can," she says, shuffling papers with an air of importance. "With the budget like it is and the bishop threatening to close more churches, what else can you do? I just feel bad for Father M. There's no rest for him these days."

"*No rest for the weary...*" Father Macedo emerges from his office. He's dressed in black pants and the short-sleeve, button-down shirt he wears every day but Sunday. A ring of faded tattoos curls down one forearm. Today, like a lot of days, he's not wearing his collar.

"Isn't this a surprise! Good morning, Carlinha. You've had a haircut, I see."

I shrug awkwardly. I guess this haircut is going to be a whole thing.

"What can I do for you and ... ?" He looks at Danny, who rises quickly to his feet, stammering something.

"This is my friend Danny," I say, stopping him before he can make a complete idiot of himself.

Father Macedo is the only living person who calls me by my full name (aside from Ma when she's pissed). He's not your typical priest, though. Ma says he used to be some sort of activist rebel, like my grandfather but with less talk and more actual fighting for stuff: rights for immigrants, guys on death row, that sort of thing. He grew up here in New Avon, and Lord knows what made him stay—or why after years of doing real work, he decided to become a priest—but he's the only person I've ever met who's basically always smiling, so I guess it's worked out for him.

He's also a straight shooter, which I appreciate.

"We'd like to help out," I tell him. "With Tess's case. Ma says you're getting a ton of mail, and we thought, since it's still summer, we could do this"—I arrange my face into its most virtuous expression—"this *service*."

Father Macedo cocks his head ever so slightly, but his smile doesn't fade. "An intriguing offer. Shall we discuss?"

He leads us into the conference room—the one that got hit by Hurricane Paperwork. It's large and dim, dark wooden panels broken up by a set of narrow, murky windows. In the center sits an enormous round table, strewn with envelopes. An assortment of crates and boxes balance haphazardly on chairs, filled to the brim with more unopened mail. All letters about Tess? Jesus. It's worse than I imagined.

Father Macedo closes the door behind us. "Carlinha, of course I'm glad to have your assistance—yours too, Danny—but are you sure this is the best choice right now? These past few months haven't been easy. Your mother was rather worried about you Sunday."

"Right. About that. I'm sorry I ran out of Mass and all that. I wasn't feeling great and—"

Father Macedo dismisses it with a wave. "No need to explain. This week's events have stirred up a lot of emotions. You never have to apologize for what's in your heart."

If anyone else said that, I'd roll my eyes, but Father M is so goddamn sincere. Steady smile, eyes like bits of granite worn by the sea. The expression in them now brings the taste of salt to my mouth. It's too much. I shift my gaze to the wall behind him, a row of gilt-framed portraits of white-haired men. The largest I recognize as Bishop Landry. With that square jaw and thick nose, he's always reminded me more of a gangster than a holy man. *It's the hat,* Tess said. *Who can trust a guy in a pointy hat?*

Ask Ma, and she'll tell you something else about our bishop: He's a downright bully.

"The Masses and ceremonies are tough for me right now," I tell Father Macedo. "But I can't just sit around and feel sad all the time. I want to be doing something to help Tess." I give him the same puppy eyes I used on Danny earlier.

It's probably the worst kind of sin—lying to a priest—but what I've said isn't a lie. Not exactly. We just have different definitions of *helping.*

Danny steps forward, clearing his throat. "Me too, Father. I didn't know Tess as well as Callie. Obviously. But she was always so kind, even to people like me who didn't deserve it."

What is he talking about? He didn't deserve *kindness*? I want to yank Danny's hands out of his pockets and tell him how ridiculous he sounds right now. He made Tess laugh when no one else could. Of course he deserved her kindness. Why is he being so weird?

Father Macedo's gray gaze bounds from Danny to me. I have an uncomfortable feeling he's picking up on more than he should. "Before we commit, let's take a look around, shall we?"

He gestures toward the table and shows us his system, which is not much of a system at all—three messy stacks of envelopes, three cardboard boxes standing behind them, one marked NO, one UNLIKELY, and the third INVESTIGATE. I look around for a fourth box marked YES! SHE'S A SAINT! but there isn't one. I allow myself a sliver of hope.

"A cause for sainthood can be a painstaking process," he tells us, "and we've barely begun. We've received a lot of mail from those who've learned of young Teresa's example. They are all very enthusiastic. But, between us, some events are more extraordinary than others. At this stage, it falls on the local parish to discern which rise above the rest."

He points out two more boxes of emails that Mrs. Driscoll has printed. "Right now, we're collecting every possible testimony, trying to sort through them as efficiently as we can. If we have enough evidence, we can petition the Vatican to consider Teresa's cause on an accelerated timeline."

"You mean like they did for Mother Teresa?" I say. "Isn't that pretty unusual?"

Father Macedo's brows arc. "I see you've done your research."

I don't know what to say to that. Of course I've done my research. She's my sister.

"Shall we review a few together?" He pulls a crate from a chair, and the three of us sit. Father Macedo hands me a letter and something that looks like a stealth murder weapon. "A letter opener," he says.

I turn the piece of metal over in my hand, then shove the sharp end into the flap. The envelope tears almost in half.

The letter inside is dated several weeks ago. It begins with a whole long story—the woman didn't go to church for years, lost her faith in God, blah blah, until her husband lost his job and she got sick. That's when she decided to visit Tess on our front porch.

She told me I should have faith in my husband, that things would turn out okay. And after she died, I kept hearing those words: HAVE FAITH. Last week, after a year of searching, my Ryan found a job. It's a true miracle.

I pass the letter to Danny. "Definitely a no. Tess would never say that stuff. She might tell her to stay positive, or not give up. But why would she tell this woman to have faith in a guy she'd never met?"

"Not to mention that finding a job is hardly a miracle," Danny adds. "Maybe he just had to look in the right place, and when he did, bingo, there was a job."

Father Macedo skims the page, placing it in the UNLIKELY box. "Interesting insights."

I grab the next envelope and stab it with my shiny new tool. Father Macedo reaches over to help when Mrs. Driscoll shouts from the other room, "Father! Bishop's on the line!"

His lips tighten and his tattoos twitch ever so slightly. If I didn't know better, I'd swear the old priest was saying a silent curse.

When Father Macedo's gone, Danny moves to the chair beside mine. "Think we convinced him?"

"I don't know, but that was good, what you said about that guy and the job."

"You too." Danny flashes a grin. Not the Crest kind, thank God. This one's more lopsided, genuine. "You and me make a good team."

"Yeah," I say. "We do." The room is suddenly too warm, too quiet.

I push my chair back to see what we're dealing with exactly. The UNLIKELY stack is the tallest, and the INVESTIGATE box is nearly empty. A good sign. I pull it closer. The envelope on top has been opened with a perfect slit, two pages folded neatly inside.

My boy had asthma his whole life. He could never play sports with the other kids. I brought him to every doctor and even prayed to Saint Bernadette, but nothing helped. Then I heard about Teresa da Costa and tried praying to her. A miracle! Yonny's asthma is almost gone now. He's been riding bikes with his brothers, even playing basketball some nights at the neighborhood court. It's all thanks to Teresa.

The second letter is from Yonny: *Thanks for making me better. I hate asma. I like bikes.*

It's touching, I guess, but doesn't sound all that miraculous to me.

Father Macedo's voice has quieted in the other room. At the sound of shoes padding across the foyer, I stuff the letters back where I got them and return to my chair. He appears a moment later, mouth set in an uncharacteristic frown. The cloud passes swiftly, though. He takes in the two of us, the disaster of a room, and clasps his hands in a brisk rub.

"Are you kids ready to learn your task?"

From the Journal
of
Tess da Costa

February 20

It's been three weeks since Ana Langone went missing, and I still haven't cracked the code.

THE SAVIOR CANNOT PROTECT.

HOME IS NEAR.

SHE RESTS ON A PILLOW OF STONE.

INTO THE DARKNESS COMES THE LIGHT.

Oh, how I wish the last one were true! The side-eyes I've been getting from church folks are ferocious. Last Sunday, a guy walked up onto our porch and spat at my feet. Literally spat! Old Mrs. Khoury said she's seen him spit on statues downtown where she works. It's not you, she told me quietly. That man's a spitter.

That made me feel a tiny bit better (and also? sad for the guy), but my alarm bells were clanging again the next morning when we found a prayer card tacked to the front door—me, with a forked tail, surrounded in flames.

I've decided the thing to do is avoid people. School and back, no stops in between. Even that feels risky these days. Yesterday I swore I saw that black car again, trailing me home from the bus stop. If Callie had been there, she'd have told me I was imagining things. That I'm paranoid to think it. But Callie wasn't there. It was just me, all alone, a shiny dark car sharking behind me through traffic, and I found myself walking more quickly, then running till it felt like my heart would explode.

Ma isn't helping. She's been a stressball all week, one ear plugged into the church gossip line and both eyes on me. Why didn't I pick up the phone earlier? Did I remember to send a thank-you note to the Sisters for their gift? Is that really what I'm wearing? Don't I have jeans that are a little more modest?

She hasn't said it, but I'm pretty sure the bishop's fish-faced pal got to Ma too.

Callie, meanwhile, has gone MIA. She missed the late bus today and didn't bother to text, which means she probably cut out early with Karen again. I barely see my little sister these days. She wakes up at the last possible second for school, spends afternoons doing God knows what, and stays up on the computer long after I go to sleep.

I think she and Ma had a fight over the weekend, but I don't know what it was about. (Probably Church stuff. Probably me.) I can't say for sure because it's been days since we really talked. I never even had a chance to tell Callie about what went down with Brother Andrew on Saturday. I want to talk with her so bad. I want her to tell me I'm being silly and then, if she's up to it, do her impression of the bishop in his ridiculous hat so we can fall on the floor laughing and forget about everything else for a while. Callie's the only person who can make me laugh like that—laugh so hard I crack open and all of the bad stuff gets whooshed away.

Today she's really pushing it. Any minute Ma will walk in the door and I'll have to make up another tired excuse. The thing is? Ma's going to find out that Callie quit the math team eventually. Her report card will give away the rest.

It didn't seem like a big deal the first time Callie cut out of school, or the second or the third, but I'm starting to think I should go with the truth next time Ma asks: Callie is hanging out with her "friends," doing stupid pranks and probably drinking, even though she hates beer and most of the pranks sound more desperate than fun, if you ask me.

Callie strolls in as I'm thinking it through, a goofy grin plastered on her face. Is she drunk? Wait till you hear what Karen made me do, she says. And then she's telling me the story—something involving a statue and shaving cream—and she's cracking herself up, but I'm only half listening because I don't know who this girl is and where she's put my sister.

Why are you doing this? I whisper.

Huh? She stops midway through a bit about how Karen is the best kind of person because she will say whatever's on her mind, unlike certain fake people at school, not to mention the hypocrites at church, and—What did you just say?

Me: Is this what you care about now? You skipped class to play with shaving cream?

Callie, squinting: Are you mad 'cause you had to take the bus by yourself?

Me: No, I'm mad 'cause you're ruining your life and you don't even see it. It's like you're trying to be the anti-saint or something. It doesn't make sense. What about college? What about all of the things you were going to do? You used to care about real stuff, Callie. Bigger stuff than stupid pranks.

Callie's cheeks have bloomed red. Look who's talking, she says. This is how you want to spend your life? She waves angrily at the room, and I notice for the first time that it's taken on a sour, hermity stench.

News flash, she says, I'm not the only one who's changed around here. Okay, so it's not Ma she's angry with. It's me.

I can tell she wants to say more, but she chokes it down, and then we're just staring at each other, wide-eyed, because neither of us wants to do this. We are sisters who don't fight. We disagree sometimes, sure, and tease each other mercilessly. But we never fight out of anger. We promised we'd never let something get between us, not like Ma and Wendy.

Callie fidgets with her sleeve and that's when I notice something else. Is that my sweater?

She looks down, confused. You said it didn't fit anymore.

Actually, it was Ma who said that. She said the V-neck was "too revealing" on me, not appropriate for school. (Saints aren't supposed to have cleavage, you know.)

The last time I wore it, D told me I looked beautiful. Amazing. I almost ravished him on the spot. And now my little sister is here, looking totally terrific in my favorite sweater, all slim & smooth where my body curves, bold & brave where I am weak. While I curled up here, cowardly, she spent the day doing laughtastic things with those friends of hers and D and . . .

And I don't know why I never thought of it before, but . . .

Tess?

. . . a whole bunch of moments click into place: The way Callie used to talk about "D and them" but now she only ever mentions what

Karen said, or sometimes that Carlos kid. But never D. I remember the way she went all quiet the first time I told her about us, and I figured it was just surprise—I was shocked too!—but maybe it was something else.

I slump back on the bed, out of breath.

How didn't I think if it until now? Is it possible that my sister had a thing—<u>has</u> a thing?—for my boyfriend? The thought sinks in quickly, losing its strangeness. Callie and D. They're together all the time. It makes more sense than him & me.

Tess, what's wrong? Callie has pulled the sweater over her head. She shoves it back in the bureau—wrong drawer, but whatever. I wouldn't have borrowed it if I thought you'd be mad, she says. I'm sorry I yelled.

She stands there, all sharp collarbones and scooped-out belly. Looking sad & sorry and like her real self again.

I'm sorry too, I say. I'm not mad about the sweater. I just had a weird day is all. A weird couple days actually.

I think back to that horrible priest with his nasty threats, the worry that's been eating me ever since.

Callie sits by my pillow, puts a hand on mine. Tell me, she says.

So I do. I tell her all of it, and for once, Callie doesn't make jokes or try to find answers. She just listens and holds my hand tight, and it turns out that today that's the exact thing I need.

19.

The next morning, Thursday, Danny and I sift through a mountain of letters in the church conference room. I make it through twenty in the first hour. Recovery from a bad flu, two friends who patched up a fight, a guy who made it five days without a drink (slipped up on the sixth, but who's counting?), and an adored cat who survived a run-in with a wild turkey out on Cape Cod. I pause for a second on the last one—did that say *turkey*?—then drop it in the NO pile too.

Really, this is the crap people pray about. *Miracles*, my ass.

Danny is reading more slowly, partly because he's got all the letters in Spanish (he speaks better than he reads), and partly because he's taking the whole thing too seriously if you ask me. Every so often, he tips his chair against mine to read a bit aloud, seemingly unaware of all of the shoulder bumpage that's happening, or the fact that I'm trying to get work done too. (FYI, scoring a visa to bring your mom up from Honduras is *not* proof of divine intervention; it's proof of a good lawyer.)

Hundreds of unopened letters sprawl out before us, not to mention the stacks we still haven't untouched. Most were sent shortly after Tess died in April. A smaller number have been sitting here longer, addressed to a living Tess c/o the church. Judging by the size of the box delivered this morning, I'd say Ma was right: There's definitely been a surge of interest since Ana was found Sunday.

The brassy old clock over the door ticks steady and loud, reminding me of how little time we have. Quick math: We'll need to read three hundred letters a day if we want to finish before school starts up again in three weeks.

School. The thought sends a shudder through me. All of the work I still haven't touched. Those packed hallways, pitted parking lot, whirling lights taking her away . . . I'm not sure I'll ever be ready to face that place again.

But maybe . . . and here's where my thinking gets a little swirly . . . maybe if Danny and I do a knockout job with the three weeks I have left—like, a good enough job to shut this sainthood case down for good—maybe then I'll feel differently. About all of it. Maybe I'll be ready to take on other battles, like finishing high school.

Wishful thinking? Perhaps. All I know is this that these letters are all I can think about right now. Right now, this fight—Tess's fight—is the only one that matters.

On Friday we start making phone calls. A handful of claims are less clean cut than the rest, and Danny and I agree we need to be extra-careful with those—nail down their shortcomings and document thoroughly in our reports to Father Macedo.

Asthma boy, it turns out, had three brothers who outgrew asthma before him. (Another for the NO pile.) And the girl who quit heroin all on her own clarifies that it happened *last* June, when Tess was still alive. I have to explain that the Vatican only cares about postmortem miracles.

"Post who?" she asks.

"After death," I say, and the line goes quiet. "But it's still great what you did," I hurry to add. "I'm sure Tess would be happy for you." The call ends with a disappointed click.

Most of the calls go similarly. But there's one that gets confusing—an old woman had severe tremors in her limbs, believed the end was approaching, was suddenly cured, and now thinks Danny is the Pope's assistant calling to give her his blessing—???

She lives nearby, so we decide it'll be easier to follow up in person.

Mrs. LaVoie opens on the first ring. Stooped spine, skin thin as paper, eyes like pools of black ink. Her apartment is tiny and cluttered, but her white hair is immaculate.

"Come right in," she says. "I've been waiting since you called."

She brings tea and lowers herself between us on the couch.

"It was terrible. I was so frightened. I prayed to young Teresa every day for a week, and when I finally got an appointment with that specialist, I said twenty-five rosaries in thanks."

Danny and I exchange a look.

"What did the doctor say?" we ask at the same time.

"The doctor?" Mrs. LaVoie seems confused, like we've changed the subject on her. "Oh, he wrote me a prescription for a new type of pill. He wasn't a very kind man, if you ask me. Doctors used to be much more understanding. They took time to really listen."

"Did you take the medication?" I ask.

"Of course, dear. I'm not taking any chances, old as I am. Here, it's this brown one." She points to the Wednesday slot in her pill-box. "Or maybe it's the green." Her fine hair trembles. "For the life of me, I can't keep them all straight."

I place my cup in my saucer—ready to leave, another big fat NO—but Danny gives me a *sit, girl* look.

"Is there anything else we should know?" he asks.

Mrs. LaVoie takes it as a cue to run through a list of ailments. There are many. So many. (After the first few, I conclude that old age is deeply unfair. Shouldn't people this woman's age get a pass on pain? Haven't they earned it?)

When Mrs. LaVoie pauses, I glance again at the door, but Danny ignores me. On purpose. He has more questions: about the wedding ring she wears on a chain around her throat, what it's like living without sugar, and how often she gets visitors these days. (Not often.) Something Danny says prompts her to break out an album filled with photos of her son. He was a good boy, she tells us, a Boy Scout, spent summers working down on the docks to save for college. The bullet that struck him was meant for some-one else—a case of wrong place, wrong time—but bullets don't discriminate between good kids and bad, Mrs. LaVoie discovered: They kill everyone equally.

"Folks left flowers at first," she recalls. "My Lenny was so loved by so many. But you know how it goes. The next thing happens. People move on. Everyone but the mother."

It's been more than thirty years since Lenny LaVoie died. His mother's grief is still so huge, so alive, it sends quivers across my skin.

"You know that won't count," I tell Danny once we're outside, walking back toward the car. "She took medication and the shaking stops? I feel bad for her and all, but we could have spent that hour getting through fifty other claims."

"Callie. We were the first people to visit her in *weeks*." He gives me a *what's wrong with you* look, which I match with one of my own. I mean, really. Since when is Danny such a Good Samaritan?

The truth is, though, I'm glad we stayed. Glad and slightly unsettled. Maybe it was the extra cup of tea, or the way Mrs. LaVoie's eyes rippled as she talked about the flowers, but I've felt a little unsteady since we got up to leave.

"It's like her whole life was based on being a mom," Danny says. "She looked so happy in those pictures and then, bam: One instant, all of it's just . . . gone."

"Yeah." My steps falter. "One instant."

"Oh. God. Callie. Shit." Danny reaches for me. "I wasn't . . . thinking."

I shake my head, push him away, avoiding those probing brown eyes. I'm not this easily rattled, am I? It's probably just lack of sleep. All week, each time I've closed my eyes, I've seen those damned birds, a whirling yellow light.

"Hey." Danny's arm slips around my shoulder. "I'm an idiot.

You shouldn't listen to me. Ever." He pulls my head in toward his shoulder, and for some reason I don't resist.

Good Danny. So loyal. So kind. (*A Taurus, you know . . . Perfect for a prickly little Scorpio like you.*) I should push him away. It's the smart thing to do. I should suck back the tsunami of ache like I've done so many times before. But his other arm comes around, locking me into place, and suddenly I'm not smart, or tough, or brave. I breathe in the clean scent of cotton and let my eyes close. Hugging is good, I tell myself. People *need* hugs. And Lord knows I haven't had many lately. Tess was my top supplier. I wish I'd paid better attention, held her a bit longer the last time. I don't even know when that was. I didn't record it, didn't realize it was an event.

Behind my lids, I see Mrs. LaVoie and her boy. "It's crazy, isn't it?" My voice is muffled by Danny's shoulder.

"What's that?"

I tilt my face toward his chin. "How she has to work so hard to keep a memory alive, when all we want is for everyone to leave Tess alone, for them to forget her."

Up close, Danny's lashes are small paintbrushes, leaving a spatter of tiny freckles across the warm palette of his skin.

He nods. "Yeah. Crazy."

There it is again. That word Tess hated. But the only one I know for a situation like ours.

Something unfolds in the pit of my belly right then, and a hundred questions bubble up. I want to know if Danny feels as twisted or as lonely as I do. I want to know if anyone ever hugs *him* now that Tess is gone. Does he ever wake up forgetting she's gone? His head tips closer and a question passes behind his eyes. The next second, his lashes flicker and arms go stiff. They drop away without warning, leaving me shivering in the summer heat.

I try to read his face—What just happened? Or *didn't*—but his eyes are trained on something behind me. "Hey, yo, Carlitos."

Oh shit. I grasp my forehead—oh, *nononono*—turning slowly, and there he is: our loyal-yet-dumb friend Carlos, the one I called a loser three days ago. Guess where he lives? Yup, that's right. Sometimes this city is way too small. Carlos stands a few paces from us, not even trying to be subtle about what he's just seen.

"Hey, D." One side of his mouth curls slowly.

"What's up, man? You look . . . sharp."

"Thanks, bro, got some hours at work. A date later." Carlos adjusts a clunky watch on his wrist and gives me a pointed look. *See,* his eyes say, *I'm no loser.*

I feel my jaw unlock. Too many weird things are happening right now. A job? A date? Since when does Carlos care about being on time? It's not just the watch, I realize. His eyes are clear, face shaved, hair trimmed in a crisp line. He's even swapped that ratty Red Sox jersey for a shirt with buttons. Actual buttons. *Carlos.*

"You think Mandy'll like it?" he asks Danny, ignoring me.

Mandy? It takes a second for the words to connect. Carlos finally asked out our glossy-lipped friend Amanda.

Danny claps him on the back. "She'll love it, man. No girl can resist that style."

"I look good, right?" Carlos brushes off his shoulders, spins for effect. "Maybe once you land a paycheck, we could do a double date. You know, if your girl is done being a pendeja."

"She's not my—"

"I'm not his—"

Girl, we say at the same time.

Carlos raises a brow. "'K. Whatever. We can check in on that later. I got places to be y pues . . ." He looks at Danny and then me. "Have fun doing whatever it is you *wasn't* doing."

And just like that he's gone, leaving Danny and me and a giant swath of sidewalk. We study the cracks carefully.

"We should head back to the church, don't you think?" Danny says after a bit.

"Yeah. The letters won't read themselves."

We shuffle toward the parking lot and crank the car's windows wide, letting the wind fill the silence. Nothing happened, I remind myself. It was just a hug. There's nothing wrong with hugs. But even though that's true, I can tell something's shifted between us.

We spend the rest of the afternoon on opposite sides of the conference room. Danny doesn't interrupt me once, or lean over to read bits aloud like he did earlier. I scan through the letters quickly: twenty, thirty . . . fifty more for the NO pile. The only sounds are cars passing on the street and the patter of Mrs. Driscoll's fingers on her keyboard in the other room.

Then, as the clock approaches five, and Mrs. Driscoll starts making sounds like she's packing up, Danny shoots up from his chair.

"What the . . . You gotta take a look at this one, Cal." He holds out a letter.

I get up to take a look.

she left me belly hungry in the dark
only one that loved me   gone
did you see her   my angel love?
long hair   brown eyes
                              big heart   sweetest smile
every day shes there
                    watching   protecting
                    takes the belt for me
he hurts her   not me
hes the monster   not me
these people they don't know
             i only loved her   my angel

We read the letter—or is it a poem?—three or four times, trying to make sense of it. The handwriting is so strange—at once
childlike and violent—and those words: *monster*? *belt*? *angel*?
We're both afraid to say what we're thinking, but I can't help seeing those swooping lines in the darkened apartment, their motion
as dawn crept through the boarded-up windows.

"You don't think . . . ? It couldn't be . . . ?"

"No," Danny says. "No way." We study the page, looking for
a name, something, but there's nothing on the reverse side and no
return address. The envelope has one of those inked-on stamps,
dated last December, long before Tess died. Before Ana was even
taken.

"The angel thing must be a coincidence," I say. "Catholics love them almost as much as saints."

Danny is still reading it, silently.

"It could be a prank for all we know," I say, although nothing about the letter seems particularly funny.

We debate it a bit longer and finally drop the letter in the NO box. But when Danny goes to find Mrs. Driscoll's keys, I scoop it back out of the box and make a quick copy, sticking the original in my bag.

In case we're wrong. In case the angel turns out to be Ana.

He's near. The girl can feel it.

She feels his sorrow creeping around the edges of the apartment, rising through the floorboards, sinking into her skin. His sadness is pushy, persistent. Like him.

Sometimes she thinks her grandmother feels it too. She sees it in a quick look, a new line of worry, a hug that lasts longer than it should.

Other times, the old woman is tuned into a different channel entirely. She scrubs dishes while he circles, runs the vacuum while he cries. He draws closer, and she hands the girl a cup filled with juice, announces that her tired bones are due for a shower.

As the water runs, the cries grow louder. The girl wishes he would hush. Maybe he'll go away if she talks to him. If she lets him know she hasn't forgotten. She'll never forget.

She studies the front door: one lock, two bolts, chain undone.

Upstairs, the water flows.

The girl reaches for the first bolt. Clunk. The next, thunk. One more click, and the door opens with a sharp inhale.

20.

On Saturday morning I slip outside before Ma's alarm. A thin fog hangs low over Cranston Street, kissing the parked cars and wrapping the whole neighborhood in a gentle mist. I step down from the porch, balancing Tess's shoe box full of journals in both arms.

One hundred and thirty days have passed. It's time.

Last night, after Ma gave me the latest miracle rundown over dinner (Dr. Gillis: still avoiding calls; Ana Langone: mute as well; *Newsline* piece: moving forward anyway), I locked myself in my room, telling Ma I was exhausted. Instead of getting in bed, I pulled out the creepy letter/poem Danny found and laid it beside the items we found in the Walnut Street apartment. Four days since we found them. Danny has nudged me a few times, asking what the plan is, but I keep putting him off. If they're talking jail time for the Shrine Smasher, I can only imagine what a Crime Scene Snatcher would get. (Or what would happen if one girl turned out to be both.)

The angel letter was written on a different type of paper than the sheets in the manila envelope. I couldn't tell if the handwriting matched—different-color pen, so many cross-outs: Was it the same person? Hard to say. I went over the other items too, but they remained just as inscrutable as the last time I looked. Two little kids, a social worker, a long list of names.

And Tess. Why did the kidnapper keep her prayer card? Where did he get it? I looked at her face for a long time, wishing she could answer, or tell me I'm being ridiculous. What I wouldn't give to hear my sister tell me I'm in over my head with this, to have her tug me back to shallower water.

As dawn broke, so did I. So many days since I last heard your voice. My head's gone all out of whack. I needed your words to snap my world back into focus, so I pulled a chair to the closet and reached for your hiding spot.

Which brings me to now: creeping across the yard to the driveway, slipping past the landlord's car and into the old shed. It's still dark inside, and I notice with surprise that your lamp has been knocked over, its neck broken. I give Rudy a stern look. He wags his tail innocently.

I backtrack to the porch and snatch up a couple of votive candles and a fresh booklet of matches, bringing them to the shed. Rudy settles into his doggy bassinet as I light the candles.

My collection continues to grow. Three more shrines last

night after Danny dropped me at home. I don't know why I keep doing it or how to stop. Or if I even want to. I stare at her shoe box, considering, then finally pull off the lid and drop it to the floor.

The top layer is photos and sentimental scraps: a flyer from last year's Cranberry Festival, a few notes in handwriting I recognize as Danny's, a strip of photos we took down by the waterfront (me making devil's horns, you doing an impression of a chipmunk), another set of you and Danny (laughing, making faces, kissing). Some items go all the way back to middle school. The two strangest bits are a flattened Milk Duds box and a pen splintered in two. I run my fingers along its jagged edge. It's an odd thing to hold on to, even for you, Tess.

Rudy smacks his tail, and I get the hint, digging deeper, pulling the journals out, and setting them on the trunk. There are five in total, dated consecutively, beginning the year you turned thirteen. The most recent stops in mid January.

Rudy gets up for a stretch, and I check the dates to be sure. Two months are missing. I know you kept writing, though. Some nights you'd wait until you thought I was sleeping, and I'd hear your pen scritching beneath the light from your phone.

Rudy noses my chin, and I rub his shoulder. *Do you know where she put it, pup?* He butts my chin more aggressively, whining. He wants out.

I rock forward slowly, blowing out the candles and giving the journals one last look. *Did you hide it, Tess? Destroy it? When?* The second I unlatch the door, Rudy bounds toward the street.

I run after him, catching him at the front fence—latched

tight, for once. My heart unclutches, and I crouch to give him a good rub, but his yips turn into a growl.

"Rudy?"

He snaps at the fence.

The street is quiet, soft folds of fog just beginning to break. There is nothing—absolutely nothing—for a dog to get worked up about.

Is there?

I shoot to my feet when I see her: a little girl, planted in the damp grass across the street. Her long hair is pulled back and she's wearing what looks like overalls. She isn't like the pictures in the paper. She doesn't look like I remember either—a kid full of sparkles and laughter. Ana Langone is thinner now, her mouth a narrow line, like one of those dolls you know is supposed to resemble a child but has all the wrong angles and proportions.

At first I think she's scowling at me. Then I realize her attention is fixed on something in the street. But there's nothing to look at there: just a bunch of parked cars, that old utility truck, the usual trickle of folks headed to work. Nothing unusual. Nothing out of place.

Except for Ana.

Rudy barks when I close the gate behind me, continues barking as I step into the street. I'm halfway across the Langones' yard when the front door bangs open.

"Ana!" Maxine Langone steps onto the porch in slippers, wet hair clinging. When she sees me, she straightens, pulling her robe tight around her waist.

"What in God's name?" She sees Ana and hurtles from the steps.

The old woman's movements aren't graceful, but she's faster than I would have guessed. She scoops her granddaughter up in her arms, buries her face in her long curls, scolding or cooing, I can't quite tell.

After a bit she raises her head, remembering me.

"Callie, from across the street." I walk toward them, pointing lamely toward my building, where Rudy is still barking like a madman.

"I saw her sitting there. I didn't mean to scare you—"

"Hush. Don't apologize." Mrs. Langone props Ana on her hip. "She's the one scared me half to death. An escape artist, looks like. Always been too smart for her own good."

It's something Ma used to say about me—the *too smart* thing—but Mrs. Langone says it differently: with pride.

Ana perches stiffly in her grandmother's arms, her eyelids spasming queerly.

Mrs. Langone kisses her head. "Doctor says she has dry eyes from not enough sleep."

Ana ducks out from the kiss, and the spasms stop.

"She hasn't said anything? Nothing at all?"

Mrs. Langone shakes her head, whispers a no, and I want to ask if she's worried about that—if the doctors are too—but I know from her face that she's far more than worried. She's something closer to terrified.

Ana lifts a small hand, stretching it toward me. Does she want me to take it? I step closer and her fingers snap onto my palm.

Her skin is soft, dry, bones fragile like a tiny animal's. She's just a little kid, six years old, but something in her expression is ancient, frightening. She may be home safely now, but it's clear that Ana Langone is not the girl she once was. I wonder if she'll ever be.

I want to ask Mrs. Langone if she really believes in miracles. How can she place faith in a God that would let this happen to a child?

An engine rumbles to life, and Ana's hand unclenches. I turn to see what's captured her attention. A gray Dodge pulls from the curb, and a neighbor—what's his name again?—waves. Another walks by, head bent to the ground. Voices drift from an open window. The fog has melted, giving way to a fiery sun.

Rudy watches us quietly. Whatever was bothering him has passed.

I follow Ana's gaze to the spot where this street merges with the next, a stop sign, empty intersection. Nothing out of place.

"Sorry to bother you," I say again, although Mrs. Langone just told me not to. I can't help it. I feel like she deserves an apology from someone. A big one. As big as they come.

"I appreciate your keeping an eye out," she tells me.

I wait as grandmother and child move toward the house. I don't turn around until I've heard the bolt plunk into place.

From the Journal
of
<u>Tess da Costa</u>

March 4

Since I woke up this morning, it's been one line, over and over.

SHE RESTS ON A PILLOW OF STONE.

SHERESTSONAPILLOWOFSTONE.

SHERESTSON

a PILLOW?

of STONE?

By fifth period, my head is pounding, the pain pulsing with the words. SHERESTS ONAPILLOW OFSTONE. The hallway is pure misery. Slam of metal lockers, screeches, hoots. And somehow it's the whispers that get me the worst—silent, slit-eyed looks that fork me right between the eyes. They think I don't hear what they say, but I do.

She's a Jesus freak.

An attention whore.

A psycho lunatic.

She probably snatched that little girl herself.

It's no worse than what they've been saying for the past two years (at New Avon High cynics reign supreme), but put it together with the mean little gifts I've found on our porch this week (smashed eggs, pee-soaked socks, etc.), Ma's stress, and the rumors swirling at church: folks accusing us of running a scam, of toying with people's faith . . . and I just can't anymore.

I just . . . can't.

D asks if I'm up for the library—we haven't had time alone in two weeks—but I tell him not today. His shoulders droop, my head throbs.

Wash, rinse, repeat.

When the last bell rings, Callie is waiting by my locker. (She's behaving this week.) I tell her I want to walk home. Another thing I can't deal with right now: a crowded, stinking bus, all of those eyes on me. Callie loves walking, hates people. She doesn't take much convincing.

The street that leads home is icy and slick. I notice a car paused up ahead: black, tinted windows, a shiny silver grille. I grab Callie by the sleeve and suggest a shortcut through the old Methodist cemetery. She shrugs. An adventure. That's cool.

Naked trees, naked tombs, bodies lying frozen in the ground. We slip along the narrow paths, and Callie chatters loudly, her breath an icy cloud.

—the idea that anyone could call that school an institution of education is a joke. Why don't they call it what it is? A breeding zoo. A holding cell? A godforsaken piece of—

I keep her going with an occasional mmm-hmm and aghh—I know! because she's been good to me this last week and it's what sisters do. Also, I'd rather think about anything other than my achy head and this creepy place: so many names and numbers etched in stone.

We're far from the street now, but I still have a sense we're being followed. Paranoia, Callie would call it if I told her. But what if she's wrong? Brother Andrew said he'd be keeping an eye on me, but he never said whose eye it would be. Maybe he's gathered a small army of skeptics to do his bidding. Like, that lady over there. The one kneeling by that grave, wearing sunglasses on a dreary winter day. Mourner or spy?

Tess?!

Callie's breath is ragged, eyes chipped with concern. I realize I've been walking extra-fast.

I slow my pace and we emerge, finally, on the far side of the cemetery, where Granite Ave crosses Quarry. In the distance, the church spire rises against a steel-colored sky.

I look left, right. But there's no one. Nothing.

Nothing except a feeling climbing up through my bones.

SHE RESTS ON A PILLOW.

A PILLOW OF

stone.

I stare hard at the walk signal, a blinking hand warning us not to cross. When the light goes green, a thought tugs me forward.

I drag Callie with me.

But—

She points in the direction of home.

I need to see something, I say. I can't explain more than that. It's an instinct, so fluttery—so faint—I don't want to lose it. My GPS may be spotty, but when it does its thing, I have no choice but to follow. Also? If it's right, and if it leads me to Ana, then maybe I can let go of this fear once and for all. Maybe I can prove I'm not, bit by bit, losing my mind.

Frostbitten asphalt, slick patches of ice. Three more blocks, past

Chestnut Street and Walnut, and the road hooks right, bringing us to an enormous gate: Bedford Stone & Gravel. A PILLOW OF STONE. The feeling pulses in the roots of my teeth.

What is this place? Callie's eyes are huge.

A dark car edges around the bend, and I tell her to hush. The front gate is locked, but the chain hangs limp. I pull Callie through and duck behind the wall, watching as the car turns up another street. Dark blue, no gills.

The path into the quarry is lined with pyramids of gravel, dusty pebbles mixed with rosy quartz and deeper tones of gray. I study the mounds, check my body for a stronger signal, but the feeling's grown faint.

The path ends after a few yards, earth slicing away without warning, the whole world disappearing into a gaping pit. I teeter at the edge, measuring the drop with my eyes (hundreds of feet? thousands?). My arms lift. One move and I could put a stop to all of this—is that what Brother Andrew meant? I taste the possibility of flight.

Tess! Callie yanks me back to safe ground. Her whole body is trembling.

I wasn't really . . . I mean, I wouldn't . . .

You better not, she whispers, keeping an arm around my waist. We look out across the crater together. It's as big as several football fields, the earth bitten into sharp ledges. Toy-sized trucks stand motionless on distant platforms, abandoned by their tiny humans.

You think Ana's here, don't you?

I don't answer. The feeling is gone now, leaving me as stranded as those trucks.

She rests on a pillow of stone, Callie whispers.

I cringe, hearing how silly it sounds. I shouldn't have told her. I shouldn't have brought her here. How many stones must there be in this city? How many rocks in this world?

Callie holds a hand over her eyes, squinting into the gravelly depths.

But there's nothing. It's all sand and stone and ice. No sign of a little girl. Just signs that my sanity is slipping.

Callie returns to my side, blowing on her purpled hands.

We should make a list, she says, of places to look, places with a lot of stone.

I want to cry then, but my tear ducts are frozen. What is she doing? My logical little sister. If she thinks she can make me feel less foolish, she's wrong.

You need gloves, I tell her. And a hat.

We should go over to the old fort or down to the seawall—they're both made of granite.

Let's go home, Cal.

Isn't there another quarry, too? Out past the park?

Home, I tell her. We're going home.

Only if you promise me you won't do this again without me. You can't do stuff like this by yourself.

I haven't, I say. I won't.

You used to tell me everything, she says. It's better when you do that.

I don't say anything. Because is it really? I don't see how it's better when it's two of us worrying, instead of one.

Callie laces her fingers through mine, pulling them into her pocket. Beside us the chasm yawns wide. We can pretend it's not there, this gulf between normal and crazy, but that doesn't make it less real.

THE SAVIOR CANNOT PROTECT.

For the first time, it strikes me that the lines I've been hearing may not be about Ana. Maybe they're about us. Only, who is the savior in this picture? And who needs saving?

Promise me you'll tell me everything, Callie says, gripping my hand tighter. There's only one answer she'll accept.

Cross my heart, I say.

That's all it takes. Her face relaxes and she leads me back to the street, chattering on about something—the difference between stone & gravel, boulders & rocks—and I'm saying huh and wow and I never thought of that!, but the whole time I'm thinking it's easier to lie to Callie than I'd thought.

21.

The mailman delivers two full crates on Tuesday. It's been nine days since Ana Langone was found, and the letter-writing fervor is picking up speed. Yesterday we found a letter from Hawaii. This morning: Latvia.

"Been with the US Postal Service for thirty-seven years," the mailman tells Danny and me. "Never seen anything like this."

We stack the new boxes beside the ones from yesterday, and I try not to let my frustration show. It's like Jesus with the bread—the more letters we read, the more appear to replace them. Ma says twelve million people tuned in for the *Newsline* piece about Tess on Sunday. (*Twelve million!*) It was a shorter segment than originally planned and there was no interview with Dr. Gillis, but apparently twelve million Americans don't care about silly details like evidence.

Danny is quiet today. I can't tell if it's all beginning to wear on him too—if, like me, he's wondering how long we can keep this up and whether it will make a difference—or if he's still feeling awkward because of what happened last week. The hug, Carlos, all of that.

I slip the letter opener into the next envelope, slicing it cleanly. (It took a few paper cuts to get the hang of it, but I've become a pro with this thing.) I skim quickly—another nonbeliever who was lost and confused, anger, alcohol, bad relationships, blahblahblah, heard about Tess-slash-Jesus: And voilà, he's a whole new person!

Another one for the NO pile.

I reach for the box at my feet and pause. The edge of an envelope peeks out from beneath the others, just three letters showing, but the way the lines cut across the paper—crude, uneven—makes my spine go rigid.

One slip of my little knife and a page slips free.

> my angel she loves yellow
> yellow lemon
> yellow sun
> she loves me too
> silly billy funny bunny you so sweet big kiss for you
> one two three bitty bones
> little angel flaps her wings
> i put my ear to listen
> the wings move inside
> fast

fast   faster

my angel waits quiet
watching
big eyes   see me
        keep me

   right

here

I call to Danny, and he takes the letter from me. It's happening again—those connections that probably aren't real. *My angel she loves yellow.* I see flashes of that horrible yellow dress, Ana's face the other day as she held my hand, eyes on the street.

Bitty bones. Wings flapping.

I press both palms onto the cool table, wait for the horror flick in my head to go still. It can't be the same guy. Can it? All that twisted emotion spilled out on the page. The person who wrote this letter couldn't cross a street without drawing attention to himself. How could he hide a child for months?

"We had a mail machine like this at my old job." Danny's holding the envelope up to the window. "There's a zip code here, so we know it came from someplace local. I don't know what these numbers mean."

I join him by the window, and he points to a string of digits at the bottom of the inked-on stamp. His fingers are even more chewed up than usual. It's been a few days since I've been close enough to see.

"You think it's like a company code or something? Could we trace it?"

"The police could." Danny runs a torn-up thumb along his lip. "Callie, we should really—"

The door bangs open before he can finish saying what it is we should do.

"Have you kids seen Father M? Where did he go off to now?" Mrs. Driscoll stops in the center of the room, hands planted several inches above the waist she lost track of years ago. She peers under the table, like maybe Father Macedo's playing hide-and-seek.

"Where could that man be? Oh, this is not good. Not good at all." She waves her manicured fingers and the air around her stirs.

I lay an arm across the loose papers on the table. "He left a while ago. A sick parishioner, I think?"

"I'm sure he won't be long, Mrs. D. Can we help you out with something?" Danny says gently.

Mrs. Driscoll tugs at her rings, uncertain. "The woman on the phone says they found something. At the Langone house. Said it's a sign from God. Proof of the miracle. The reporters will be there any minute."

"She said *what*?" Danny and I step nearer.

"Plain as day, right in the yard." Mrs. Driscoll's pink lips crimp in distress. "I told that man he needs a cell phone. Priests need to keep up with the times."

Danny places a hand on her shoulder. "Don't worry, Mrs. D. Callie and me can take care of this. We'll go over there now."

She doesn't look convinced.

"We'll take lots of notes," I say, "and pictures." I pull out my phone to show her. "Father M won't miss a thing."

Mrs. Driscoll looks up at Danny, who smiles broadly. The air around her begins to settle. "What good kids you are." She pats Danny's arm. "How about I make some iced tea for you when you get back?"

"I love iced tea," he says.

"I know you do, sweetheart." Mrs. Driscoll winks, heading back to her desk.

"Good God," I say, when she's out of earshot. "That's some talent. Is it only old ladies or do you specialize in drama queens generally?"

Danny gives me a significant look.

"Hey." I smack him with a stack of letters, but it only makes his brows dance.

Maybe that's all it takes to keep things easy between us: Jokes. Teasing. Two things I know how to do.

"All right, Captain Charming. Enough messing around. God called. We got work to do."

A crowd has gathered by the time we arrive, white news vans flanking the house. I have to lean against Danny's car for a second to get my bearings. I lift my cropped hair so the hot sun can drink up the dampness at the base of my neck.

The last time I saw so many reporters in one place was Tess's funeral. Hundreds of people came to say their good-byes, their faces a blur in the cold April drizzle. This crowd is smaller. Judging by the number of people wearing flip-flops and slippers, I'd guess most came from nearby, drawn by the noise.

Danny tilts his head in my direction and I nod, pushing off the car. Together, we make our way into the crowd. All eyes are on a woman up front with a helmet of wavy bronze hair. She's attempting to crouch, but her pencil skirt isn't cooperating. She wobbles, pointing at something by her feet. I can't quite see what it is, but someone in front of Danny is holding up a phone with a nice big screen. The grass by the reporter's feet has been shaped—plucked, it looks like—into a circle with rays radiating outward. Like an eye, or a newly risen sun.

"We're here in New Avon, where people are asking: Is this a trick of Mother Nature or a sign from God?" The reporter teeters back to standing.

"The real miracle is that her hair spray doesn't melt in this heat," I mutter. Danny sniggers.

I elbow deeper into the crowd, with Danny close behind. I'm trying to picture the yard as it was the other morning, without all the people, without stiletto-heeled reporters stabbing up the dirt, but it's tough. It's only when I reach an opening, with a direct view of the house, that I realize: It must have been her. Ana. The symbol they're gaping at is in the same spot where I found her the other morning.

But . . .

Why would she . . . ?

Another reporter is interviewing a cop to my left. "We think it may be a religious symbol," he's telling her, "possibly ancient. It

could connect our guy to a religious sect of some sort. The FBI is sending one of their cult specialists to check it out."

The FBI? I'd laugh if this weren't so messed up, if the truth weren't even more disturbing: A traumatized six-year-old is trying to tell us something. She's begging us for help.

I picture Ana as she was the other morning, her tiny hand reaching for mine, those eyes too old for her face, and my rage meter spikes. She was just a little girl. These assholes are missing the whole point.

Somewhere off behind us, a guy is blustering about crop circles and alien life-forms. I roll my eyes, nudging Danny. "These guys are idiots. Aliens? A cult? It was Ana who made it. Don't they see?"

Danny doesn't respond. I look up and discover a guy with way too much facial hair glaring down at me. Whoops. Wrong elbow. I inch back, bumping into someone else. I spin the other way, knocking against more elbows. Danny's nowhere in sight.

A whisper moves through the crowd. At the sound of Tess's name, I turn.

Aren't you Teresa da Costa's sister? A microphone appears.

"Uh." I put up a hand, try to back away, but bodies form a wall, pressing me forward.

Did you say you believe Ana Langone created that symbol?

"Well, yeah. She was sitting in that same spot the other day."

Do you know what the symbol means?

"No, I—"

How did you crack her code?

"I didn't. I—" The sun beats against my scalp. I search for a break in the crowd, for a glimpse of Danny, but I'm wedged so tight I can't move. It's just like my nightmare, that hallway packed with bodies, pressing, keeping me from reaching Tess. My breath grows jagged. The questions don't let up.

Is it true that your family has a history of mental illness?

"What?" The question comes from somewhere to my left, unexpected. "Who told you that?"

A source had informed us that your mother was institutionalized.

"My *mother*?" I feel like I've stepped into some alternate universe, everything upside down and melty. I make a face at the reporter with the scrambled facts. "It was my *grandmother* who saw *visions*. It was totally different. She—"

Shit. I stop myself too late. All they need is one little hint, Ma warned me.

So it's true then that schizophrenia runs in your family?

"No, that's not what I—"

I'm cut off by another question, pitched so fast I can't catch it. There are more microphones. Beads of sweat burst from my forehead, rolling toward my eyes. For a strange second, I feel like I've been split in two. One part stands on this little patch of earth, hemmed in by muscle and grit, while the other floats somewhere up above, watching, understanding that there's no way this will turn out well.

Miss da Costa, do you hear voices too?

What's it really like having a saint for a sister?

Did you resent the attention? Does your skepticism stem from jealousy perhaps?

The last question catches me below the ribs. "Are you kidding me? You think she *wanted* this? You think anyone would choose to be followed around by assholes like you? All Tess wanted was to live her life like anyone else, make her own decisions, make mistakes, and . . . be happy." I swipe at my stinging eyes. "We used to be happy."

The reporters pull in tighter, microphones outstretched. They've forgotten all about that rising sun or God's eye or whatever the fuck Ana drew in the grass. This scene is better, practically made for television: heartsick girl, guts laid bare for the world to see.

I could claw out their eyes for looking at me that way, like my sister, my *life*, is just another two-minute news clip. I feel my temperature surge.

"The ones you should be grilling are these nuts." I thrust a finger at the crowd. "Yeah, that's right. You! You're the whack jobs! If anyone around here had half a brain cell left, they'd see that none of this is miraculous. It's sad is what it is. Ana can't even talk! Her life's been wrecked. And you're thanking God? What happens when the cameras go away, huh? What's she left with then? She'll never get past this. She'll never be normal or happy. She'll probably wind up some messed-up old lady, broken and all alo—"

An arm circles my waist. "Shhh. Not another word, Cal." Danny speaks low into my ear.

"*Now* you show up? Where the fuck have you been?"

He wheels me away from the reporters, who've broken out in excited chatter. *You heard it here, folks . . . da Costa family worn thin . . . sibling rivalry? . . . as tensions boil over on Cranston Street . . . left with one question . . . What would Saint Teresa say?*

I try to pull away—I want to batter in their faces, make them stop—but Danny holds me tight, using his body as a shield to guide me through the crowd. There are more people than when we arrived. Cameras flash. Eyes narrow. Someone says something about manners. Someone else says something about kids today.

I raise one arm above my head and give them all the single-finger salute.

22.

They won't air any of that," Danny says, pushing me up my front steps. "You're a minor. I'm pretty sure it'd be illegal."

I'm sweat-soaked, humiliated. And still shaking with anger.

Danny nudges me forward, offering advice like I'm a child: *Don't go outside, avoid the windows, don't answer the phone.* He'll check on me later, he says, then mutters something about an errand he just remembered he has to do.

An errand? Rudy howls from the first-floor window. Danny's leaving me *now* to go do errands? I turn as the screen door claps shut, but he's already halfway down the steps. He's forgotten all about panicky Mrs. Driscoll back at the church. I guess both of us drama queens will have to deal with shit on our own.

The phone's ringing when I get upstairs.

"Carlinha da Costa? *South Coast Gazette.* Could I get your thoughts on a story?"

"Are you kidding me?" I slam the phone back into its cradle. It begins ringing again almost immediately. "No comment," I tell the second caller, not even listening to the spiel.

No comment. That's what I should've said to those other reporters. *No comment. No comment. No comment.* So simple. Straightforward. Anyone with half a brain cell would've known to do that.

The third time the phone rings, I yank the cord from the socket. The silence is so abrupt that for a second I think I've unplugged my brain. (Bliss.) The next second, my cell phone starts buzzing. *Unknown caller.*

"You fuckers are really persistent, aren't you? How'd you get this number?"

There's a pause on the other end. "Callie?" It's a woman's voice. "It's Ms. Chisholm from New Avon High? I haven't heard from you in weeks. I've been getting worried."

"Oh, uh. Sorry about that, Ms. C. This really isn't the best time."

"I'm afraid there's not going to be a better one, Callie. Summer grades are due. I did everything I could, but you have to meet me halfway. If you don't turn in something—"

I pull the phone away from my ear. I don't mean to be rude. Ms. Chisholm was my favorite teacher back when things were different. She took it upon herself to fix things when she heard about my situation last spring. No one understood why she did it, least of all me.

"Do you realize what will happen, Callie? This isn't just a matter of repeating tenth grade. It'll be on your transcript. Colleges don't—"

"Ms. C. Really. Now's not a great time."

I've turned on the TV and am flicking through the stations to see if they've aired anything yet. Danny's probably right about how things are supposed to go, but this is New Avon. No age rule stopped reporters from tagging along after Tess during that first wave of interest. Tess got really good at smiling and stepping out of the way, a trick I wish she'd taught me.

Ms. Chisholm sounds tired. "Don't you still want to go to college, Callie? You're such a bright girl. You could go places if you'd just pull yourself together and try."

Tess said something similar last winter. She worried that I was trying to turn myself into the anti-saint, as if cutting classes with Karen and slacking on homework were all about her. It seemed incredibly self-centered when she said it—like I didn't have thoughts or desires of my own. But maybe she was right. Maybe these past two years and all the ways I've changed really are just reactions to her. Like, something in my head told me that if Tess couldn't be a normal kid, then I'd screw up for her, in every way possible. Like, I was somehow trying to restore balance to the universe, or add a few sins to a pot flavored too heavily with virtue. But I lost myself in the process. In trying to be Tess's opposite, I forgot how to be me.

Is that all I am now: a twisted reflection of my sister?

"I don't want to scare you," Ms. Chisholm is saying, "but I wonder if you realize how many students never finish high school. It starts this way: one bad quarter, a failed year. Soon it's impossible to catch up." She pauses, seeming to finally notice the silence on the other end. "Callie?"

I want to say the right thing. I want her to know how much I appreciate her caring. I do. But my mind's filled with other things right now.

"Thanks for trying, Ms. C. Please don't call me again."

I put my phone on silent and scan through the channels from top to bottom and back again. The doorbell buzzes, and Rudy lets loose his fiercest bark. From the front window, I see a reporter scamper back to safety. I consider going downstairs to cover my tracks in the shed, just in case, but the camera crews seem to be packing up. I watch as the van doors slam shut and the last of the news vehicles drive away.

A breeze carries the faint odor of salt up through the open window. September is right around the corner and it's still hotter than hell. There's a fresh current, though, beneath the heat, promising a change coming soon. Maybe another storm. Maybe just a sprinkling of rain.

Maybe a different kind of heat.

The local news comes on at five. The same stories rotate on all the channels: a brush fire across the border in Rhode Island, an insurance salesman indicted for ripping off a bunch of old people, city bus drivers discuss a strike. A clue in the New Avon kidnapping.

By now, they've all concluded that it was Ana who made the pattern in the grass. They don't say what tipped them off, but Mrs. Langone confirmed that she found the child sitting in the yard a few days ago.

Is it a silent plea, the reporters wonder, or a sign of the child's mental deterioration? Psychologists have attempted to interview the child with no success, they say.

There is no mention of me and only a brief aside about the miracle rumors that were circulating earlier. They show a clip of a guy waving his arms and talking about aliens, and the news anchors chuckle. There'll be a remix on YouTube by nightfall.

Ma's key slides into the lock just as the local news switches to national. I turn off the TV and prepare for a tongue-lashing. She must have heard everything by now.

She opens the door, looking absolutely flattened. "I hope you're up for takeout. You won't believe the day I had."

I jump up to grab the bag from her outstretched hand. Has she really not heard? The bag releases a puff of garlic, and I take a peek inside. "Chinese. Yum."

Over dinner, Ma tells me about a reporter who called her this morning with odd questions about the family's medical history. She was in the middle of a busy shift and didn't have time to call back. A summer flu outbreak has hospital staff stretched to their breaking point, she tells me, and the company that handles laundry is in some sort of dispute with management. The nurses and maintenance folks got the worst of it. "Not what you want to see," Ma says. "Gastric distress and a shortage of bedding."

"Ew," I say, and she laughs.

We fall quiet, munching on our noodles, and I wonder how much longer we have until this moment of peace comes crashing down around our heads. Any second, it will happen: a call on her cell phone, a neighbor stopping by to fill her in. Ma will hear about the whole insane incident this afternoon, including the thing I told them about Grandma. The thing I promised never to tell.

Ma dips an egg roll in sauce. "Father Macedo says you've been really helpful these past few days."

"He did?"

I wait for the list of warnings and reminders she must have rehearsed, but Ma takes another calm bite. "I'm proud of you, Cal. Tess would be too, knowing you're here on her side."

I look at Tess's chair and wonder what she'd say to that. It doesn't make sense that two people who loved Tess could have such different ideas about what it means to be on her side. If Ma knew what I'm really up to . . . If I could help her see the truth. But no. I've flapped my mouth enough for one day. It's a battle I won't win.

"I hear that boy's helping too." Ma gives me a funny look, and I stiffen. Here it comes: the comment.

"Danny's been a good friend," I say.

"Mmm." Her brow stays pointed. "He reminds me a little of your father, you know."

"Ma!" Is she serious? "You don't even know Danny. Why would you say that?"

"Just be careful is all I'm saying. You can think you know someone, and then . . . well, you know the rest of that story."

The thing is, I don't. Not really. All I know is that my father, Ma's high school sweetheart, got out of New Avon the second he had the chance. Even Tess was too young to remember much. She had a weird guilt complex about it, felt like he'd left because we made their lives difficult. I think that's why she always tried so hard to make things easy for Ma, to keep the peace. Not that Tess missed him either. As far as we were both concerned, Nick de Souza had no more claim on this family than a total stranger might. He didn't put food on the table, clean our scrapes, or kiss away tears. That was Ma. She was all we ever needed. She was more than enough.

Still, there are moments, like now, when I wonder about Nick, what he was like, which of his flaws I inherited, what it was about him that caused Ma to fall in love in the first place. It's a hard thing to picture: Ma in love.

She's scooping the leftovers into one carton. "What do you say to some TV?"

I look toward the small TV on the counter and bite my lip. The six o'clock news is done, but you never know what snippets they'll air on commercial breaks.

"I was planning to, uh . . . do some homework. I'm pretty behind."

At least one part of that is true.

"Oh, right. Your homework. You really should get a move on that," Ma says, but she looks strangely sad about it.

"Ma?"

She shakes her head. "It's nothing. It's just . . ." She looks up at me with an expression eerily like Tess. "I guess I was hoping we could spend some more time together. It's been a while since we watched one of your shows. What's that one I like: *The Real Detective*?"

"*True Detective*."

"Right. We'll watch it another time. Go do your work."

I hesitate. Homework, of course, is not on my agenda, but a TV night? We haven't watched any of our shows since April, and it seems wrong without Tess. At the same time, it may be the closest thing Ma and I have left to normal.

"One night won't make a difference," I say. "I'll go set up the TV."

Ma beams.

While she gets dessert, I grab the pillows. A few minutes later, we're curled up in our PJs and it's almost like old times. Except not really. The little sofa is too big, the room far too quiet without Tess's commentary. My sister had something to say about every wardrobe choice, every line of dialogue that didn't ring true. It was annoying at the time, and now it's just . . . quiet.

"Those slacks look terrible on him," Ma whispers after a bit. "Are they trying to make him ugly?"

I nod, try to say yes, ugly is the point of the show, but my vocal cords aren't working. Ma scoots closer, reaching an arm around me. In her soft gaze I see it: She felt it too, that wave of memory, the sudden loss of voice. I nestle into her shoulder, breathe her warm-baked scent.

Nineteen weeks.

How could you leave us here, Tess? How could you?

From the Journal
of
Tess da Costa

March 13

I stay in bed a few extra minutes while Callie showers, listening as
Ma bustles off to work. I feel like someone beat me up in the night,
somebody with cinder blocks for fists. My bones feel so heavy they
could sink right through the mattress and into the apartment below.
That would be awkward. Why, good morning, downstairs neighbor! I'm
gonna get up off your floor annnnnny second now, just as soon as I
can figure out which of these achy bits is my feet!

When the shower stops, I pull myself up one tired bone at a time.
By the time I'm standing, my head is slamming. It's been happening
more and more lately—headaches of the skull-bashing variety. It's
probably the dry air, lack of sleep. Winter seeking her final flu-ish
revenge. I check my blinking phone, ten unanswered texts from D, a
black crack of lightning across my vision.

It's a coffee morning for sure.

I make my way slowly toward the kitchen, keeping my spine straight
so my brain won't slosh against my skull. I need a minute before I can
work up the energy to reach for the coffee filters—deep breath, tippy
toes, reeeeeeeeach.

The box is . . . empty.

I toss it on the floor, decide crying would hurt too much. I open the next cabinet slowly, give a quick pep talk to my tired bones, but the scritch-scratch of cans and all that stretching—ooof—I slump into a chair to catch my breath.

When I look up, Callie is standing in the doorway. What's the matter, she asks. But there are no words to express the sadness of no coffee.

Tess? She comes closer, clutching her towel. Your face looks weird. You're so pale. Even your lips—

I'm just tired, I manage, the words too slow to be snappish. It's only a headache, I tell her. I'm fine.

There is a page in the How to Be a Sister Etiquette Guide that identifies the moment when a little sister should back the hell off— hint: this is it—but Callie has never done well with rules.

How many headaches has it been this week? she asks.

I lift my head one thousandth of an inch, just enough to give her a good, steady glare. I dunno, four? Five? You wanna be number six?

Callie's hair drips onto the floor. Puckers appear below her eyes, so small someone else would never notice.

Callie, I—

She doesn't wait for my apology, just reaches above the fridge and pulls down a new box of filters, tossing them on the table with a thwack. She's gone before I can flinch.

It all goes downhill from there. Late school bus, drizzly rain. It's not cold enough for snow, but it's wet enough to make my joints wail. I've had two cups of coffee and four Advil. My brain is still sluggish and sore. (On the upside, the voice has gone quiet, like even it can't stand being in my head today.) At the bus stop, I keep an eye out for dark cars and fish-faced spies. This is when they come for you. When you're already on your knees.

A man appears on the opposite curb. He isn't very spylike, though. In fact, he seems a tiny bit familiar. Ugh. Is it . . . ? Yes, it's that dough-faced guy from the library, the one who's missing a sister and definitely a sense of appropriate boundaries. He stands there in his short sleeves & misted-up glasses, the smeary lenses pointed at me.

Callie is at the other end of the stop, talking with someone from school. I want to ask her what she thinks, does this guy make her feel squicky too, but she keeps her head angled away from me. She's still pissed.

I check the street to make sure he's alone. There are no cars parked on this end of the street, no shiny sedans with silvery fins, just a little white truck with hazard lights blinking. Maybe it's because there are other people here, but Mr. Dough Face doesn't approach me this time. He just stands there, watching and . . . crying?

We arrive at school after the first bell. The halls are hot & crowded, slippery & steamy and filled to the brim with jeering kids. It's all I can do to keep from raising my fist and shaking it at them like some crotchety old lady.

D finds me after homeroom. He's planted himself by my locker, hovers there while I spin the lock, spin it some more, turn it every which way until it's my head that's spinny and still the thing won't open.

I decide maybe I don't need books after all.

You don't look okay, D's saying. Are you sick? Or is it still the missing kid? It's been over a month, Tess. You know it's not your fault—

Thanks but I don't need a shrink, I snap. (The caffeine gave me some bite.)

A pang shoots across D's face. Too late—I'm on a roll. I don't need people seeing you here with me either, I tell him. (I glance over my shoulder at my rude classmates, who for once don't seem to be paying attention.) That's the last thing I need right now, I tell him. More attention, more gossip.

The final bit comes out a little too loudly, a little too growly. The girl at the next locker widens her eyes.

You've been sending a lot of texts, I say more quietly.

But D's already backing away, his face all torn edges and crumpled corners.

Don't look like that, I say. Stop. I just need space. I need time to think. I bang my hand against the locker, regretting it instantly. My eyes begin to leak.

I get it, he's saying. You're right. You don't want to waste your time on me.

Oh, but I do! I want to tell him. You are wonderful! The best time drain around! And no one—no one!—should ever treat you the way I just did. The way I do.

D, please, I—

When I release my throbby skull long enough to look up, he's already been swept away by the second-bell tide.

237

23.

The sound of the front door buzzer makes us sit up on the couch. It's ten forty-five—too late for reporters, but who else would show up this late? Panic sparks in my belly as Ma pulls on a robe to go downstairs. I consider following, but then I notice the blinking light on my silenced phone: a missed call and four texts, all from Danny.

CAN U TALK

WHERE R U?

IM COMING OVER . . .

The most recent announces that he's here, waiting outside. Shit. Shitshitshitshit. I fumble with the phone's tiny keys, but before I can warn him to go away—and hurry—Ma's back upstairs.

"It's that boy of yours." Her lips are pursed, but I can't tell if she's annoyed about the interruption or annoyed that it's Danny. "I asked him to wait outside." She points to the upstairs porch.

"I told you, Ma. He's just a friend."

The truth: I'm a little pissed at Danny too, for yanking us out of our small-screen escape, for turning Ma back into, well, *Ma*. What could be so important that he couldn't wait till morning?

I pull myself up from my nest on the couch, and Ma's gaze sweeps over my tank top and boxers. "Put on a robe," she says. "And make it quick. You might want to tell *your friend* that decent people don't just show up at the front door in the middle of the night."

"It's not really the middle—" I bite down the rest. Not worth it. "I'll tell him," I say.

I step out onto the third-floor porch a couple minutes later, bundled in a thick bathrobe that belonged to Tess. Another rainstorm has come and gone, leaving the air heavy with humidity. My head is still slurred with images from the show we were watching: clapboard churches, savage murderers, good guys with twisted pasts.

Danny straightens when he sees me. "Aren't you hot?"

I shrug. Sweat has already begun to gather behind my knees. "My mother," I say as explanation.

"She hates me, doesn't she?"

"Not just you. All men."

"You think she knows? About me and Tess?"

"Nah. She thinks I'm the one you, uh . . ." I swallow, scratching one toe with the other. The rest of the sentence hangs in the air between us. "What was this urgent thing you had to tell me?"

"Right. That." Danny turns to look out over the railing, but there's nothing to see. Just quiet apartments and a dark, shimmering street. He grips the rail, and maybe three crime-solving episodes was too much for one evening, but I think I recognize something in his posture: those rigid lines, taut skin, a messy story pushing up, begging for release.

"I drove over to Plainsboro after I left you, to the Channel 4 studio, 5 and 7 too. Turns out Channel 5's down in Providence, so it was kind of a long trip. It was a ridiculous plan, actually." His arms fall by his sides.

I step closer. "You did *what*?"

"It was a total bust. I couldn't even get past the front desks. I did see one of those reporters, though. From earlier? She was talking in the elevator, seemed upset, like the story wasn't working out the way she hoped. I did the only thing I could think of and told all the receptionists that they interviewed a minor and your mom would sue the networks. They seemed to pay attention to that."

"My mom doesn't have the money to sue anybody."

"They don't know that." Danny shrugs, a small smile emerging. Sorry-not-sorry.

I'm tempted to grab him around the neck and kiss him. For doing all that. For me.

The thought must show on my face—and then the thought after that. At the same moment, we step apart.

Around us, crickets chirp and air conditioners hum.

"So that's what you came to tell me?" It was a sweet gesture—brave, even—but not exactly breaking news.

Danny squints out at the street. "When we got separated earlier, there was a reporter who approached me. She wasn't one of the high-heeled ones, so I thought she was a regular person at first. She asked if I was Danny Delgado. She asked me how well I knew Tess."

"She knew your name?"

He nods. "She had a picture of me and Tess at the library. She said there were more."

"Someone was following you? And taking pictures?"

"Following Tess."

Just then a car door slams, making my heart thud. We both check the street, instinctive. But it's still quiet, empty.

"She was always so careful," Danny says. "I thought she was just embarrassed by me. But if she really had reporters trailing her? That's—"

"Totally fucked up," I say.

"Yeah."

For the first time Tess's paranoia doesn't seem so far-fetched. "I doubt it was a reporter who was following her," I say. "Someone else probably gave them the photos."

"Someone like who?"

I have a guess, but it sounds too out-there. In her last weeks, Tess became convinced that Bishop Landry and his fishy assistant were gathering dirt on her, looking for a misstep. I told her she'd been watching too many spy shows. Real Church officials aren't half as demented—or intelligent—as the ones on the screen. Now I wonder if she was right. But *photos*? Would a bishop really be that creepy? And why hang on to them until now?

Because now the threat of sainthood is real. I get it suddenly:

how a twisted bishop's logic might work. If he truly didn't want my sister canonized, this would be the time to play every card he has left.

I suppose I should be glad to have a powerful Church leader on our side of the fight, but somehow it's not very comforting. Somehow, it feels worse.

"Callie, what if they know other stuff too?"

"Stuff like what?" Are we back to the sex question? Something worse? Was Tess *pregnant*?

"Danny, just say it."

He takes a breath and I wait for it: the real reason he's here.

Another breath and then, "I dumped her," he says. "I think."

The crickets are going wild now, singing a freaking symphony. I have to squint to see Danny's face, to make sure I've heard him right. "You dumped my sister? You. Dumped *her*." It's a simple enough statement, but none of the words makes sense. "You're not sure? You *think*?"

Danny sinks into a porch chair, catching his hair in both fists. I lower myself into the one beside him, the one Tess preferred because it didn't complain so much.

"It was confusing," he says. "I've thought it over a thousand times—it's, like, all I think about—and I still don't get what happened. We were going to talk more the next day, but . . . then . . . there wasn't. A next day."

"Oh."

The reality of what he's saying sinks in fast. The night before Tess died I'd come home late to find her slumped on her bed—not unusual. But that time was different because I'd had a hard day too. A math test bombed so thoroughly it shocked even me, and then a clash with Ma as soon as I walked in the door. I needed my sister to talk me through it. I'd needed her for months, but she was disappearing.

She barely glanced up as I entered the room. "Not now," she said. "Headache."

I saw the slug tracks of tears, the quiver of her chin. I knew the right thing to do was fetch her the Advil, maybe a glass of water too, to sit down beside her and listen. But I'd been listening. Sometimes it felt like all I did was listen. That night, I snapped. I let it all go. All the stored-up bitterness I'd been holding back.

I called her things I'll never be able to take back: *selfish, pitiful, weak*.

The next morning, she was up early, acting odd, *smiling*, which made no sense then and even less sense now. Danny had dumped her. Her kid sister had chewed her to bits. She must have felt horrible as she pulled on her school clothes. Her heart must have been bruised to a bloody pulp as I handed her the toothpaste.

The next thing I knew, she was gone. Gone down the stairs, gone on some sort of errand before school. And then just . . . gone.

I'm still stumped by one part of what Danny said. "I thought you loved her."

"I did! Of course I did. I still *do*. But things were never easy with us. It's like I was a distraction or something, something she kept separate. She was using me and I wasn't enough. She was so important, and I . . ."

"You what, Danny?"

"I wasn't good enough." His head drops into his hands.

"Well, that part's true anyway."

Danny looks up, confused.

"What? She's my sister. No one could ever be good enough. But she loved you. I have no doubt about that."

"Well, I'm an idiot then. The world's biggest."

"Probably not the *biggest*."

Both of us smile then, but if mine's anywhere near as pathetic as Danny's, then the two of us have struck a new low. Danny burrows his head back in his hands.

I should hate him for what he did, for hurting my sister, my sister who sighed each time she said his name. I should hate him for being such a complete and total fool. Instead, I drag my chair closer and place a hand on his shoulder. Because I get it. I wasn't the only one Tess pushed away. A small part of me is happy I wasn't the only one, but most of me just feels sad, sad for Danny, sad for all of us.

Danny makes a choked sound, and I grip his shoulder more firmly.

"No one can blame you for looking out for yourself, you know."

"They can blame me for hurting her," he moans. "And for some of the stuff we did. What if they think I'm just some asshole guy who was out to score with a saint? I've been reading up on Catholic virtue, Cal, and let me tell you, the things we did—"

"Whoa, stop right there." I raise my palms before he can say more. "I think you had the right idea keeping some things private."

Danny lifts his head and peers at me in the darkness. I can't tell if he's about to laugh or cry. I'm not sure he can tell either. "I loved your sister, Callie. I doubt the Pope would care, but I did. I loved her so much."

"I know." I reach again for his shoulder, but he catches my hand, folds it between both of his. They are warm, living things. Five fingers, flesh, bones, muscles, blood. Nothing extraordinary, nothing special, but their warmth seeps into mine, causing my fingers to twitch.

"Is that why you came over?" I say. "That's what you needed to get off your chest?"

Danny nods. "Yeah. That reporter really got to me, I guess. My head's been spinning ever since. Sorry I came over so late. I hope your mom's not too pissed. But, Callie?" His hands grip mine tighter, his eyes seeking mine in the dark. "Is it okay if I call you sometimes? Like, if I really need to? Will you pick up?"

"Of course. Will you pick up for me?"

"Always." His fingers travel over my knuckles and up to my wrist, finding the soft center of my pulse. The crickets are humming more softly now. A warm breeze whispers across the folds of Tess's bathrobe, filling the air with her scent. It occurs to me that it might not be so strange, whatever this is, happening here. Maybe comfort comes in surprising places. Maybe love can be passed from one person to another, like a torch, or a chain that loops outward, linking one heart to the next and the next, until it swoops back to where it began.

Danny's fingers slip back and forth across my wrist and his

face goes soft, like he's thinking the same thing. Would it really be so bad? Him and me? Would Tess blame us? Even on her worst days, all Tess ever wanted was for the people she loved to be happy.

I can see the words gathering behind his eyes, but before they get to his lips, a light snaps on and we're drenched in a yellow glare.

"Callie?" Ma's voice blasts through the window. "Get in here! You're on TV!"

24.

The three of us stand frozen as the television pans across the Langones' yard. It stops at a glossy-haired woman with magenta lips. *It was quite a scene here today in New Avon, Jed.*

It's the third time they've shown the same clip. A girl lurches forward, her face fierce and tight, hair poofed by the heat. *You! You're the whack jobs!* she screeches. The girl is me, they keep saying, a monster version that I hardly recognize.

Beside me, Danny smacks his head. "You idiot! Fox. How could you forget about Fox?"

On my other side, Ma is losing her shit, but in a terrifying, motionless way only a daughter would be able to see.

None of this is miraculous! TV Callie screams. *Jesus Christ, you people are [BLEEEEEEP].* She raises a finger to the crowd.

Investigators have verified that the symbol left in the Langones' yard was indeed man-made, or to be more accurate, child-*made, and while this isn't the first time New Avon believers have been called on their bluff, this time the skepticism comes from a surprising corner.*

Again, that clip. My face: ugly, shiny, torn with rage. *What happens when the cameras go away,* TV Callie shrieks. *She'll never get past this. She'll never be normal or happy. She'll probably wind up some messed-up old lady, broken and all alo—*

I sound worse than the alien guy. Why was I going on like that about a little kid I barely know? It's like I wasn't even talking about Ana anymore, but—oh.

I grab my stomach. I can't watch. "Turn it off. Please."

But Ma and Danny are still mesmerized.

None of what the reporter is saying makes sense. She calls me Tess's *older* sister. (Does she think I'm eighteen?) She mentions pedophiles, a summer drought, and mass delusion in the same sentence. She links Danny to Tess, calling him her *secret lover,* botching his name but following it with a clear photo of him with an arm around Tess. They're on the library steps, and some other guy stands beside them. It's not exactly the stuff steamy scandals are made of. But it makes the point.

TV Callie snarls: "It was my *grandmother* who saw *visions.*"

At that Ma makes a sound so small, so peculiar, my skin goes cold. She turns, eyes blown wide with hurt. The one thing she made me promise never to tell.

"Ma, I can—"

She swats the air to hush me.

"—explain," I whisper.

But I can't really, can I? And anyway, she isn't listening. Reporter

Barbie's pink lips turn sober: *According to local sources, instability runs in the da Costa family. Our team decided to dig deeper.*

The next shot is of a telephone, the old-fashioned kind with a cord and a dial. A recording plays over the image, choppy and scrambled. It sounds like someone is barking. Panting. A girl giggles. Her laughter is followed by a deep woof.

My knees unlock. That can't be . . .

But yes. It is.

The Sisters of Mercy informed us that this was just one of many prank calls originating from the Delgado residence.

Sister Lucretia smiles apologetically. *I'm sure they mean no harm. Most times, I hang up before they're through. But this one got caught on the machine while we were at church. The Sisters were quite startled to discover it. It was more (cough) graphic than they're used to.*

The recording plays again: more panting, grunting, whining. This time, it's punctuated by snorting laughter and a great big: *Ca-a-a-llie for the win!*

"Oh, God." I sink into a ball on the floor.

"*Nuns?*" Ma is clutching the place where pearls should be. "Callie, those women have been nothing but kind to us. I raised you better than—"

"It was supposed to be . . . a joke."

My voice has no fight left. Of all the stupid things I've done, to have *this* be the one that comes back to bite me in the ass? Honestly, I'm disappointed in myself too.

And from Ma's face, I know this prank call is only a cherry

on the shit sundae I've made. It's the Grandma betrayal that she'll never forgive.

The TV continues to jabber. *In related news, the St. Thomas Aquinas parish is offering a reward to anyone with information on—*

Ma hits the mute button, and my eyes pop at the image on the screen: a shrine, pummeled. Oh, Lord. Imagine the fun the Fox team will have when they uncover *that* ugly truth.

Ma's attention has shifted to Danny. "Is it true what they said? You and Tess?"

Danny opens his mouth, but all that comes out is a raspy breath.

"Ma, it's—"

"Callie. *Not now.* I'm asking your friend here a question." She places herself between Danny and the television, pinning him with a look that could kill a much larger mammal. "Is it true? Were you sneaking around with my daughter? Do you know what this will do to her reputation?"

Danny's shoulders tremble, and one hand pushes through his hair. Over and over.

It would be so easy to not say anything, to let this story stick: all the proof they'd need to decide Tess was no saint at all. But one look at Danny's wide-open face, those eyes of his that show everything—I can't stand it. I snatch his hand from the air and bring it down to my side. His palm is cooler than it was earlier. Clammy. It stiffens in my grasp.

"Those reporters messed everything up, Ma. You heard them say I was the older sister. They got it wrong about Danny, too."

I grab his hand tighter. *Shut up,* my hand tells him. *Go with this.*

"You were right, Ma. About us. You saw right through me." I gaze up at Danny with the type of smile I've seen other girls use on boys, puffing my chest up for effect. His mouth opens in full-blown panic.

"We've been together since last summer. Right, D?"

I tug on Danny's wrist, and his throat muscles convulse. "Rig—" He can't get it out.

Ma's eyes narrow. "And the photo of him and Tess?"

"Bad timing?" I say. "I must've run inside to get something. She was only there to get me because I cut class that day. She thought she could talk sense into me. She wanted to save you the worry."

Ma looks back and forth from Danny to me. It's a believable story—bold, specific—but will she buy it?

Her posture shifts. "How many things have you lied about exactly, Callie? Is there anything you say that I can believe?"

I stare at the floor, trying not to think about where we were an hour ago, nestled on the couch. Ma and I are back to square one, our natural, warring state. The worst part is, I know a part of her is probably happy about it: Tess remains unblemished. As for me? She already knew I was a lost cause.

"It's slander," she says to the TV. "I won't stand by and let them make up lies about my child. Tomorrow I'm going down there to give them a piece of my mind."

"I can go with you," I say in a small voice. I picture it fleetingly: the two of us, shoulder to shoulder, telling those plastic-faced morons where they can shove their "news."

Danny and Ma look at me like I've grown two heads. "What you're going to do, young lady, is keep your damn mouth shut. In fact, you're grounded until further notice."

"Grounded?" I think of the boxes of letters at church, the creepy one Danny and I still haven't properly discussed. I don't have time to be grounded. More to the point, Ma doesn't *believe* in grounding. "Ma—"

Her eyes are pure murder. I hear the thin ice creaking, and for once, I take my cue. "Okay," I say. "Grounded."

Ma lobs one more death glare at me before clomping out of the room, muttering something about her goddamn sister being right once again.

Danny's hand comes back to life, and he squeezes mine gently. "You just took a bullet for me, Cal. You didn't have to, but you did."

His expression is warm, grateful, a different kind of warmth from earlier on the porch. I wish I knew what he had been about to say before Ma interrupted us, but that moment is gone now. Everything has shifted again, new layers of sediment, new questions added to the mix. Are the reporters following us now? What happens when they find out what we're really up to? Didn't Danny say the reporter had more than one photo?

Danny drops my hand, turning, like he's finally seeing the room around him. Our living room. "What's with all the dead flowers?"

I try to see it the way he must: all the prayer cards and dried-up bouquets: yellow-brown roses, blackened leaves, spindly baby's breath. One hundred percent creepy. It wasn't always this way, I want to tell him. Instead, I push him toward the door, and as I reach for the knob, I remember a detail the newscaster left hanging.

"Who was that guy with you in the photo? At the library?"

Danny shrugs. "Just some dude. He wanted a prayer. For his sister, I think." He scratches his chin. "Yeah. I'm pretty sure he mentioned a sister."

All day they ask questions. All day the girl sits patiently, blinking for yes, staring hard for no.

They show her a photo of the front grass, lines nearly as crisp as the original. It's beautiful. Perfect.

Have you seen this somewhere before?

Have you seen it recently?

The girl opens her mouth, but the air is locked tight.

Please try, they tell her. *Give us one word. Anything.*

Her brow folds. She pushes every thought, every bit of energy into the void where her voice used to live, but all that comes out is a sizzle of breath.

The questions turn into pleading, and the girl becomes angry. Frustrated. She *has* tried. She *did* try. Don't they see? Look at the picture! How much clearer can she get? She takes their photos and tears them in half.

They get the hint, leaving the girl and her grandmother in peace.

Silence stretches then, velvet fingers wrapped around their home and the next. Soon the whole street is hushed, people tucked inside, dreaming restless dreams.

But not all of them. No. Not her monster. The girl can feel him near, waiting.

There's no mistaking it now. She's seen him.

From the Journal
of
Tess da Costa

March 20

How many headaches has it been? How many days of a voice clanging in my ears, thoughts spinning out of control, doubts mashing my insides to a jelly?

Jelly is heavier than you'd think. It sinks to your feet when you walk, leaving you light-headed & wobbly. When I lie down, the jelly seems to expand, spreading my skin thin like a balloon. There's a point when the jelly takes over completely, squeezing out all other thoughts, and you stop caring whether everyone is watching, what the voice is saying, or whether you're a big fat disappointment to them all. You stop caring if they'll see the truth about you because you can see it now for yourself: You need help.

I lie to Callie, tell her I'm seeing D after school. She shrugs, whatever. It seems like everything I do lately makes her eyes roll. She's started showering at night so she can avoid me in the mornings and putting on headphones before falling asleep.

I haven't seen much of D either. He's stopped texting, like I asked, and even though I know it's my turn, but every time I should apologize, say something. Anything would be better than silence, but every time I pull out my phone, my brain scrambles and I forget how to breathe.

Aunt Wendy acts like she's been waiting for my visit. She pours two sodas, and we sit knee to knee on Grandma's old sofa, the one with red flowers and wandering vines. Wendy finally had the plastic covers removed.

Nothing else has changed. Grandma's crystal angels still wink at me from the cabinet, wedged among family photos and trophies. Even Vovô's horrible brown recliner is still sitting smack-dab in the middle of things where it's always been. It takes only two seconds, and I'm back on Grandma's lap, her gentle hands on my face, those brown eyes that see everything.

Wendy isn't expecting my first question. Where did you hear that? she asks. She doesn't confirm or deny.

It's true then? Grandma was like me?

Wendy sighs, tells me what she remembers about my grandmother: the times she seemed to disappear in the middle of the playground or the grocery store—right there, but gone. Grandma fretted about the visions she had, tried to make sense of them and couldn't. There were days she didn't get out of bed. Your grandmother was very sad most of her life, Wendy tells me. They thought the hallucinations were related to the depression. She tried to hurt herself more than once.

Oh, I say. I didn't know.

Wendy grabs my hand. Have you? she whispers.

I shake my head. No, I'm not going to kill myself. It's nothing like that.

Wendy's hands relax.

But I do feel sad sometimes, I tell her. I'm sad right now.

I tell Wendy how a little part of me always knew about Grandma. I picked up on the clues, little things Ma has said and not said, the way she can't even say Grandma's name without crumbling. Sometimes, she gets the same expression when she's looking at me.

I just wish she'd told me, I say.

Wendy's face gets superserious then. Fierce, you could say. Wendy and Ma squabble sometimes, but they protect each other too.

She thought it would make you worry too much. I disagreed, but— Wendy tips her head, studies me—maybe she was right.

Do you think I'm crazy, Auntie?

Wendy's lashes flicker. That word is not in my vocabulary, she says. Your grandmother was simply ill. She asked for help, and the doctors did the best they could. We all did. The treatment she got wasn't perfect, but she got better. A lot better. After many rocky years, I really believe she found peace toward the end. You and Callie brought her so much joy.

I picture my grandmother, the way her eyes turned to warm chocolate each time she looked at me, and I know Wendy's right.

I wish I could talk to her, I say.

I want to know how it felt. What did she see in her visions? Did she believe she had a gift? Did they give her headaches sometimes? Did she feel as scared as me? As exhausted? Did she sometimes wish it would all just go away?

I wish I could talk to her too, Wendy says. I wish it every day.

We're silent for a while. Wendy pats my knee, tries to appear calm, but in those da Costa eyes I see a battle raging.

I pull together the last bit of courage I have and blurt out the thing I came here to ask: Auntie, will you take me to a doctor?

25.

Grounded is a new feeling. Within ten minutes of waking up Wednesday morning I decide I hate it. I circle the apartment like a trapped animal: nothing new in the fridge, no messages on my phone, same awful bullshit on TV.

Ma, in a fit of despotism, left notes taped everywhere reminding me that I am not to leave the apartment for any reason, under any circumstances.

Even a fire? I wonder, plucking a note from the stove.

Not that I plan to cross her on this. I keep hearing that sound she made last night—tiny, guttural—as she watched me share her most painful secret with all of New England. This morning, the comments sections on the local news sites were littered with nasty opinions about our family. Several people—including a few Ma once called friends—didn't even bother disguising their names. Ma looked so small as she left for work this morning, and for the first time, I was glad Tess wasn't here, that she's been spared this latest version of hell.

No, I'm not planning to do anything stupid. I'll stay in this third-floor cage, doing my penance, if that's what Ma needs. I've caused enough damage for one week. I got lucky, too. The reporters could've linked me to the shrines.

Speaking of which, I hesitate at the back door but decide a slight stretch of Ma's rules is worth it in this case. I'll be back upstairs in ten minutes, saving both of us further humiliation.

Rudy hears my steps, meeting me at the back door with a pathetic yowl. *You're better off inside, pup,* I whisper. *You don't want to see this.*

In the shed, door firmly shut, I light a candle and take stock. Something's not right, but I can't put my finger on exactly what. Has my beach chair been moved? Has old Mr. Flaherty ventured outside for the first time this decade? Was *Ma* checking up on me? Panic sends up a tiny flare. But no. Ma would've said something. If she'd seen all this, she'd probably have disowned me.

A car speeds by, bass thumping, and I get to work.

One by one, I take down the photos from the wall's inner ridge, popping them free from their frames. There are twelve total, from twelve different shrines. I went a little overboard the last couple times and snatched bonus items—a handful of notes people left her, a tiny statue of a girl saint, a horrible homemade crucifix that would've made Tess laugh. I toss the letters into the pile with the photos. I'll have to get rid of the rest separately. First, though, I need to figure out what to do with her photos—anyone who saw prints this size, these particular shots, would know exactly where they came from. Should I shred them? Dispose of them in an anonymous dumpster? My gaze drifts toward the sputtering candle. No, burning is better, more thorough. I clear a space on the floor and scoop the photos and letters into a tight pile so the flames won't spread.

The candle has sunk too low in its holder to be of much use, so I reach for the matches. There are only four left. That's odd. I thought the booklet was full the other day.

The first match breaks and the second won't light.

I look at the booklet more carefully. The sandpaper's worn through at the center. I press the match to the end that's still gritty. With a quick pull, it hisses to life.

Tess, age twelve, sits atop the pile, wearing a thin smile and a shirt I helped her pick out for her birthday. I squat down, bringing the match nearer to the photo's edge, and her smile grows more nervous. *Tess. Who could've expected this? You and me, here?* The flame creeps toward my fingers, its heat growing intense. Fuck. I drop the match, sticking my scorched thumb in my mouth.

I chuck the last of the matches across the shed, annoyed at my own weakness. The booklet skitters wide, landing on Rudy's cushion. I picture him there, blinking up at me doggishly. He'd understand my hesitation, wouldn't he? But I also know that Rudy would do anything to protect his girl, no matter how much it hurt.

I rise from my crouch, reaching again for the matches, resolved to get it over with. And that's when I see something odd about Rudy's cushion. It's too flat on one side, a pointed corner jutting out, like something's been wedged inside. Something the size of a small book. *Tess.* I run my fingers around the edge, finding the zipper. Out slips a slender volume, blue and white stripes, the same one I saw her scribbling in this past winter.

And that's not the only thing. Tucked beneath Rudy's cushion is a piece of orange paper, covered in a chaos of black pen. The dark slashes—immediately recognizable—make my throat catch.

they call me so many things
ugly stupid toomuchtrouble
    broken nogood headed nowhere
nobody loves a boy like me
they don't know
my angel loves me
    sees me
    says i'm good like her   good like G-O-D
it was them did this
them made my angel so sad
    took her away   left me nothing but a stone
talk to HIM please
tell HIM i'm good not bad
tell HIM give me back my angel
i can't wait   no   not much longer

It's been scrawled on the back of one of Tess's mementos—the flyer she kept from last year's Cranberry Festival. Which means whoever wrote it was here. In this shed. Going through her things.

My gaze jumps from the beach chair to the depleted matches, the candle burned low, the broken lamp. Heart slamming, I open the door an inch, then a few more, to find an empty driveway, a calm street, cars zipping up the block, a straight-shot view of the little duplex across the way.

There's no sign of where he came from, or where he's gone, but those final words have left a quiver in my fingers: He can't wait much longer. Or what? What will he do?

My phone pings. Danny.

WHERE U AT? NEED TO SHOW U SOMETHING.

THINK I FOUND ANGEL DUDE.

It takes all my concentration to make my shaking fingers find the right buttons. I text him back: I THINK I DID TOO.

26.

Danny climbs out of his car and we're both talking fast, pelting words across the car's hood. Him about mailmen and tracking codes. Me about creepy messages, stalkers, and angels.

I pass the latest note to Danny, and he goes quiet, frowns. He flips the page over and frowns. I consider explaining the flyer it's written on—sentimental Tess, the shoe box, etc.—but it's a messier story than I want to get into right now.

"I think he wants our help," I say. "Or Tess's help. Or . . ." I scratch my nose. I have no idea whose help he's seeking, actually. But I'm ninety-nine percent sure it's him, the kidnapper.

"You found it just now? At your house?"

"In there." I point to the shed at the end of the narrow driveway, and Danny makes a move to go see. I skid to the right, blocking his way. I don't need anyone—least of all Danny—seeing how deep my shit runs.

"You haven't finished telling me your thing. About the mail-man or whatever."

"He prefers to be called a *mail carrier*," Danny says. "I showed him the envelopes the first two letters came in, and he traced the stamp codes to the same spot."

"Are we going there now? To check it out?"

Danny looks at me. "Aren't you grounded?"

"Yeah, technically. But . . ." I look up at the third floor, then back toward the shed. There's no sign of anyone lurking now, but I don't want to be here alone when he returns. I don't want to cross Ma either, but . . .

I reach for the car door. There's still hours till she gets home. "This is more important," I tell Danny. "I'm coming."

We get in the car, and Danny makes a wide U-turn, directing the car toward the city's East End. I lean back into the seat, clutching my messenger bag with Tess's journal tucked inside and saying a small prayer that Ma never finds out about any of this.

We take a sharp turn onto a narrow side street, where a flock of lazy pigeons takes one look at the shitbox gunning toward them and rises up in feathered confusion. Danny bangs on the blinker again, and we emerge on deserted Acushnet Ave: New Avon's no-man's-land—nothing but weed-infested lots and abandoned factories as far as the eye can see.

"Where are we going exactly?"

Danny grins. "I was wondering when you'd ask."

The car picks up speed and Danny rakes back his hair all dra-matic. He's having way too much fun with this.

"MassBay Energy."

It takes me a second. "The electric company?"

Danny nods. "I checked both of the envelopes to be sure. They both came from the same mail machine, sent on different days."

"The electric company." A tingle plays across my scalp. I'm not sure if it's surprise or the exact opposite. I picture the little utility truck that was on my block earlier this week. Was it him? Right in front of our noses the whole time?

"You think he works there?" I ask Danny.

"That, or he knows someone who does."

We're still missing puzzle pieces, critical ones, but it feels like the full picture is on the verge of appearing, just waiting for us to snap the right clues into place.

We arrive at a series of low buildings, flat roofs and faded brick. They huddle together, windowless, separated from the street by a wide swath of parking lot and a long chain-link fence. We follow the fence until it cuts away to the water.

Danny turns the car around, and we double back more slowly.

There are dozens of cars on the other side of the fence, but there's no clear entrance. Giant signs warn SECURE AREA NO TRESPASSING, and the snarling wire promises punishment to anyone who disobeys.

We pull up to a small brick building sandwiched between barricades. The windows are shuttered. I get out of the car to see if there's a buzzer or someone inside. I've only taken two steps when I stop short.

To the left, behind the guardhouse, there's another small parking lot. This one isn't dotted with old sedans and shiny SUVs like the others. It's filled with white trucks in varied sizes and stages of disrepair. They're all marked with *South Shore Electric*, in yellow and blue, and a large logo: a bold circle, lines radiating outward, like a watchful eye or a newly risen sun.

27.

We're in the car, speeding back toward Cranston Street, and I piece things together as best I can for Danny. "Remember when South Shore Electric got taken over and all those people lost their jobs?"

"Uh. Kinda?"

"The logo must have changed. That's why no one recognized the old one when Ana drew it in the grass." It wasn't a signal from God or aliens. It was Ana, showing us a clue right in front of us.

That little white utility truck. Was it there on the morning I found Ana in the grass? Was that what she was staring at so intently? I trace my memories back to that morning, but the days have scrambled in my head. I remember the broken streetlight, but that was days ago, or at least I think it was. I have no idea how many times I saw that truck, or if it was even the same one.

"I'm not surprised no one saw the connection," Danny says.

"When a traumatized kid starts doing weird shit, you don't think: Oh, she must be drawing a logo! It's not the first idea that springs to mind anyway."

"Right."

But it's not the only clue we had. Or not the only one *I* had. There was also that phrase Tess heard, over and over, like a signal stuck on repeat. *Into darkness comes the light.* I kept telling her those messages likely had nothing to do with Ana, but maybe Tess knew better. Maybe that voice really knew things we didn't.

"*Into darkness comes the light.*" I whisper the words aloud.

"What's that?" Danny gives me an odd look. I explain as best I can.

"I told her they could've meant anything. Or nothing at all." But the argument is less convincing now. If Ana's kidnapper was *literally* in the business of making light? Maybe I was the silly one, refusing to see things that didn't fit my logic.

Danny is chewing his nail, and then, without warning, he hits the turn signal and veers right toward downtown.

"Wait. Where're you going?"

"The police. This is some serious shit, Cal. We need to tell someone."

He's right. Of course he is. Still, it makes me nervous, especially since we haven't come up with a plan. "How much do we tell them? Do we mention our little break-in on Walnut Street?"

"Let's start with the logo thing. And the letters he sent to the church. That may be all they need."

An annoyed-looking sergeant with a pathetic beard meets us

at the front desk of the downtown station. Before Danny's gotten three words out, he cuts him off. "Tip line's closed on that case."

"But we have something you'll want to see," I say.

The cop's expression doesn't change. "Sure you do. Like I said, we're not taking more tips."

"But it's a pretty big—"

He cuts Danny off with a swipe of his hand.

I blurt out a bunch more questions—Have they arrested someone? Did he work for the electric company? Where did they find him?—which the sergeant meets with a bloodshot glare. "This is police business, kids. We don't need your help. Also? You interrupted my lunch."

I crane my head to see if I can catch the attention of another—kinder—cop back there in the office, but the few heads I see are bent low over their computers.

Danny tilts his head toward the door. Deflated, I follow him out to the car.

Neither of us knows what to make of the cop's response. Was he just being a dick or are they really done looking? Did they find the kidnapper or not? Danny thinks they must have a suspect. We turn on the radio, but there are none of the announcements you'd expect, and nothing comes up when I do a search on my phone.

We head back toward my neighborhood, unsure what to do next.

"What if he shows up again?" I ask. "What if they're chasing the wrong guy?"

I pull the letters from my bag: *i can't wait . . . not much longer,* he wrote. The wind whips at the page as the car picks up speed.

We arrive at my house with a lurch and a squeal of brakes. I open the car door cautiously. The air is still and the pavement glistens in the moist heat.

No little white van. A good sign. Or at least, I think it is. I look up the narrow driveway toward the shed. The door is closed, unlatched. Did I leave it that way? I shoot a nervous glance back at Danny, and he comes around to my side of the car.

Together, we make a move toward the shed, and I'm thinking about how I'll explain its contents to Danny when a shout sends me up onto my toes.

"Callie da Costa! What exactly don't you understand about the word *grounded*?"

Ma stands rigid on the front porch. One pierce of those hazel eyes, and I feel the earth give beneath me.

"You're home early," I squeak.

Upstairs, I prepare myself for the tongue-lashing and maybe even another slap, but Ma is eerily quiet this time. She sent Danny home, waiting for his car to slip around the bend before yanking me inside. Now she disappears into the bathroom, her silence broken only by the sound of cabinets thunking open and shut.

The phone rings, and I stare at it, not sure what to do. I consider which would piss Ma off least—picking it up or letting it ring. She reemerges before I have to decide, tossing a bag onto the floor with a rattle. It lands beside her old suitcase. A suitcase?

"Ma? What's happening?"

The phone is still ringing. Two dark spots burn in the centers of Ma's cheeks and her mouth is pinched shut. I've never seen her like this. Her silence is unnerving.

"Ma. I know I wasn't supposed to leave, and I wasn't going to, but then something happened. If you'd just let me . . . explain."

The phone stops ringing. I search her face for some sign that she's seeing me right now, hearing me, but she is pure granite.

"Is it because of those reporters? Are they still calling? You know I didn't mean to tell them that stuff, Ma. They said it was *you* who was crazy, not Grandma. I panicked. I didn't . . . I wasn't trying to hurt you, I swear."

The hard edge of her jaw unlocks. "And the shed? Did you not mean to do that either?"

Now it's my turn to go silent. To gasp a bit. Ma saw. She knows.

"I'm told decent mothers keep tabs on their children. At least, that's what numerous people have suggested on my voice mail today. One even went out of his way to find me at the hospital, caused such a ruckus Lena had to send me home."

I close my eyes. "Ma, I'm so sorry."

"—and of course, you weren't here when I got home. Why would you be when it's the one thing I asked of you? I thought, maybe I should take their advice, see what my child—my own flesh and blood—has been up to when I'm not watching her night and day. I was expecting to find beer cans, Callie. Marijuana wouldn't have surprised me. I didn't expect—"

She chokes and her eyes—bright, brittle gems—say the rest: She's seen what I've done and thinks I did it on purpose. I realize how it must have looked to her—the frames and silly gifts discarded in a heap, Tess's photos tossed on the floor like garbage.

"I don't understand what could make you so cruel," Ma whispers. "Why you'd want to hurt me like this. Did I neglect you, Callie? Is that what this is: a jealousy thing?"

I lower my head. "No, of course not." I never envied Tess for all that unwanted attention—for being pushed into a role no sane person would choose. I prickle at the idea Ma would think it. But it would've been nice if Ma could've seen me too. That's it. *Seen* me. The way I really am: not a saint, not perfect, so far from it. A regular girl who sometimes feels mixed up and ugly. I wish she could've seen all that and loved me anyway.

Ma's looking at me now, eyes aglow, but there's no love shining there. Just hurt and regret and confusion. She looks as lost as I feel.

In the other room, her cell phone tinkles. She doesn't move. I glance down at the suitcase. "Are you going to turn me in?" I don't think criminals are allowed to bring luggage to prison, but I can't guess what else Ma could have planned for me.

"And have the whole city know it was my own kid who did this?" Ma snorts, then sighs, pressing her fingertips into her forehead. "Callie, I don't know what to do anymore. I've tried everything with you. I'm exhausted. I need a break."

"So what? Are we going somewhere? Like a vacation?" That was what Aunt Wendy thought we should do way back when Tess first heard the voice: get away until the chatter died down. A smart idea in hindsight.

Ma shakes her head slowly. "No. It's just you who's going. Why don't you go pack whatever else you think you'll need."

The girl sits patiently as the visitor puts away the crayons and brings out the dolls. The boy doll is shiny and always shouting. The visitor speaks softly to the girl doll, who is frightened of everything.

She has questions, same as last time.

Do you remember how he spoke? What he wore? What he fed you?

The girl frowns, concentrating on the spot in her chest where she last remembers feeling her voice, but no sound emerges.

Can you tell me what this means?

The visitor places a picture on the table, a circle, lines shooting out like a sun. The girl stares at it hard, breath coming faster. Her tongue quivers, then arcs in her mouth.

Do you remember anything the man told you? Anything at all?

The girl's throat unzips then, and her eyes pop wide as a sound escapes: one word. Two syllables.

The visitor drops the dolls, asks the question again. But the girl is tired, depleted. Her tongue has curled back in its nest. She pinches her lips, looks toward the door.

It's been another long session, and one word is all she has.

28.

"Well, well, well, if it isn't New Avon's favorite prankster." Aunt Wendy props open the front door with a round hip. She's a shorter, plumper version of my mother—darker eyes, lighter hair, twice as tough.

Ma didn't give any details about her plans for me. After she handed me the suitcase, it was like she'd run out of things to say. Like she could no longer bring herself to bother. The car ride over was silent, and as we drove up to a familiar white duplex, my big-voiced mother said not a word. Before I fully grasped what was happening, I was standing in the driveway, bags at my feet, while Ma backed out into the street, honking at anyone stupid enough to cross her.

Wendy clucks at my predicament. "I hope you ditched the paparazzi, hon. 'Cause my roots are a mess."

She watches, not offering to help, as I wrestle my belongings into an awkward armful. Two thoughts occur to me as I squeeze past my aunt and trip over the threshold: First, if there really is a God, she had a wicked sense of humor when she made two da Costa women. Second, a trip to juvie probably would've been a vacation compared to this.

I drop my bags on the rug by Vovô's old brown recliner. Wendy took over my grandparents' apartment after they died, but she didn't bother to redecorate. The living room is exactly as I remember it. Same floral couch and rose-petaled rug, same lacy scraps dripping from chair backs, crystal collectibles sparkling in the cabinets. And in the middle of all this fancy pretense, Vovô's cracked vinyl chair, taking up all the space it wants, like that ill-mannered relative who won't stop reminding everyone where you really come from.

I run my fingers along the worn brown pleather, wishing the old man were here to defend me now. If anyone could sympathize with the mess I've created, it'd be him. Always one to take the unpopular position, Vovô really let go after my grandmother passed, arguing at full blast. His daughters told him he needed to relax, watch his health, drink less. They said he wouldn't last long the way he was going. They were right. Vovô died two years after the woman he called his better, gentler half, his coração.

I get it now, why the loss had such an effect on him. I only wish I were an old man so I could get away with crappy behavior the way he did.

Wendy has decided to turn my downfall into an opportunity for free labor. First, she has me dust Grandma's knickknacks, one by one. Then I vacuum the apartment top to bottom (and *revacuum* it because she likes all the lines to run in the same direction). And just as I'm trying to figure out how I can steal a moment to check in with Danny—find out what he's been up to since our search got cut off—Wendy puts me to work on dinner.

I slice the carrots slowly, aiming for dials of exactly a quarter inch. (My mother's not the only da Costa with control issues).

Wendy tosses garlic into a sizzling pan and lowers the heat. "Your mother told me about that boy you've been seeing. I hope you're using protection."

I bring the knife down on the next carrot, nearly catching my finger. We were doing so much better with silence.

"I'm good, thanks," I say, hoping it'll shut the topic down quick.

Wendy takes a gulp from her wineglass. "Well, don't be afraid to ask him to do his part is all I'm saying. Girls can get funny about speaking up, but it's not worth the risk." She scrapes at the browning garlic. "Your ma made that mistake. Twice."

I turn to stare at my aunt, but she's busy adding the onions, doesn't seem to even see the problem with what she just said. A mistake? Me and Tess? I suppose I shouldn't be entirely surprised. Wendy is always giving opinions no one asked for, but this is a new level of rude, even for her.

I return to chopping, more aggressively.

After a minute, Wendy peeks over and chuckles. "The apple really doesn't fall too far, does it?"

I put down the knife. "What the hell is that supposed to mean?"

I spent the last two hours cleaning this woman's house and I'll do my part with dinner, but if she thinks I'm going to stand here and let her poke at me like this—if she thinks being my aunt gives her the right—she's got another think coming.

Wendy raises a brow. "It means you're a glutton for drama, like your ma. You're the spitting image of her, Callie, in more ways than either one of you realizes. Mona's always made things more difficult than they need to be. Her whole life she's been like that, running up against everybody, getting prickly over every little thing. She'd needle our mother, especially. It put your grandfather through the roof. The three of them got into a cycle."

Wendy takes another sip from her glass—it was a tall pour—and it's all I can do not to show her exactly how prickly I'm feeling right now. How dare she tell me what I'm like. Or pretend to be the expert on my mother. I picture Ma the other night, raw-eyed, telling me about Grandma's illness. Somehow I doubt Ma meant to needle her mother. Maybe she tried to be good. Maybe she couldn't help causing trouble.

"I have to say, I never thought I'd see the day when wild little Mona would turn into a church girl. No one saw that part coming." Wendy sets down her glass and sighs. "I miss my little sister sometimes, you know?"

I go back to chopping. If Wendy wants my pity, she's taking the wrong approach.

"She must've really reached the end of her rope to call me today. I knew as soon as her number popped up it'd be about you. She's always worried over you, made herself sick about every little hurt you felt, used to call me for advice all the time."

"She did?" I look up despite myself, and Wendy nods.

"It started when you were real young. You had a teacher—

second or third grade—who said you were too impulsive, always shouting out answers and getting upset when she punished you for it."

"Miss Jeffries," I say. I'd forgotten about her.

"You were too advanced is all it was. That teacher didn't know what to do with you, and neither did your ma. I told her you were a good kid and you'd turn out fine, but I think it scared her to see so much of herself in you. All of that fire. She wanted you to have it easier than she did. Wanted you to fit in without so much struggle. Tess had an easier time that way. But you can't tell a sun to act like the moon, I always told her. Sometimes the sun burns too hot, but you gotta let it shine. You gotta let it be the sun."

Wendy puts a hand on my shoulder, but I keep my head bent over the counter. I don't want her to see my face. She really thinks I'm the sun?

It's a lot to take in, and I'm not sure which parts to believe. Something tells me all of it is, and that's going to take some time to process.

Wendy gives her veggies another stir and flicks on the radio. She rotates past rock and pop stations, and I'm hoping she'll land on something mellow, maybe that Portuguese station Vovô liked so much. Some of that old-timey crooning might settle the swirl in my chest.

She pauses on an announcer's voice:

Earlier today, New Avon police arrested José Lara in connection with the Ana Langone kidnapping. Lara is a registered sex offender currently employed by Santos & Santos Inc., a janitorial service based in Braintree. He'd been on parole at the time of the abduction.

Wendy clicks her tongue against her teeth. "'Bout time they found that bastard."

It takes my brain a second to catch up. "A sex offender?"

"I know. Poor child."

"But she wasn't raped. The police said Ana wasn't raped."

Wendy's brow furrows. She reaches again for the dial.

She finds a similar announcement on another station. This one offers an additional detail. Police received a tip from the child. Ana gave them the guy's name: *Lara*.

They're interviewing a woman who lives near the apartment where Ana was held. Her voice has the gravelly tone of a chain-smoker. It sounds like the woman we talked to: Lew's sister Myrna.

It could be him, she's saying. *His hair was dark like that, bit of a belly. That's what I've been saying all along. A sex offender, huh? How many more criminals are wandering these streets, I wonder. Do we women need to be worried?*

"Callie!" Wendy lifts the knife from my hand. I've completely massacred the celery.

"Why don't you take a seat while I finish this up, eh?" Wendy elbows me out of the way, clucking at the mess, insisting it won't matter. "The sauce will still taste the same."

Wendy turns the radio to another station, and Amália Rodrigues's smoky warble fills the kitchen. It's one of Vovô's favorites, a song played so often in my childhood that I can almost make sense of the Portuguese. Amália weeps for a lost love, lost time, an old home she may never see again. Wendy sings along, belting the notes as Ma does in church, like it's a prayer she doesn't want God to miss. A psalm for lost souls.

Before bed, I unpack the items I'd thrown into my messenger bag earlier. Tess's striped journal comes out first. There hasn't been time to look at it since I found it in the shed this morning, and anyway I'm focused on a different question now. I lay the other items out on the bed: the three strange letters, the photo of the girl in the yellow dress, another photo of her with her baby brother, the social worker's business card, the page torn from some sort of church booklet. I flip the last one over, scanning the long list of names until I find the small scribble beside that one name: *Lara Tilsbury.*

Lara.

Is that it? Could that be what led them to José Lara? A single word? I do a quick search on my phone, but once again, the only Lara Tilsbury I find is an old woman in Arizona.

I stay up into the wee hours, studying the clues I've got from every angle possible, trying to get them to add up to a janitor named José. When my head finally hits the pillow, I'm met with a familiar scene: droning teacher, birds pecking hopefully, an ambulance pulling into the school lot. But this time, the dream takes a new twist. When I step out into the hall, I'm faced with a mob of mail carriers. Their letters are sharp as knives. One slices off my hand. Another takes off my kneecap. A third cuts out my heart.

Blood spatters the concrete as I run.

From the Journal
of
Tess da Costa

March 25

The doctor runs eleventy thousand tests and asks a gazillion questions:

What age were you when you first had this experience?

Can you tell me about your emotional state at the time?

Is the voice ever angry?

Has it asked you to do things that make you uncomfortable?

Do you feel compelled to obey?

The whole time she's asking these questions, I'm nodding, shaking my head, bouncing my foot, and fiddling with the pen I used to fill out all of her surveys.

Dr. Wolff, meanwhile, has the ultimate poker face, a face made of steel.

Ahhhh, mmmmm, she says after each of my answers, nodding significantly . . . or maybe not significantly. (Is it significant that I'm not a fan of exercise? Or that I'm a sucker for gooey sweets?) I don't know if I'm saying exactly the wrong things or the right ones, whether she thinks I'm beyond repair or hears this same stuff every day of her life.

You have trouble sleeping? Ahhhh, mmmmm.

But no fluctuations in weight or appetite? Mmmmm, I see.

Low energy levels? Shortness of breath? Ahhhhhhhhhhhh.

Please, lady, I want to scream. Just tell me: AM I CRAZY???

She calls Wendy (aka "my mom") into the office after a while. Wendy found me a doctor in Boston, one who definitely doesn't know Ma and clearly hasn't heard my story either.

The good news is I don't believe we're dealing with schizophrenia or another more acute disorder, she tells us. I'd like to continue meeting with Teresa, but—the doctor takes off her glasses for this part—it's not her mental health that is of most concern to me at the moment. There are other symptoms that trouble me more—the persistent headaches, the breathlessness. Her blood work looks fairly normal, but there's still a possibility that we're dealing with another underlying condition, something more serious.

Wendy squeezes my hand.

She should be seen by a physician, Dr. Wolff says. The sooner the better.

Clickclickclick goes the pen in my hand. I glance at Wendy to see if she's getting all this, but now she's the one nodding and going ohhhhhh and ahhhhhh.

So I'm not crazy? Is that what you're saying? I level my gaze at the doctor. Sometimes a girl has to cut through the BS.

Her mask drops away for less than a second. Mmmmm, she says. That's not a word I like to use. Auditory experiences can be triggered by a number of factors and are not necessarily a sign of poor mental health. Whatever we discover, my goal will be to help you achieve the best possible health outcome.

I sit back in my chair. Clickclickclick. Whatever _that_ means. She should've gone into politics, this one.

I'm going to prescribe a low-dose medication that will help with your anxiety, she tells me. Just a week's worth of pills to get you through until you can see your physician. You might find you feel groggy or a bit sluggish after taking them, but it will help you sleep better and calm those anxious thoughts you described.

Wendy is looking at me now, and I can see she's having anxious thoughts about <u>my</u> anxious thoughts, which makes me have <u>even more</u> anxious thoughts, which—

The doctor interrupts our little exchange: I don't think anxiety is a surprising response to the circumstances Teresa has described. But her stress level is quite high and until we can resolve the source, I suggest we work together to give her body a rest.

She hands Wendy a card. Then we're standing and saying good-bye and it's over and I don't feel any better, or any clearer. After fifty quadrillion tests, all she can say is that I'm <u>anxious</u>??? Maybe they should give me a medical degree because I COULD'VE TOLD YOU THAT.

In the car, Wendy is quiet. You know we can't keep this from your mother, she finally says. We agreed to one appointment.

I stare out the window at a bunch of birds soaring through the clouds. Spring is coming. It's almost here.

Tess, did you hear what Dr. Wolff said? It might be serious.

Yeah, I say. I heard.

I see the worry gather across Wendy's brow. Maybe I should feel something more than I do. But mainly I feel frustrated. I went to the doctor for answers and left with more questions piled on the heap.

Wendy wants to stop at the pharmacy to pick up the zombie pills that Dr. Obvious prescribed, but I tell her I'll do that later, after I've spoken with Ma. And Callie. God, Callie. For the past week she's been walking around like a dark cloud ready to burst and I have no idea why. A groggy head is not what I need right now, no thank you. What I need are answers, and let's start with the big ones: Where did this voice come from? Why did it choose me? Why is it failing me now?

Almost eight weeks since Ana Langone went missing, no sign where she's gone. At church, they've basically given up on me.

At school, I'm a joke.

And at home . . .

I never asked for this gift—this curse?—but now that it's failed me, a strange part of me misses it. It was so much easier when they all believed in me, even if I couldn't understand why. It was better than feeling sore and broken and sad. Even though it's not logical, I keep thinking that if I could just trace it all back to the day Ana went missing, if I could just make sense of those phrases I heard—for weeks, I heard them, and now? hardly anything—maybe this would all stop, maybe things could go back to normal, and we'd all be okay.

HOME IS NEAR, the voice told me.

INTO DARKNESS . . .

SHE RESTS ON A PILLOW . . .

THE SAVIOR CANNOT . . . PROTECT.

Something snaps in my hand. I look down and find the remains of a pen—the doctor's pen. Terrific. I'm a klepto now too? I try to piece the bits back together, but it's beyond fixing, all stabby slivers and pointy shards, like Humpty after his fall. Like me.

29.

Nothing's going to happen. I'll be fine. Call you in an hour." I unclick my seat belt and blink brightly at my aunt. "And the hour after that."

After some negotiation I convinced Wendy that the church would be the safest place to leave me while she's at work. She agreed, with conditions. The first one: I have to check in with her every hour.

"My phone's charged, I won't leave the building, not even for lunch," I tell her, waving the sandwich she made me pack.

"And watch yourself around that Danny kid," she says. "I don't want to hear about any funny business going on in the confessionals."

I roll my eyes as I climb out of the car. This woman.

I watch from the annex steps as Wendy spins the car into reverse. The sky is a swampy gray, the lot still damp from another late-night rainstorm. Through the windshield's thick glass, with her hair pulled back, I could swear the woman waving at me was Ma. I give a small wave, wishing it was.

I send the real Ma another quick text before I go in, another apology. She's ignored the last five.

Mrs. Driscoll's desk is still tidied from last night—she's off on Thursdays—and Father Macedo's office is dark. Danny won't be here for at least another hour. For a while, I'll have the place to myself. Enough space to drown in.

The conference room is in much better shape than it was when we started a little over a week ago. Danny and I replaced Father Macedo's "system" with plastic crates and hanging folders we found in a supply closet. The hundreds of letters we've read are labeled, alphabetized, and filed exactly where they belong. Meanwhile, the boxes of unread letters continue to grow.

I hunt for the spot where we left off, pulling a fresh crate of mail over to the table. It'll be good to fill my head with something else for a bit—something that isn't Ma's stony silence, or the constant media updates about the man they've arrested.

Danny texted me shortly before I fell asleep last night. He'd been listening to the radio too, and found out from a Spanish news site that Lara immigrated as a young man. He spoke little English and definitely didn't write it. Meaning: He couldn't be the same guy leaving those creepy letters.

So either the letters weren't written by Ana's kidnapper . . . Danny texted.

Or José Lara isn't our guy, I texted back.

We decided we'd talk it all through this morning, at church, and I promised not to do anything rash in the meantime. Not a hard thing to promise. I'm through with being the loose cannon. From here on out, just call me Cautious Callie.

A thin haze seeps through the conference room's narrow windows, and the ticking clock fills the silence. I find my rhythm quickly: slice, open, scan, drop. Next letter. The letters have all begun to sound the same, one story crashing into the next, like waves against a rocky shore. Maybe it's lack of sleep or the hangover of guilt from what went down with Ma, but for the first time, I feel their desperation—all that *hope*—pressing against my craggy layers and seeping through my cracks.

The outer door groans open and I drop the letter I'm holding, grateful for a break. But when I turn, it's not Danny who appears in the doorway. It's Father Macedo.

"You're here early, Carlinha." If he's angry with me, it doesn't show. "I've been hoping we could talk, just you and I. Join me in my office? I'll be along in a moment."

Father Macedo disappears into a back kitchen, and a second later, I hear the coffee grinder whirring. I make my way to his office on the other side of the foyer, feeling a bit like a kid who's about to get in trouble. I wouldn't blame Father M for thinking I need a little discipline.

I pick up a pile of bulletins on the chair opposite his desk, and prepare to explain what he must have seen and read since my Fox News debut. I take a closer look at the pages in my hands. The texture of the paper is familiar. Sure enough, I flip through the pages and find, at the back, long rows of names in tiny type. On the very last page, middle of the second row: *Lara Tilsbury*.

Father Macedo places two mugs of coffee on the desk.

"Do you know this person? Lara Tilsbury?" I point to the booklet.

"The name doesn't ring a bell. She's likely a family member of someone in the parish. That's a memorial listing, a way for parishioners to remember loved ones who've passed."

I squint. Lara Tilsbury's dead?

Father Macedo takes his chair, pushing one of the coffees toward me. I shake my head. I'm keyed up enough as it is, and the heavy lines that have appeared on his face aren't helping.

"I've gone through all your reports, Carlinha, and I've pulled out a few I was hoping we might discuss."

"Oh." My hands relax. That's all he wants to talk about? Not the pranks or the outburst on the news, or whatever else Ma must have told him by now. "I didn't do a good job?"

"You've done a fine job. A very fine job," he says, and in his gaze there's an expression I recognize—a teacher speaking to a favorite student—but there's a tightness around his mouth that doesn't quite match. "I think, perhaps, you've been a little *too* rigorous in some cases. I'm concerned you may have missed the point of this exercise."

"Wasn't the point to clear out the junk so you can focus on the serious claims?"

"I wouldn't call any of it *junk*, Carlinha. Every story matters in its own way. All provide evidence of the faith Teresa inspired, even those that one wouldn't deem miracles." He pulls a folder from his desk. "What about this boy with the asthma? This didn't strike you as significant?"

I sit taller. Asthma boy's who he's worried about? "I was careful, Father. And respectful, like you said. I called the kid's mother, and it was obvious right away that there was another explanation. He had three older brothers who outgrew asthma. He didn't need Tess to help him. A claim like that would never hold up at the Vatican. There's way too much room for doubt."

"I see. Is that why you're here? Because you have doubts?"

The question catches me off guard. I start to shift in my seat, but Father Macedo's granite gaze pins me in place.

"I had a sense of what was on your mind when you first volunteered to help," he says, "but I thought that reading these cases and meeting these people might cause a change of heart. That's what I hoped, anyway."

"Wait. This was a trick?" So much for straight-shooting priests. I should've known better. This one might have tattoos and a soft spot for social justice, but he still takes his orders from a guy in a pointy hat. (*Never* trust a guy in a pointy hat.)

"I prefer to think of it as a learning opportunity. You've done an important service here. You've helped me prepare for the inevitable questions from my superiors."

"But?" He's using the past tense. Is Father Macedo . . . *firing* me?

"I spoke to your mother last night. It seems I may have misjudged your emotional state."

I stare at the fists in my lap, feeling my cheeks flame hot. He knows about the shrines then. The fact is, I never intended to help his cause, not really—Father M and I both had some tricks to play—so it shouldn't be a surprise that I haven't lived up to his expectations. Still, it *is* surprising how ashamed I feel now, knowing I've let him down so thoroughly, having him see what a mess I really am.

"Are you angry, Carlinha? Is that what this is? Are you angry with your mother?"

I picture Ma, with her head held high, eyes bright with hurt, doing the best she can with a daughter like me. Ma worried for me, Wendy said. All she wanted was to make my life easier. She loved me and tried to protect me, and I burned her. Again and again.

"I was," I admit. "Really mad. But I'm not anymore. I don't think."

"Are you angry with Teresa?" Father Macedo's voice is soft as a well-worn blanket. "That would be quite normal, you know. Grief makes us feel and do strange things."

I squeeze my fists tighter, feel my face close up too. My sister was my best friend. My sister left me here alone, with no sense of what comes next or who I'm supposed to be without her. Am I angry with Tess? Maybe. Probably. Yes.

"You don't believe she's a saint, do you?"

I look up then. The easy answer to that one is no, but nothing feels easy right now. I've read that word, *saint*, hundreds of times over the past week, heard it evoked by lonely old ladies and by sneering reporters. *Saint*. What a word. It's like calling someone a hero. Or a monster. When you step back and really look, what do words like these even mean?

Father Macedo's firm edges have softened. "You do understand, there are many in this community who take great comfort in Teresa, in the belief that someone they trust is looking out for them. Even as we struggle with our own questions, we need to respect their truths too."

It would be easy to roll my eyes at the idea of *truths*, plural, to tell him that no stranger's need could ever trump a sister's. But I'm thinking of Mrs. LaVoie, sitting alone in her apartment, a grief so huge it swallowed her whole. Even if I don't agree with her belief in my sister, I get why she clings to it.

"It's a lot of pressure to put on one girl," I say. I mean Tess.

"That's a thought that kept me up as well."

"It did?"

Father Macedo nods. "You should know that your sister wasn't entirely unhappy, Carlinha. She struggled, but she also knew moments of grace. We had several long conversations, including one on the morning of her passing. I don't think she'd mind my sharing the essence with you. After some searching, Teresa had discovered that her followers weren't looking for her to become someone she wasn't. They wanted her to be herself, to be present, to share in their lives. She had come to see their trust in her as a gift."

It sounds like more convenient Church talk, but in my mind's eye, I see Tess on that final morning, smiling inexplicably as she asked for the toothpaste, and a feather of panic flutters in my gut. Is that where was she headed? To see Father Macedo?

I don't want to believe him, but I do.

"She used to tell me everything," I whisper.

"Yes, well. Some journeys are hard to share with others, even a sister. Teresa understood that faith is complicated, for all of us. She had to find her truth on her own. Carlinha, perhaps it's time for you to find your truth too."

My head lifts. I don't like the sound of that.

"You've been working hard, my dear, during a difficult time. I should have known better than to ask so much of you." There he goes again with the past tense.

"Are you seriously firing me? Who will go through all those letters? If you're not going to really question what these people say, what's the point? Why should anyone believe in anything at all?" I hear the hysteria in my voice. I know my protest is weak against his. The fight has been lost, but I still can't process what it means. Doesn't he realize this case is all I have left?

Outside the church bell chimes, and Father Macedo eases back his chair.

"Carlinha, I think it's time for you to step away from this case."

30.

I'm back in the conference room, spinning. I grab on to the table, a handful of letters, my bag, not sure what comes with me and what stays. Or what happens now. Without these ridiculous miracles to fill my days, I'm back to square one. Back to endless rounds of truth or dare in a musty old basement. Back to long nights, alone, no one to turn to, in a room meant for two.

Except, no. I don't even have that. Because now my friends hate me and I've been banished to a guest room across town. Ma may forgive me in time, like Wendy says. Then again, what does Wendy really know about situations like ours? Has she ever encountered one like it before? One daughter tapped for saint-hood, the other hell-bent on making trouble. Ma tried to love me, did the best she could, but I made it impossible. I pushed her away, betrayed and humiliated her. I deserve every bit of her wrath.

I slump into a chair. The table has gone blurry. My phone blinks—a message from Wendy, not Ma.

I ignore it. What now? Where do I go? What comes next? Questions, like so many waves, crash against me. I don't hear Danny come in until he's there, at my elbow.

"Callie?"

I tuck my head, push my fingers into the soft flesh below my eyes. "Hey," I say. "'Sup?" It comes out cracked, stupid.

I feel Danny trying to assess what's going on, glancing from Father Macedo's office across the way, back to me. Father M is on a phone call. From the sound of things, it's not going well.

Danny closes the door gently and pulls a chair next to mine. "What is it? What happened?"

I lift my head, see all the letters we still haven't touched, and have a sudden urge to retch.

Then I look at Danny. He glances down at his plaid shirt, self-conscious. "Just came from a job interview, or what was supposed to be an interview. Carlos's manager took one look at me and said he couldn't have employees who don't, quote, *exhibit integrity and professionalism*. I guess he saw me on the news. I didn't point out that it's a shitty mall job. How much professionalism does he think he's going to get? I wish you were there, Cal. You would've laughed in this guy's face."

I want to laugh now or make some kind of quip—ease the sting like a good friend would do—but my face is too stiff and my throat's barely working. "He fired me," I whisper.

"Father M? Why? What did you—" Danny catches himself. "I mean, why would he do that?"

"Because I suck at this. Because my only real talents are pissing people off and pushing them away. My mom threw me out too. Did I mention that?"

"What? Oh, Callie." Danny lays one arm on the table. The other circles around me, and there it is again: that warm, sturdy nest. Clean boy-scented cotton, a wide plane of chest calling for me to lay down my achy head. And I do. The tears rise without warning, surging up and spilling over my banks. Danny's arms tighten.

"Shhh. Shhh. It's all right. Shhhhh." One hand strokes my hair, while the other runs up and down my back.

Get it together, Callie. Pull yourself together, a voice whispers inside, but I can't. I don't have it together. Not even close.

After what feels like a small eternity, my shoulders stop shaking. The leakage slows. I sit back in my chair, and Danny finds a box of tissues. Together, we sop up the mess.

"Your mom's going to forgive you, Cal. She probably just needs time to cool off."

"You don't know that," I say. Danny has no idea how stubborn the da Costas can be. "You might want to think about getting some distance from me too. You already lost a job thanks to me. Who knows what I'll fuck up next."

Danny pushes a soggy curl back from my face. "First of all, I never had the job. And second, there are more stores in that mall and crappy jobs in this city. I've only just started looking. Don't you think someone will want me?"

He looks so pathetic as he says it, a crooked smile, hair all tufted on one side, combed flat on the other. It's meant as a joke, rhetorical, but I can tell by the way his gaze wavers that it's at least partly a real question: Danny is scared about what comes next too. He feels small inside, unchosen and unworthy. Like me.

"Of course someone will hire you," I say, reaching to smooth the collar of his shirt, all wrinkled and damp from my tears. *Danny.* In a shirt with a *collar.* It barely even fits—too tight in the chest and too short at the wrists. He must have wanted that job badly.

"I'm so sorry. I messed it all up for you."

"No. It's not your fault," he says again. He's such a good friend, and such a terrible liar.

My eyes are leaking again. Danny grabs more tissues, leans in to brush my cheek, a touch so light it sets off a pulse beneath my skin. He's there: lashes like brushes, spatter of freckles, eyes all dark-roasted concern. I push back the tears with a rough swipe, but a drop escapes, dribbles down to my lip. Danny's eyes wander there.

Shhhhh.

And then it happens. Lips on lips. Soft, at first, tentative. Then more insistent. Mouths cracked open. Salty and strange, greedy, confused.

Danny's lips are on mine, and my belly flutters, then flops. A little pebble comes loose somewhere inside me, and the tears flow faster. The dam is broken now, and there's a voice inside my head. It's saying something but I don't know what.

31.

The kiss stops as suddenly as it began, with the scrape of a chair and Danny tugging at his hair. "Callie." His pupils are enormous, black. "Callie, shit."

Not quite the words you want to hear when you've just kissed someone for the first time.

"I'm such an asshole. Callie, I'm so sorry."

I hunch low in my chair, and he keeps saying it: "I'm so sorry." And: "We can't." I want to tell him to stop, it's only making this worse, but all I can manage is a wet snuffle.

The room grows still, no sound except the clock's steady tick and the low thrum of Father Macedo's voice on the phone. Danny doesn't try to mop me up this time. I can feel him staring at my messy, snotty face. If I could melt into this chair, fuse my atoms into its wooden grooves, I'd do it.

"This is so weird," he says. "You and me . . . these past couple weeks. I get so confused."

I nod. I get it. It's not me Danny saw a few moments ago, not me he wanted to kiss. It was Tess.

"It's the haircut," I say.

Danny cocks his head. "You don't look *that* much like her. The way you act sometimes, though—it's spooky."

"You think I act like Tess?"

"I wouldn't look so happy, if I was you. Your sister could be stubborn. She took things too much to heart. She could be a real pain in the ass."

My smile spreads wider. It's true. Maybe he does know the da Costas after all.

Danny's gaze has gone soft. His arm rests on the table beside mine, close enough that I can sense its exact temperature. My fingers unwind, a small fraction of a movement. It's messed up, him and me. Or maybe it's not. I still can't decide.

Danny sees my fingers, and his arm slips from the table. "Callie . . . we can't."

There they are again, those words. But this time, I hear the words beneath them. It's not *we*—it's *I*: Danny. It's not *can't*—it's *won't*. Really, I shouldn't be at all surprised. Danny didn't choose me back then. I didn't mind it so much that time, and this time . . . well.

I pull my knees up against my ribs. The room has grown chilly suddenly.

Danny blinks, like he's seeing me for the first time. "Oh, God. Callie. Do you—"

I hug my knees tighter. "Don't. Please." I think I might fall apart completely if he says it out loud—that he knows what's in my crooked little heart and feels sorry for me. Because it's sick, isn't it? Being this lonely, falling for the first person who seems to see you, who feels some of the same pain you feel. It's a sign of serious damage, isn't it? Coveting thy sister's one true love?

Danny swallows loud enough to hear. "It's not that I haven't thought about it."

I lift my eyes. He *has*?

Danny scratches his chin, not quite looking at me. "But you know we can't. For so many reasons."

"Right," I say, even though I can't think of any right now, aside from the big one: Tess.

"I mean, look at me." Danny points to his plaid chest. "Your sister was pretty much the only good thing I had going, and now? Barely finished high school, no job, no plans. My mom has to give me *gas money*. Do you realize how sad that is?"

Not as sad as being kept back in tenth grade, which is about to be me.

"You'll find a job, Danny. You said it yourself. Someone will want you."

I bite my lip, wishing I'd phrased that differently, but Danny doesn't seem to notice.

"Maybe. If I'm lucky," he says. "But even so, I wouldn't wish myself on anyone right now. The stuff with your sister really messed me up. You don't even know." He lowers his head, lets it hang heavy, like suddenly it's become too much to hold.

Fact: I *do* know what it's like. How it is to feel completely scrambled inside, a total disaster. I could write the owner's manual on that feeling. Danny's a mess. I'm a mess. Both things are true. And even though I know he's right—*we shouldn't*—and I know it's not going to happen—he *won't*—part of me wishes he'd pick up that head of his and lean over and kiss me again. Right now. Danny Delgado can't fill the space Tess left, but I wouldn't mind if he tried.

"I just wish I'd understood her better," he mumbles, "or been more patient. Maybe she'd still be here, none of this would be happening, if I'd . . ."

"If you'd what?"

"I mean, I know she had that condition and everything, but she was gone so suddenly. It's stupid, but . . ."

I loosen my grip on my knees. Is *this* what's been eating at Danny? It's not just that he dumped her. He thinks her death was his fault. He thinks he broke her heart. Literally.

My feet plunk back on the floor. "Danny. No. Dr. Gillis said the heart attack would've happened no matter what. It wasn't anything that happened. It was just a matter of time. None of us could have stopped it." Even as I say it, I realize the doctor's words hadn't fully registered until now. None of us could have saved her. No one. Not even me.

Danny's brow crimps. "When did he say that?"

"When we went to the hospital. He asked about my 'headaches' and I—"

"You've known this for more than a week? Callie, what the fuck?"

I pull my head back, startled. "I didn't mean to keep it from you. We started talking about other things, arguing, then that thing with Karen, and I—" I don't know what I was thinking, looking back on it.

Danny shakes his head in disbelief. "You don't get it. You think this has all been about you, don't you? This whole thing. You call the shots, you decide what to tell me. I'm just here to rescue you or comfort you, or whatever. When it suits your schedule."

He sounds bitter, way too bitter, like this isn't just me he's talking about. But I know he's right too. In the beginning, this was all about me: *my* grief, *my* sister. Things have changed. I've seen pieces of Danny I'd never seen before—like that other night on the porch, like the pain on his face right now. I've seen a similar ache in Ma and even in some of the people we interviewed. I might have thought my grief was the biggest— the most important—when we started, but I know now that I'm not the only one with a great gaping hole where love used to be.

"I'm sorry. I should've told you. I get it now."

"Do you? Get it?" Danny's eyes have gone pitchy like the other day. "You think you know what I'm feeling? I really doubt that. You've never even been in love, have you?"

The words land hard, unfair. Have I ever been in love? Of course I have. I fell in love the moment I was born, the second Tess leaned over my cradle and peered into my face, her mouth wide open in wonder. My big sister. My universe.

But, of course, that's not what he means. Danny presses the heels of his hands into his cheeks, folding forward, nodding ever so slightly, like he's praying, or breaking.

I gather my things quietly, slipping out before he can make it official: He's through with me too.

The people take the old woman's hands and smile. They look at the girl too. Quick, edgy glances. They don't touch her, though.

She really seems happier, they say.

And: *Look at her color.*

Plus: *You must be so relieved.*

When they think the girl cannot hear, they add: *We got him now, the sonofabitch. That monster's gonna rot in hell.*

The girl wonders who they mean. They can't be talking about her monster. She peers out over the street, cocks her ear to the wind, hears his howls.

He made a promise a long time ago. He said he'd never let her go. And he meant it.

The girl watches as the people smile, hands clapping, mouths flapping, their nightmares gone limp in the daylight, terrors left unguarded.

She sees it in their eyes: These people don't know a thing about monsters.

32.

The church cemetery stretches for several blocks in both directions, reaching back all the way to the highway. Narrow, swooping walkways, enormous gray stones topped with towering crosses. The paths fan out to tendrils where the oldest stones, markings faded, sink into the earth like a bad set of teeth.

I place a quick call to Wendy to keep her at bay, and I walk back and forth, up then down, from old section to new, wishing I could get lost or at least shake off the truths pressing on my head.

I'm alone.

Tess isn't coming back.

No one, not even Danny, can fill the place she left.

I walk for a long time, walk until my feet burn and my legs grow loose enough to march right off my body. Until my pace slows to a defeated shuffle and then, finally, a full stop.

Teresa Inês da Costa, 1999–2017.

An ancient willow leans down, weeping over the polished stone and the small mountain of flowers and offerings. I haven't been here since that day in early April, a shivery blur of handshakes and hard-packed soil. Father Macedo gave one of his longer sermons that morning. He told a story of a man who lost his whole family quite suddenly, and with them, the very definition of himself. My attention was scattered. His words made no sense. All I could see were the rows and rows of stones. I tried to count them, to wrap my head around so much loss. So much heartache in one little city. Entire generations of pain. How can anyone bear it?

If there was a lesson about faith at the end of the sermon, I missed it. The next thing I knew, the crowd had drifted back toward the main path and their own lives, leaving Ma and me at the grave site, the earth raw and pitted beneath us.

I made a promise that day that I'd be back as often as I could. I'd sit with Tess, talk to her, keep her company among all those strangers. Come springtime, I'd make sure her little plot grew as lush as all the others. But in the weeks that followed, I found I couldn't do it—I couldn't do much of anything—and then later, as her shrines cropped up all over the city, the whole idea of a cemetery began to seem redundant. Why visit a grave when the whole city had become her tomb?

Now, as I stand here, I understand the difference. I feel it in the deep quiet and the dappled shadows. I see it in the bright clusters of lilies that lie across her stone. Ma. How often has she come here without me?

I sink to my knees and then my stomach, laying my face against the cool blades of grass, still damp from the rain, shutting my eyes against the images that want to come up: Ma's stony chin, frothy yellow dresses, Danny's salty lips.

Oh, Tess. I'm so, so sorry. I didn't mean to do it. I didn't want to feel this way.

I lie in the grass for a long time, letting the dampness soak through my clothes to my skin and squeezing my eyes against the image of your face, steady, unblinking, on that last night when you let me pelt you with insults. Maybe my sanity's worn thin, but for a moment, I swear I hear your voice in my ear: *I love you, Cal. Always.*

The giant cracks and gaping holes inside me yawn wide, wide, wider—so big that for a second I think I will split right open, all my insides spilling out onto the dirt. Then, slowly, they begin to close.

When I open my eyes, my vision is fuzzy, my head cranked at a strange angle. Straight ahead, another headstone glistens. It's smaller, one bouquet to Tess's thirty. The flowers are fresh, though, and the plantings well-tended. A pair of names is carved into the smooth stone: *Marlena Jacinta Figueroa da Costa & Francisco Patricio da Costa.* Above my grandparents' names an angel unfurls its wings.

I sit up. Green grass, gray stones, black pavement. The colors grow more crisp, the lines bright and sharp.

They . . . left me nothing but a stone, he wrote in the most recent letter.

A pillow of stone, said Tess's voice.

A memorial booklet with one name marked in pencil.

By the time I'm upright, the pieces have already tumbled into place. A *grave*stone.

It doesn't take long to find it. The groundskeeper points me to the main building, to a computer they set up for lost and confused mourners, searchable by the first and last name of the interred. A quick scan of records, and I have the name I want: *Lara Tilsbury, 1982–1989.*

His Lara. A name he must have whispered to Ana. A name she repeated to the police.

Did you see her, my angel love?

His angel is dead.

I find her stone set among other modest memorials. Fresh daisies, a pair of neat shrubs. The inscription at the top reads: *Behold, an angel. May she rest in God's arms.* There's a framed photo latched to the base. A little girl smiles, dark hair, saddle shoes, yellow dress foaming about her knees.

It's the girl from the photo Danny and I found on the day we began our search. At her feet rests another letter.

From the Journal
of
Tess da Costa

March 29

Wendy called twice on Wednesday, three times yesterday, once already today. My head is pounding so hard on the last call that I can barely hear what she's saying. Have I told Ma yet? No, not exactly. But I will. Just give me the weekend, I beg her. What's a couple days, really?

It takes some negotiating, some promises—I'll drink plenty of OJ, get some fresh air, get to bed on time, all of those things. And if I haven't talked to Ma by Monday morning, yes, Wendy can step in.

She finally agrees.

Time. That's all I need, right? Time to clear my head. Time for the last three Advil to kick in. Time to figure out what I think. Time to figure out what to say to Ma.

Fact: Dr. Wolff, a respected psychiatrist, has no idea what is wrong with my head. Instead, she thinks something might be wrong with my body? Finding out what it is will require a trip to another doctor, which Wendy says we can't keep from Ma. She says it was wrong to go around Ma in the first place.

She's your mother, Wendy reminds me. This is your health.

Right, I say. Of course. I know.

But Ma's been so stressed out lately. They've cut staff on her floor and increased her hours, and more cutbacks are coming. She's been dealing with stuff at church, too, things she won't tell me. And bickering with Callie like you wouldn't believe. The trick is finding a moment to slip it in—oh, hey, by the way, I went behind your back to see a psychiatrist and guess what? She knows nothing but wants you to bring me to a doctor which I know is going bring up all kinds of questions and maybe even cause you and Wendy to fight, so maybe we should just forget about all of this? Just, like, pray or something and hope it all goes away?

It's been nine weeks, and Ana Langone is still missing. So many prayers unanswered, so much heartache and disappointment. Meanwhile, the voice has gone AWOL, and I never thought I'd say this, Dear Diary, but . . . I think I miss it.

I almost confess all of this to Callie as we climb into bed. I want to. I want to tell her everything, have her break down my worries and tell me they aren't as bad as I fear. But she clicks off the light and rolls toward the window before I can get in a word. She hasn't said it out loud, but something changed when I snapped at her a few weeks ago. She's sick of me and my stress.

The truth: I'm sick of me too.

March 31

I still haven't found the right moment to tell Ma. Today, fewer people visit our porch than at any time since this all began two years ago. Ma says it's probably because of the cold, but her mouth has gone flat, unconvincing.

We're all losing faith.

She brings me hot tea and an extra blanket, and Rudy plops himself on my feet. (Callie stays inside.) Together we look out at the odd little group—less than a dozen people—who've come to see me. Despite the sharp wind. Despite a sky that threatens snow. Despite the obvious questions: Why haven't their prayers been answered? What kind of God can't protect an innocent child?

I've given them so little these last few weeks. All my energy has been focused on a few phrases that went nowhere, nothing leftover for them. They've kept showing up, though, even when I had nothing to tell them, even in the bitterest cold. Today they raise their eyes to the porch, hopeful.

There is Mrs. Tavares, who bakes me the most delicious little cakes (she hasn't seen her own grandchildren in years), and Mr. Cardozo who, each week, tells me a new story about his cat, Otis, the only friend he has left. Mrs. Khoury takes her time walking up the path, insists on kneeling, never complaining, even as her joints disintegrate, folding her into a tiny paper crane.

I take the bent hand she extends to me and apologize. The voice has been quiet this week, I tell her. I don't have anything for you.

A year ago, Mrs. Khoury's pain improved suddenly, and she told everyone it was because of me. But now it's back with a vengeance. She doesn't fret about it, of course, but I see it there in her trembling chin. And I'm helpless to do anything. Completely, utterly helpless.

That's okay, dear, she says, squeezing my hand. I don't expect magic at my age. I'm here to see you. Here to pray with you.

Something shifts in me when she says that. I get it, suddenly. Mrs. Khoury didn't come here today expecting a miracle. The others didn't either. For them, that's not what all this is about. Mrs. Khoury, old Mr. Cardozo, and the others just want someone to listen, to care, to pray with them.

And those are three things I can do.

I tell Ma to go inside, I won't be long, and I give these sweet people the best that I've got.

After the first round of prayers, my energy begins to lift. By the third round, my headache is gone and as we all murmur amen, I hear the voice for the first time in days: LOVE, it tells me. IN THE END IS LOVE.

I know somehow that this message isn't for Mrs. Khoury or the others. This one's for me. And I think I know what it means too: The voice is telling me not to be afraid, reminding me that even in the worst moments, when nothing makes sense and doubt and worry make everything bleak, there is still love in my life. Right here with this small group of believers. And inside with Callie and Ma.

I ask Mrs. Khoury & Co to give me their blessings before they go. Because today, the tables have turned. Today, their faith has healed me.

When I get upstairs, Ma has the popcorn made and Callie has The Exorcist queued to play. Ma asks how I'm feeling, and for once I don't have to lie. I tell her I'm okay. It's true. For the first time in weeks, my head doesn't hurt. My questions and stress have packed their bags and gone on vacation. They'll probably be back at some point, but I'm going to enjoy the break while I can. I sink onto the couch between the two people who know me best, who've been here from the start, battling, and worrying, and dishing out love the way they know how. We snuggle together under a giant blanket, and Callie, who's taken a break from grumbling, hits play.

Tomorrow I'll tell them. We'll call the doctor together. We'll find out what's happening and what happens next.

We're all going to be just fine, I tell myself, and in this moment, I believe it.

33.

"Explain to me again where you got this?"

The police officer squints at the letter I've handed him. His desk—crammed with coffee-stained papers and a computer left over from the Age of Gray Plastic—is one of dozens in the enormous, tanklike room. Around us, cops click away at keyboards, interrupted every so often by the scratchy belch of a radio.

"I found it at the cemetery, less than an hour ago," I tell the officer again. "It rained last night, but the letter was dry."

The officer fingers the crisp page. He isn't wearing a uniform like the others but dress pants and a button-down shirt, rolled at the cuffs. The plate on his desk reads: *Det. Eduardo Mendoza.* When I walked up to the reception counter this time, I was greeted by a different cop than the one we met yesterday. Maybe all that crying I did earlier gave me a more convincing edge—or maybe it was just the difference between getting a nice cop and a hangry one—because after about thirty seconds of my dead-angel spiel, this one buzzed Detective Mendoza.

"If the page is dry, it means he left it there *today*," I explain to the detective. "Which means he's still walking around out there."

I'm not sure how much more clearly I can spell it out.

"What makes you think he's a kidnapper?"

"Did you *read* this thing? It's practically a confession. He says he took her. He thinks he saved her. He says they'll be together again soon. Which: Hello, he's probably stalking her right this second! Don't you think you should do something about that?"

Detective Mendoza takes another gulp of coffee and scans the letter again.

my angel they take you
                    away
and away
they break me
                again
                and again
i want peace only
you only
smiling   happy
i take you, save you
so much snow, you laughing
its then that make you sad

make her smile go away
bad sound sharp sound like crying

heart breaking

put my hands say shhhhh shhhhhh stopit stopit SHUTUP

so much crying so much hurting

squeeze till she hush
till she smile with big wet eyes and I know
she love me always
my sweet sister child
we be together   soon

I tap my fingers, trying to be patient. "Did you see the part about the snow? Ana Langone went missing the morning after that big snowstorm." I can still see Tess's face when Ma told us the news.

I've explained the whole story to the detective three times already and don't understand why he isn't reacting. Four letters, same creepy-ass handwriting, same weird choppy lines about a little angel, all laid out for him on his desk. Plus, a photo of a girl in a dress matching the one Ana was found in. Dark hair, like Ana's. Sweet smile, like Ana's. But not Ana. It's his *sweet sister child*.

The guy who took Ana was trying to get back a sister he lost decades ago.

That's my theory, anyway. Maybe you have to know what a loss like that feels like to see it. I'm starting to think I caught this detective at the end of a long shift, which would explain why he's acting so slow. His face has a grayish tinge, now that I look at it, soft pouches under his eyes.

"You do realize we've made an arrest in that case?" he says again.

"And I'm telling you you've got the wrong guy. The right guy is Lara Tilsbury's brother."

His eyebrows lift. Detective Mendoza has a kind face, if you ignore the gray sagging bits. Eyes the color of autumn. He's probably somebody's dad or uncle. I might think he was a good guy if he'd listen to me.

"Did you look at the dress?" I direct his attention back to the framed photo, which I may or may not have unlatched from a grave a short while ago.

"You guys had the Lara part right," I explain. "But it's not José Lara. It's Lara Tilsbury, the kidnapper's sister. Little sister, big sister—I'm not sure. He must have told Ana about her. Or maybe he thought Ana Langone *was* his sister. In his letters, he seems confused, like he can't tell the past from the present.

"This guy is clearly messed up," I say. "Like, really disturbed." I show him the one I found at my house, his supplication to Tess, asking her to speak to G-O-D on his behalf.

The detective still isn't reacting like I'd hoped, and I didn't want to go there if I could help it, but—deep breath—I reach into my bag, pulling out the matching photo of Lara Tilsbury that I took from that shrine on Bedford Street. And the envelope we took from the apartment on Walnut Street, with the page from a memorial booklet, another photo of two kids (is the little boy the kidnapper as a child?), and the business card I still haven't figured out.

"You found this *where*?"

I explain quietly, leaving out Danny's role in everything. He's dealt with enough of my shit. I'll face these consequences on my own.

Detective Mendoza's eyes have lost their sag. He leans back in his chair. "Hey, O'B, get over here!"

Another officer appears, bloodshot eyes and an uneven smear of facial hair. Ugh. It's the same one who turned Danny and me away yesterday. I can tell from the way his eyes narrow that he remembers me too. He perches on the edge of the desk as Detective Mendoza continues with the questions.

"Let me get this straight," Mendoza says to me. "You messed with two clearly marked crime scenes. And you broke into a private residence."

I cringe. There's no dressing up those facts. "The door wasn't locked," I say, like it will matter.

Both cops frown at me. If this were TV, now would be the moment I'd ask for a lawyer. But this is real life, and a real creep is out there, seeking his dead sister in a living, breathing girl.

"You saw this part, right?" I point to the bulletin. "The little pencil mark. Same name as the gravestone. Lara Tilsbury. The guy living in the apartment knew the girl buried in that grave. It's got to be the same guy. Did I mention he left that letter *this morning*?"

The second cop—O'Brien—is still giving me a tense look. "What you're telling us is you've been hanging on to crime scene evidence—or what you *claim* is evidence—for more than a week?"

"I did try. I came in here yesterday, but . . ." *You wouldn't listen,* I say with my eyes.

His face hardens. "We got real crimes to solve around here, kid. We don't got time to talk to some rando girl about her little theories. If you wanna find a pastime, I got a good idea where you can—"

Detective Mendoza gives him the same *cool it* signal I give Rudy sometimes. He tells O'Brien to go see what he can find on Lara Tilsbury in the system, and the younger cop stalks off muttering. (Not hard to tell who's the loose cannon in this setup.)

"Now what's this about a logo?" Mendoza says to me, more quietly.

I'm telling him what we found at the electric plant, and how the symbol is just like the one Ana drew, when O'Brien shouts across the room.

"You guys ready for this?"

The desks around us go quiet, hands hovering over keyboards as O'Brien reads from the screen.

"October 12, 1989. Lara Tilsbury, six years old, killed in a domestic dispute. Mother and boyfriend charged with multiple counts of abuse and neglect. A second kid, Joseph Tilsbury, age four, is handed over to DCF. Looks like he was in state care most of his life, in and out of group homes, flagged for some sort of incident when he was sixteen, but the file's sealed on that. He was discharged from state care last fall. No prior arrests. No prints in the system either."

Joseph Tilsbury. An abandoned child. It fits well with everything in the letters. I turn to Mendoza, expecting him to be jumping out of his chair, but he's rereading one of the letters, tapping his pencil against the desk. The other cops resume their typing like nothing has happened.

"So what happens now? You go find him? Stake out the cemetery or something?"

O'Brien takes his perch on the desk. "Please. You been watching too much TV, kid. There's nothing here but a sad guy with a sad story. No indication he went anywhere near Ana Langone."

"What do you mean? What about the stuff we found in his apartment?"

"We?" Detective Mendoza's pencil stops tapping.

"Me. I mean me. *I* found them. In the room where he kept her." Kill me now. The least I can do is keep Danny out of this.

"Our forensics team was all over that place," O'Brien says. "I'll tell you what I think: You're a bored kid, too much time on her hands, maybe watched too much of that *CSI* crap?"

I glare at him. *CSI* is a terrible show. I'm not a complete idiot.

I turn back to Detective Mendoza to plead my case, but he shakes his head. "Like I said, we already made our arrest, hon."

"That's it? That's your answer? What if you're wrong? What if he's out there, trying to get Ana back?" The two cops look at me blankly.

There's a squeal and a blast of static. A shout comes from across the office, and Detective Mendoza is up from his chair, grabbing his jacket. O'Brien is already gone.

There's a flurry as the room empties out, a dozen cops rushing toward the sliding glass doors. Mendoza pauses at the last second, jutting his chin toward the pages on the desk. "Why don't you let me hang on to that stuff for a while, okay?"

"You'll look into it?" I ask.

But he's already out the door.

34.

The name Joseph Tilsbury brings up a single grainy photo: a man with large glasses and a warm grin. *South Shore Electric Employee of the Month*, reads the caption. A brief post, dated four years back, says "Joey" had recently celebrated his ten-year anniversary with the company. He'd originally been hired through a work co-op program for adults in residential care and then had moved into a permanent job. He was a quiet but cheerful presence in the company mailroom, his former co-workers said, never missed a day of work.

I stare at the photo, wondering how this could be the same person who wrote those strange letters, even as I'm now certain he is. I don't know what I expected. Gritted teeth maybe. The dead-eyed stare of a psychopath. But this guy looks . . . friendly. Kind. You wouldn't guess from the photo that he's got a disability or whatever, and the article offers no additional explanation about that. Had Tilsbury always been unstable and his co-workers didn't notice somehow? The cops said he was four years old when his sister was killed. Did he see her die? Was he injured too? Traumatized? In one of the letters he said that his angel protected him, took the belt for him. And then she was gone. He must have carried that history, that pain, where no one could see. Maybe he became good at faking normal. Or maybe the people around him were simply blind.

I look up Maxine Langone's number and dial it from the police station's front steps. Straight to voice mail. I leave a brief message, telling her to be careful, to do whatever she can to keep Ana safe.

Ma's phone goes to voice mail too.

It's lunchtime, and downtown New Avon is a noisy mess. Women in work clothes brushing past men with lingering eyes. An old dude shouts at a flock of pigeons as another beat-up car bounces across the cobblestones. At the bus terminal I see that Marcela girl who was the Portuguese Festival Princess a couple years back. Her hair's gone weedy, and she's bumming change for a smoke.

Oh, how we do fall.

That night, I lie on the guest room bed, listening to footfalls on the pavement, an unfamiliar dog's bark. Headlights spread out into arcs across the ceiling, then shrink back to slivers—gone.

My phone has no new messages: none from Danny, none from Ma. I can't stop thinking about Joseph Tilsbury, wondering where he is now, what made him do what he did, whether he's truly a monster or just a person who got dealt a really shitty life. I wonder if there are degrees of broken, if there are some kinds of pain that never heal. I'd like to think there's a hard, bright line separating someone like him from someone like me, but what if there isn't? What if we're all dancing on a line between stable and undone?

The room has grown stuffy, my head crowded with unwanted thoughts. Danny's eyes: pitch-black with anger. Ma: stony and still. Letters like angry howls. A six-year-old girl who may never get her childhood back.

And me, still here. Blood coursing. Heart beating. Brain cycling. Four months and thirteen days. Will it ever get easier?

I throw the window open wide and flick on the lamp, casting my gaze around the room for something—anything—to replace the snarl of thoughts in my head. My eyes land on the bedside table. Her journal.

I turn the book over in my hands, considering. Will it make me feel better or worse?

The hours stretch long before me, sleep far from reach. I decide I don't have much left to lose. I open to the first page.

From the Journal
of
Tess da Costa

April 1

I tell Wendy that Ma is all up-to-date on everything, that we got an appointment with my doctor and a follow-up with Dr. Wolff too. She makes a sound like a too-full balloon letting go of all its air.

Poor thing. I never should have put so much worry on her in the first place.

After hanging up, I turn off the house phone's ringer and silence the cell phone I snuck from Ma's bag this morning. I'm not proud of these tactics. I know I won't keep the da Costa women apart for long. But I don't need forever. I just need another hour or two, max. I'm going to tell Ma and Callie tonight. We'll have dinner first—my special enchiladas—then watch a little TV. We'll be relaxed when I finally say the words I've been practicing.

Ma, I'll say, Callie? Remember that time I fell off of the monkey bars and it looked a lot worse than it was?

They will see right away that it's not a big deal, and we'll make a plan to call a doctor, and everything will be fine.

Nothing works out like I expect. I forgot to defrost the chicken, for starters, and Callie is late getting home from school. The second

Ma opens the door, I can see she's all out of sorts. Her head's been hurting all day, her neck and shoulders too. She's been working so hard. She thinks she might have the flu.

I break out the heating pad and offer to massage her shoulders & feet. She's asleep within minutes.

And then it's just me sitting there, alone on the couch, no headache today—thank God—but my head's a jumble just the same. Should I wait to tell them tomorrow? What if Wendy calls Ma first?

My phone buzzes. It's D—first time he's called in . . . weeks. My insides sink, like they already know what's coming.

We haven't broken up, exactly, but after I snapped at him in the hallway at school, his texts slowed and then stopped. He didn't wait at my locker like he used to and has skipped homeroom almost every day. The ball's in my court—it's been in my court—but there's been so much on my mind that I haven't found the best way to apologize, to tell him all of this is my fault.

I'm a terrible girlfriend. The worst. Danny deserves sooooo much better than me. He deserves someone braver. Someone who holds his hand in public and laughs at all his jokes. A girl who will listen when he's hurting and kiss away those frowny lines. Who appreciates all of the little things he does, and how good he is, how loyal. A girl who will have a whole self to give him, a whole life that is hers to share and nobody else's business besides.

A girl, in other words, who's the opposite of me.

I leave Ma snoring on the couch and close the bedroom door quietly. I press the call button, and my heart trips on his hello.

Something's wrong with us, he says. Really wrong. I don't know how to fix it.

He waits for me to say something, and I want to say a thousand things, like: I'm so sorry I didn't call, I wish I knew what to do, tell me what to do, and I will.

But I don't say any of that. There's a long pause while I try to find the right place to start. I press one hand to my chest to keep it from cracking.

It seems like you don't want me around anymore, he says. Like you have more important things to deal with. I'm only getting in the way.

He gives me enough time to say Nononono, you've got it all wrong. Of course I want you! Of course you're important! But I don't say that either. I don't say anything. Because he's right. I <u>do</u> have other things. I <u>have</u> acted just like he says.

Tess, I don't know what else to do.

We're both quiet for a minute. My tears drip silently onto the phone.

You're breaking up with me? I say, to be sure I'm getting it right.

I guess? I mean, yeah? I think maybe I am?

. . .

Tess?

. . .

I can't say anything else. My heart shatters right then, taking my stomach with it and maybe my spleen. D mumbles something else into the phone, something about tomorrow, and the phone goes quiet.

I hold my knees to my chest for a long while, squeeze my eyes and my bones and the muscles in my toes. I squeeze anything I can get a grip on, which isn't much. I want to call him back, take it back. Everything.

Maybe I should. Maybe I will. Just as soon as I sort myself out, as soon as I'm ready to be the type of girlfriend he deserves.

Callie comes home a while later. Her face is twisted up, fists clenched at the world. She's muttering something about X, Y, and Z. Literally. She's talking about variables, and algebraic solutions and her awful Pre-Calc teacher, and, honestly, the last thing I can handle right now is more problems, especially the math kind.

Tess?

She stops her rant and peers more closely at me. I want to tell her right then, I start to, about the doctor, the zombie pills, D, my aching head and, now, my broken heart. But the sound gets stuck.

Not now, I tell her. Headache.

Her whole face flattens, then hardens into a new shape. I want to say I'm sorry for that too, but I can't.

So it's Callie who does the talking. She lets it out, finally. I am selfish, she says. Pitiful. I take things too much to heart. I always told her not to let people get to me, that she should be herself, always, and now look what I'm doing! Is this me? No. I'm letting all of these bullies and Jesus freaks tell me who to be. She doesn't even know who I am anymore. When's the last time we did something fun, just the two of us? When's the last time I told a joke?

All she does is try to help me, can't I see that? The past two years, that's all it's been. Lately, nothing is enough. It's all TessTessTessTessTess.

By the end of her speech, her shoulders are shaking with sobs, and I know she's right. About all of it. I've been a disaster lately. I've let the pressure turn me into someone I never wanted to be. Callie needs a big sister. She deserves a best friend who will listen to her too. And that's what she's going to get. Just as soon as I can stand.

She stomps out with a bang, and I use what's left of my lungs to whisper: I love you, Cal. Always.

I'm not sure she hears me, but that's okay. I'll tell her again tomorrow. And the day after that.

I have a lot of work to do, a lot of messes to clean up. I remember the words I heard yesterday: IN THE END IS LOVE. And I know I can do this. I just need to make some decisions, have a few conversations. Tough ones.

But first things first. My pillow calls to my aching head. There's a lot to do tomorrow, and I'm overdue for a good night's sleep.

35.

My cell phone wakes me. Tess's journal lies splayed on my chest, and my eyes burn. I read the whole thing in one swallow, then went over the last entries several more times before finally drifting to sleep, her words wrapped around me, holding me close.

It's Detective Mendoza, calling to make sure I'm safe. He was up late too, doing more digging on Tilsbury. "I can't share too much with you, but I can say we've confirmed your theory."

I sit up in bed. "You have him? You've arrested Joe Tilsbury?"

"Not quite. We have a bunch of guys out tracking him now. I want you to be extra-vigilant, Miss da Costa. If you see anything, anything at all—"

"Of course. I'll let you know right away."

"Promise me you'll be careful too. On that note, can I speak to your parents?"

"She's . . . not available. Look, I really don't think you need to worry. It's Ana he's after, not me."

"I'm afraid we can't assume anything about a man in his state. Based on those letters, we think he may have formed an attachment to your sister. He's likely seen you too and may think you can help him."

It sounds like a stretch. Still, to be safe, I fill the detective in on what I read in the journal, the weepy guy Tess called Mr. Dough Face, the one who kept muttering about wings.

Mendoza makes me promise to stay inside and call him if I think of anything else or see anything suspicious. "Please be careful," he says again. "The longer this man's out there, the more likely it is he'll do something drastic."

When I turn on Wendy's TV (she's gone to work), the story is already all over the news.

Breaking news in the New Avon kidnapping case. A source tells us that police have identified a new suspect in the abduction of six-year-old Ana Langone. Joseph Tilsbury, also of New Avon, Massachusetts, was among hundreds of adults discharged from the state's assisted living program last fall in the wake of severe budget cuts. Tilsbury was an employee of South Shore Electric until a merger with MassBay Energy prompted layoffs in December. Those who knew Tilsbury speculate that the combination of changes may have contributed to a rapid downward spiral.

Early this morning, police recovered a stolen electric repair vehicle that they believe was in Tilsbury's possession. They're still seeking his whereabouts for questioning. They've released a photograph of Tilsbury, advising residents that his appearance may have altered. Anyone with information about this man should contact law enforcement immediately.

After the third or fourth news cycle, I can't take it anymore: That same grainy photo keeps popping up on the screen, a grin that's at once heartbreaking and unnerving. I go out to the stoop for air, keeping my phone close. The August heat has given way to something milder, a breeze laced with hints of September. I watch the clouds skid around in the sky and wonder if I'll always feel this lost.

There's a lot to process. I helped lead the police to a criminal. The words Tess heard got me partway there. *A pillow of stone.* Does that mean she was right all along? Was the voice really God or something like it? The thoughts in her journal still curl around me, uneasy. Especially those last entries, her trip to the psychiatrist with Wendy. Tess was so close to knowing the truth, so close to finding a better way forward. It looks like Father Macedo was telling me the truth when he said she'd made peace with her role in the community. I just wish I'd known. I wish we'd had one more day together or one more week . . . or, you know, the lifetime we deserved. I'd always imagined us together till the end, like she promised. Two old ladies, seated side by side on a porch somewhere, her sweetness and my salt forever in perfect balance.

Instead, my final words with her were pure bitterness. And the response I didn't stick around long enough to hear?

I love you, Cal. Always.

When I read those words, they sliced me clean open. After all

I'd said? And done? After weeks of misunderstandings and shutting her out? So many could'ves and should'ves and what-ifs. And God, *Danny*. If I'd had any idea what he'd been put through, I'd have . . . I don't know. These last two weeks would've been very different, that's all I know.

A triangle of blue peeks through the houses across the street. After family dinners, while the adults settled in to laugh and bicker, Tess and I used to come out here to watch the harbor twinkle and shine, and she'd tell me about all the places we'd travel one day: London and Lisboa, San Juan and Avonlea. She wasn't sure whether the last one was real or not, but we'd get on a plane—or maybe a boat!—and find out. Her eyes shone as she spun out a web of plans and dreams—a future in which we'd each become the women we were meant to be, as sentimental or salty as we wanted, no questions asked. As she talked, I knew that I'd do anything for her, go anywhere, wage any battle. I still would.

I'd do anything for you, Tess. You know that, right?

I push the tears away roughly, and as I stand to go inside, something catches my eye. Off to the right. A familiar ponytail, swinging in time to a confident step.

I shoot up from the step, swiping my face, and shout Karen's name. At the far end of the block, my friend (or the girl who *was* my friend until recently) looks up. Her mouth flattens when she sees it's me. Tess wasn't the only one I treated unfairly. I walk toward Karen, head lowered.

"Don't," she says before I even have a chance to speak.

"Don't what?"

"Apologize. You're way too pathetic already." She shakes her head, nose scrunched. "Seriously, I know your loverboy ain't Mr. GQ or anything, but you ever heard of a hairbrush?"

"Danny's not my—" I stop myself. Not worth it. "Look, I'm really sorry about the other day."

She dismisses my words with a wave. "For serious. You been going through a rough patch, I get it. I'm letting it go this one time. But you can't go around talking to your friends like that, mucha-cha. Or one day you'll find yourself all alone."

Ha. Yeah. Don't I know. I kick my foot against the curb.

"Look, I know you don't like me shoving my nose in, but can I give you a piece of advice?"

"Do I have a choice?"

"Nope." Karen pops a brow. "Chica, it seems to me you need to decide what you want your life to be. You been dealing with your sister's situation for a long time now, but you can't spend your whole life inside someone else's story. Or you'll wind up . . . well, like this." She wiggles a finger at me.

It's basically the same thing Father Macedo said, isn't it? That I need to find my own truth. Funny how everyone's got a handy motto for how I should live my life.

"Thanks for the pep talk," I tell Karen. "I'll get right on that. Sounds simple."

Karen rolls her eyes. "Look, if this was a movie and I was your straight-talking and extremely good-looking amiga, I could prob-ably lay out the step-by-step. And it'd be a bunch of mierda. Real life's a bitch sometimes, Callie, pal. Far as I can tell, there's no shortcuts. Speaking of . . ." She flicks her wrist. "I got my own life to sort out. I don't get my hustle on, I'll miss my meeting."

"Meeting?" Is that what she calls hanging out at Danny's now?

"Yeah, up at the college. Classes start next week."

"Wait. College?" Now I'm completely confused. This is the girl who thinks math homework is a tool of the oppressor. Who cuts school. Regularly. With me.

"Pick up your jaw, kid. It's a program they got with the high school. Don't know if you noticed, but a lot of things changed last spring. I got a little wake-up call known as the future. You should come over with me sometime. It's way less annoying than regular school."

"Sure, maybe." I still don't want to think about school, or even that word: *future*. I'm stuck in the *right now*, the problems right in front of me. A mother who won't answer my texts. A sweet boy who Tess and I both took for granted.

"Cúidate, Callie, pal." Karen turns away with a salute. "Seriously, take care."

Back inside, I check my phone: still no messages. I pick up Tess's journal from the bed, flip through the last entries, and get an idea.

A shower and a quick bus ride later, I lift the metal latch on the Delgados' front gate, Tess's journal clasped to my chest. She ran out of time, never got to ask forgiveness for all the hurt she caused him, but I can. I can do it for both of us.

A television blares in the front window and the studio audience laughs. I make my way to the side of the house, where Danny's bedroom window gapes wide. His bureau is in worse shape than mine. In the middle of discarded papers and half-used bottles sits a photo of a happy kid and a messy-haired man who must be his father.

A car crawls up the street, stereo thumping. I reach for the sill and hoist myself inside.

Her grandmother is upstairs packing. After a few minutes, she calls down the stairs, "Baby? Are you there? Are you okay?"

The girl bangs a spoon against the floor to say, *Yes, I'm fine.*

The old woman comes downstairs anyway, locates her granddaughter with one eye, the TV with the other. It's been on since they woke up this morning.

The search continues . . .

They watch together, while her grandma folds a basket of laundry, eyes never leaving the screen.

There it is again: that face. Glasses just like the monster's. A rounder, happier face, though. The girl wonders if they're related, who this other man is they're seeking, how he got so lost.

"Everything'll be okay now." Her grandmother places a shaky hand on the girl's head. "It's just a matter of time, love."

Another photo comes on the screen. A child this time. Yellow dress, ruffled socks, saddle shoes. At the sound of her name, *Lara*, the girl sits forward, gasps.

They've found her. Finally. His angel.

36.

I leave Danny's feeling a tiny bit better, like maybe I did something right for a change. I wavered at the last second, holding the journal to my chest, ready to climb back out his window. But then I saw how sad his room looked, even more wrecked than mine, and thought of the look on his face yesterday as he told me how he disappointed Tess. (How wrong he was.) I have her other journals, a shed full of her rescued junk, sixteen years of shared memories. I realized he needs her words more than me. I placed the book on Danny's pillow and left.

I'm several blocks from his house when I realize I've gone in the wrong direction. My feet, on autopilot, have brought me to my own street. I look in the direction I came, the nearest bus stop now at least eight blocks away, most of it uphill. I don't have the energy—or heart—to climb back up. I just want to go home.

A familiar bark cuts through the air. Rudy? I walk toward the sound, and the barks grow harsher, more aggressive. I pick up my pace, and at the sound of a yelp, I'm running. One foot in front of the other, one breath, then another, muscles working, lungs pulling, one more block, a sharp corner, and then.

Nothing. I stop to catch my breath. My building looks the same as when I left it. The Langones' house too. No news vans, no utility truck. All around the tiny yards are quiet, no children out playing, no neighbors on stoops, no sign of trouble either, except for a scrappy old dog who throws his body against the fence when he sees me, his eyes peeled white with fear.

What is it, pup? What's wrong? I move toward the gate. Rudy froths at his mouth, his hard little nails clattering against the fence.

I look over my shoulder toward the Langones'. The house is quiet, a sedan with tinted windows parked in the narrow drive. "It's the police," I tell Rudy. "She's safe."

His barking grows more furious. Something pricks at my eyes and I rub them, feel grit scratch beneath the lids. When I drop my hand, I get a whiff . . . of *smoke*?

I unlatch the front gate, and Rudy bounds ahead, the breath ragged in his throat. I reach the edge of the yard and I see it. Jesus H. Jones.

At the back of the driveway, thick clouds gush from the shed. Tess's ugly seagull has been flung to the ground by the door, its beak split in two. I open the side gate and step onto the pavement. Rudy leaps to chest height, warning me back. I ignore him, placing a hand over my mouth to get a closer look. Flames leap up from a small pyre in the corner of the shed—the spot where Tess and I stacked our books. Fire licks hungrily at the walls, and sparks hop across the floor, nipping at bits of paper, turning them to ash. The smoke is too thick to see clearly, but it looks like the stack of photos from the shrines has already been devoured. Tess's shoe box sits apart, intact, less than two feet from the wreckage. The rest of her journals are still packed inside, along with the photos and scraps she cherished.

I jump back as something snaps and a stack of books tumbles with a sigh, sending sparks up to the roof. The flames spread faster, and I swing back toward the street, clutching at air, finding nothing but pavement and a barrel-shaped dog vaulting skyward.

Water. A hose. That's what I need, something that will put out these flames before it's all gone. Every bit of Tess, gone. But the hoses, I remember, are in the back of the shed, with the old lawn mower and a tank of gasoline.

Rudy bites at my shoelaces, dragging me away from the shed.

I follow him, dazed. Was it a candle? Did someone do this on purpose? Did Tilsbury come back?

I snatch Rudy to my chest—awkwardly—he's too big to be picked up, but I do it anyway, gripping him with everything I've got. He grunts in my grasp, his complaints are so loud I almost don't hear another sound: a soft whimper. Not a dog's. A human's.

I see him then, tucked against the back corner of the house. It isn't the cheerful face that's been flooding the news, but there's no doubt it's him—a disheveled, miserable version of the man police are seeking. He cowers, wisps of brown hair and eyes full of tears. His glasses have fallen onto the driveway and he blinks at the smoking shed.

"S-s-s-sorry," he moans. "So so sorry."

I stumble backward, down the driveway toward the street. Rudy, limbs flailing, catches my bare arms with his nails, but my heart is pounding too hard to let go.

The fire crackles, spitting embers onto the pavement. The huddled man sobs.

"The candle. It was . . . accident," he whimpers. "I'm not a bad man. I never hurt her, my angel."

He rises from his crouch, moving toward me, and I step back instinctively, twisting, pulling Rudy with me into the enclosed front yard. Tilsbury approaches the fence and something in his gaze makes me shiver. Like he's here but also someplace else. He stops suddenly, attention drawn to something across the street.

I turn just as the Langones' front door opens. Woman and child step onto the porch, suitcases in tow. Mrs. Langone has her back toward us, talking to someone inside the house. Ana sees us right away. She has a straight-shot view of my driveway, the burning shed, Tilsbury. She takes a step forward, lets out a strangled cry.

Like a puppet yanked to life, Tilsbury pulls to attention and lurches forward, headed toward the street.

I want to get the hell out of here, take Rudy inside and call for help. But there's no time. I set Rudy on the ground and move calmly, slowly back into the driveway. Rudy snarls at my heel.

"Lara," Tilsbury whispers. "I'll never leave you."

There's movement across the street. Hurried voices, a shuffle of bodies, followed by a shout. A uniformed officer rushes from the Langones' open door, her hands pointed forward, elbows locked.

Tilsbury trips forward, zombielike, straight for the gun.

They're going to kill him. Right now. In front of all of us.

I jump forward. "No! Don't!" I reach for Tilsbury at the same second he steps off the curb. His shirt pulls from my grasp, and the officer charges forward.

Rudy knocks me sideways, growling. Before I can stop him, he charges through the open gate, teeth gnashing.

Out of the corner of my eye, I see it approach: a car, big, shiny, moving fast.

The air cracks with one blast, then another. There's a sharp yelp, and I hear myself scream.

37.

A single thud, metal groaning. A crunch, soft and wet. The tang of burning rubber fills my lungs. I'm on my knees, bare skin against concrete, eyes raised to the sky.

It's so blue, Tess. A perfect, cloudless blue.

38.

Everything has gone quiet. I pick myself up slowly, and the pavement trembles beneath my feet. Or maybe it's me that's shaking. The driver's-side door creaks open and a woman steps out onto the street. She's shaking too.

"He jumped out," she whispers. "There was no time."

It's not clear who she means.

The car is stopped at an angle, its nose smashed into the side of a parked SUV. Smoke and a rubbery stench fill the air. The driver says something else I can't hear. She walks around the back and looks at whatever's on the passenger side, then turns her head and a stream of hot liquid hits the street. The sour stink of vomit makes my stomach spasm.

A cop is trying to calm the people who've gathered around. *Is that . . . ? Is he . . . ?* At least one person is crying.

A muffled sound makes everyone go quiet. A soft woof, hollow and echoing metallic. It happens again: another wheezy yelp, more jagged, coming from beneath the car.

I squeeze my eyes tight, squeeze my heart too, a silent prayer. *Make it quick. Please. Don't let him suffer.*

But the next yelp is louder, almost . . . cheerful? I open one eye. Another cop, the one who had the gun, is flat on the ground, peering under the driver's side of the car. I lower myself onto the pavement beside her and peer into darkness. My heart catches as one paw emerges from the shadow. Then the other. Bit by bit, Rudy shimmies forward. Scruffy head, torn-up ear, funny barrel-shaped body. The neighbors pull close, watching in amazement as he springs to his full height.

That freakin' dog. Rudy's stubby tail shivers. He doesn't have time to leap on me because I've already fallen on him, wrapped my arms around his scruffy, wriggly, foul-smelling body. *Silly pup, how could you do that to me? How could you . . . ?* My heart feels like it's split right down the middle. I squeeze Rudy to keep from falling into a million pieces.

A cluster of neighbors stands on the sidewalk across the street, looking at whatever's on the ground and speaking in low tones. I hear what sounds like a child's whimper. Then, silence.

Sirens cry in the distance, then grow louder, horns blasting, wails rising to a deafening shriek. A fire truck is the first to arrive. Shouts rise and water slaps hard against the ground.

More neighbors pour out of their apartments into the street.

"Callie? What happened? Are you hurt?"

Danny appears. He'd been listening to the police scanner and heard about a commotion on my street. He guides me to the sidewalk as I stoop, half crawling, my arms full of dog. I land on the curb with a thud and bury my face in Rudy's damp fur. He's bleeding.

Danny doesn't ask the obvious questions, like why am I crying, or who's that on the ground over there, or how did it happen. He just wraps an arm around my shoulder, strokes my hair, and I stroke Rudy, and neither of us says a thing.

Ma appears sometime later, still in hospital scrubs, pocketbook dangling. Her sharp eyes search every inch of me, hands hooking onto my shoulders, pulling me close. "Thank God you're okay," she whispers.

Even on a day like this, when the whole world reeks of fire, my mother smells like bread fresh from the oven. I let her hold me as long as she needs.

When she's through hugging me, there are questions.

"No, I'm not hurt."

"It's Rudy's blood, not mine."

"Just a scratch, I think."

"He didn't try to hurt me."

"Ma, I really don't know."

"I don't—" Someone hands me a tissue.

The police have questions too. Lots. I'm not sure what I tell them. I don't know how long Joseph Tilsbury was hiding there. Or what he planned to do. I warned that other cop not to shoot because . . . I don't know why I did that. Because he was a person, alive, and I didn't want him to be dead.

"Was it the gun that killed him?" I ask. "Was it quick?"

They shake their heads. The first shot slowed him, but it was the car that finished the job.

"Oh." I clutch my stomach, turn off the image that information creates.

Ma bats the reporters away from me. Cameras flash as a stretcher is wheeled away.

"Joseph Tilsbury pronounced dead at the scene," they say into their microphones. "A fire, a car crash, and a brutal end for the man police are now confirming was responsible for Ana Langone's abduction. We're live from New Avon as witnesses piece together exactly what happened."

No one is clear what the fire has to do with the accident, or what I have to do with Tilsbury, or how the dog fits in. So they make it up. Tilsbury is cast as the dangerous unhinged stalker. Me, the hero. Rudy, my brave sidekick. Tilsbury tried to burn me alive, the people say, and I stared him down, stopping him when he went after Ana Langone.

The firemen tell everyone that if it weren't for the recent rain, the shed would've gone up in seconds, taking the surrounding houses with it. "A miracle," someone whispers. Danny and I look at each other and shake our heads.

Ma has sent our addled landlords back inside, telling old Mr. Flaherty that she'll handle things. She guards the shed's smoldering remains with arms folded. "Private property," she barks at anyone who dares to come close.

"Back it up, folks. Crime scene," another voice adds. It's Detective Mendoza, forming a barrier with Ma.

"I hear you kept your cool like a pro," the detective tells me a little while later.

"That man's dead because of me," I tell him. *A man lost his life because I wasn't fast enough.* And I can't get his pitiful final words out of my head.

Lara.

I'll never leave you.

He was a dangerous man, a man who stole a chunk of Ana Langone's childhood and the peace of mind of many others. I should be glad it's all over, but when I picture how he cowered earlier, like a terrified child, begging forgiveness for the fire, it's hard to see him as a monster. It's hard to see him as anything other than a heartbroken little boy, missing his big sister.

"He's dead because he wanted to be," Mendoza tells me. "It's unfortunate that it had to happen this way, but it could've been worse. Much worse." He stretches a hand toward Rudy, scratching between his ears. "Cute dog."

I check his face to see if he's kidding. He isn't. Rudy licks his hand, and Mendoza laughs.

39.

Well, today turned out different than I expected." Danny collapses beside me on the front steps. The crowd has mostly cleared, and the ambulance is long gone, no trace of Tilsbury except for a large splotch on the pavement. It could be water, I tell myself. I don't let my eyes linger.

Rudy has gone off to investigate the ruined shed, but I'm not ready to face all that yet. All her things—*our* things—gone in a blast of water and smoke. *Ashes to ashes.* I can't look.

Ma and Detective Mendoza have been talking for a while now. They stand by his cruiser, Mendoza with one hand on his holster, listening closely, Ma touching her hair far more than she needs to. Is my mother *flirting*?

Danny coughs to get my attention. "You'll never guess what I found on my pillow earlier. Callie, did you break into my house?"

My mouth twitches and I shrug. "I'll take the fifth on that."

He laughs. "Okay. Fair enough. I promise to give it back when I'm done."

"No." I turn from the sodden driveway to face Danny. "It's yours. Tess would want you to have it."

His eyes turn a soft shade I've never seen. "Thank you. You didn't have to do that."

"Yes," I say. "I did."

Rudy has given up his recovery effort at the back of the driveway. As the detective drives away, he squats by the street and lets out a mournful howl.

"Does That Freakin' Dog ever shut up?" Ma folds herself onto the step by my feet. I can't tell if she's still pissed at me or if today's events have wiped our slate clean.

"The detective had some surprising things to tell me. Says you were the one who led them to the real kidnapper. *A regular little sleuth,* he called you."

Danny looks at me curiously.

"I found a few things," I say. "I thought I could help."

Ma places a hand on my shoe. "Well, you did good."

Her expression is soft, and I want to ask her, *Is it over? Can I come home?* But I'm afraid she'll say no.

She pats my foot. "You have some big fans in your corner, you know."

"I do?"

She nods. "Father Macedo, for one, and God knows your aunt Wendy always has something to say. They've both given me a lot to think about." She looks at me, bites her lip. "It's been a rough couple of days, hasn't it?"

I nod. It really, really has.

"Let's pick up your things tomorrow, talk it through then." She jingles her keys. "I don't know about you two, but all the excitement made me hungry. Anyone up for pizza?"

"I love pizza," Danny says.

Ma raises a brow. "I bet you do."

None of us feels like talking about what happened, so while we eat, Danny tells Ma about his job search, I describe Wendy's vacuuming fetish, and Ma catches me up on two days' worth of hospital gossip.

We don't turn on the TV once. We've all had enough of the news.

The girl sits in the sand, water lapping against her feet. High above, seagulls chatter. The girl and her grandmother have gone on vacation for a bit. After the thing that happened the other day—the girl still isn't sure exactly what it was, her monster was there one second, gone the next, all that commotion, all of that smoke—afterward, they placed their bags in a bus, which took them to a train, which took them to a boat, and the whole time, the girl kept her hands on the windows, watching as city turned to trees turned to water.

Her grandmother held her close the whole way, whispered, "Things will be better now, love." There was no waver in her voice, no clenched fist. The girl could tell the old woman believed it this time.

Now, at the water's edge, the girl tilts up her chin, watches a wisp of white cotton drift across the clear blue sky. The cloud moves slowly, grows translucent, stretching for the sun. A shadow flickers briefly across her face and she shivers. The next second, like a spell that's been broken, the shadow is gone.

She drops her shovel, turns to where her grandmother sits a few yards away, book in hand, face shaded by a wide-brimmed hat.

Ana opens her mouth. "Grandma, I'm hungry."

40.

The next afternoon, I take one look at my bedroom and walk back out. I return with an armful of cleaning products and a broom.

"Need help?" Ma is wearing the ripped-up jeans she saves for housework. She decided to take a couple of days off after all that happened.

While we mop and spray, we have the first of what will probably be many big talks, complete with apologies, a few tears, and the expected sap. Ma still doesn't completely understand why I did everything I did, but she's trying. And I still hate all of the saint stuff, but I'm starting to see that Ma's dealing with her own heartache the best way she knows how. Neither of us likes the fights we get into; we need to work on that. Father Macedo suggested we look past our differences for now and work on building some bridges. He told Ma that grief does funny things to people, that it doesn't always make sense.

No kidding.

When evening comes, I sit back on my bed, exhausted. Four months and fifteen days. Two more weeks and I'll go back to school, alone. Another two weeks beyond that and she'd be eighteen. This year will be full of painful markers. No way around it.

A breeze wafts through the window, and the last bits of sunlight cast a warm glow on the wooden bureaus and floor. No more dust. No more clutter. The room doesn't feel as bare as I'd expected. Tess's clothing and many of her belongings are in boxes now. Her bed is stripped clean, ready to go to another family who needs it. I've decided to keep her little figurines and bottles.

"Not junk," she insisted. "Treasures."

The next few days are uneventful—pretty boring, if we're being honest. But sometimes boring is good. Sometimes it's just what the doctor ordered. On Sunday, I spend a few hours looking at the info Karen brought over on the early college program she's joined. I rearrange Ma's living room shrine, swapping a few of the prayer cards for a framed photo of the three of us. After that, I try making Grandma's famous almond cake and burn it past recognition. Wendy comes over for dinner that night, and she and Ma stay up late, talking and drinking too much wine.

I spend most of Monday afternoon rescuing what I can from the ashes of the shed. Not everything was ruined—a few of Tess's romance novels made it, and a cluster of photos and one chair survived. Miraculously, so did a couple of her journals. As I poke through the ashes, I tell Rudy the story of a brave little dog who risked his life to protect the girl who loves him. He wags his tail and pants. It's his favorite story yet.

On Wednesday, Rudy and I walk the streets of New Avon. He leads the way on his new leash, a gift from Danny, and we trek down to the harbor, up to the high school, and back around through the park. New Avon isn't any more exciting than the last time I checked, but the number of shrines seems to have reached its peak. I leave the ones we see untouched.

At the cemetery, we stop to visit Tess and my grandparents. I pause at Joseph Tilsbury's grave too. The marker is temporary, the fresh earth bare. I steal a blossom from a better-loved stone and place it on top of his. It's a daisy. Yellow like the sun.

The papers have been full of stories about him—people trying to piece together who Tilsbury really was and where to place blame. Why did it take the police so long to find him? Why didn't his employer report the stolen truck sooner? Should the state be held responsible for pushing a man who was clearly unwell out on his own? If one person had noticed him, or spoken up sooner, could the whole tragedy have been avoided?

Some people say none of it matters, he did what he did, and he'll spend an eternity burning in hell for it. I hope they're wrong. I think of those lines he wrote and picture those giant, swooping wings. I hope his hell has ended and that, wherever he is, he finds some sort of peace.

I stop by the church on Friday. Letters are still arriving by the boxful, more and more of them coming from far-flung corners of the globe. Dublin. Nairobi. Paraguay. Tess never got to travel the world like she hoped. Now it seems the world is coming to her. It's all backward. Still, I bet it would make her smile.

I offer to tidy things for Father Macedo and maybe make a few calls. "I'll take you up on the first part," he says. "But I was quite serious about you taking a break from the rest."

When the letters are neatly labeled and tucked where they belong, I tell Father Macedo I'll see him soon. On the way out, I spot Mrs. Driscoll's spare keys hanging beside the mailboxes. I slip them in my pocket.

Danny has Saturday off from his new job. The pay is crappy, he says, but the ladies at the nursing home look forward to his visits already. "Their stories are hilarious. You wouldn't believe some of the stuff they used to do."

I only tease him a little.

We spend the rest of the day watching Tess's favorite horror movies in his basement. Danny sits on the couch, and I take the worn-out recliner.

"There's something I still don't get," he says between movies. "If the things Tess heard had to do with Tilsbury, then the first three might make sense. *Home is near*—'cause Ana was so close. *Into the darkness comes the light*—'cause he was using an electric company van to stalk her. *She rests on a pillow of stone*—"

"Because his sister was dead."

"Right. But the other one: *The savior cannot protect.* What does that have to do with anything?"

"I don't know." I've been wondering too, not because I've

become a believer in all things mystical, but because I've realized that maybe there are some things that defy logic, things that go beyond what any of us can fully understand, as hard as we may try.

"It could be about Lara not being able to protect her little brother, or maybe Tess who couldn't help Ana, or . . ." I pause, lock eyes with Danny. Maybe it's about us, unable to save Tess. "It could mean nothing, or anything we want it to, I guess."

Danny asks me if I plan to continue with her case, try to work my way back into Father Macedo's good graces, but I tell him I think I'm done with that. For now anyway. If those people need to believe in sainthood, let them. I can't spend my whole life fighting other peoples' faith. In the end, Tess had made some sort of peace with it and I'm going to try making my peace too.

Danny looks surprised.

"I have my own life to sort out," I explain. It's not that all of the shrines and stuff no longer bother me. Or that I've stopped missing Tess. I'll carry that ache with me always, just as I carry her words, her laughter, and her hurt. But I can't let myself become another Tilsbury—twisted beyond recognition by grief. I can't let the absence of Tess be all there is left of me.

"I have a lot of catching up to do," I tell Danny. "School starts in another week. I'm thinking about doing this program Karen was telling me about. They help you make up credits and earn credits toward college."

"For real?"

"Don't get too excited. It's community college. It's probably crap."

"No, it sounds good." Danny smiles. "It sounds really good."

As I stand to go, he gives me a big hug. It lasts for several seconds, maybe a second or two longer than it should.

He doesn't notice when I swipe his car keys from the table by the door.

That night, as I ease Danny's car away from the curb, the street is silent and the houses dark and peaceful.

St. Thomas's after midnight is a different place. The empty pews crouch low, miniature under the enormous arches, their farthest corners invisible in the darkness. A single streetlight shines through the stained glass, illuminating the altar in its multicolored glow.

I hum a couple of lines from one of Vovô's old songs while I work. It takes less than an hour to assemble. I've gone through my own collection of photos to find the best ones: the two of us doing chipmunk impressions, Tess sweaty after a bike ride. Tess caught by surprise, in a big openmouthed laugh.

When I'm through, I light a candle and say a quick prayer—to Tess, not God, since I still don't know what I think about the God stuff. That investigation will have to wait.

The candlelight flickers and shifts, mixing with the streetlight and illuminating my work. It's a dare that surpasses all others, a shrine to outshine the rest. Tomorrow, Sunday, it will be here for all to see: the photos, the letters, her funny little figurines and murky glass bottles, a patched-up seagull and a scorched paperback romance, a full-sized portrait of Tess with her great big laugh. It's the real Tess, the full Tess, unedited and unashamed. Soon they'll all get to meet her: my sister, as she'll always be to me.

I have a new dream that night. There are no birds in this one, no yellow lights. We're at a playground, Tess on the swing beside me. She kicks her feet, stretches her long legs, and her curls fly out behind her. She swoops back and her curls cover her face, then forward again, climbing high, high, higher. She arcs her throat to the sky and howls.

I try to follow her example. I pump my little legs, pull, push, rock my body in the hard rubber seat. But I don't soar. There's no whoosh for me. I kick harder, rock faster. Nothing.

Tess turns to tell me something and sees my face. Her smile fades and her swing loses height. Then my big sister is behind me, arms on either side. She pushes and pulls, pulls and pushes. She lifts me back and, with one mighty push, I fly.

Acknowledgments

You know those debut authors who go on and on in the acknowledgments? Well, there's a reason for that. First books are a special kind of journey, and I've been lucky to take mine with an incredible crew.

First shout-out goes to the 600+ brilliant writers who make up the Vermont College of Fine Arts community and have sustained me in so many ways. Rita Williams-Garcia, Tim Wynne-Jones, and Sharon Darrow have become the voices in my head when I revise. Shelley Tanaka is my courage. I'd like to think you'll find traces of Louise Hawes and Martine Leavitt in this book too. You'll definitely see: Liz Cook, Alicia Potter, Adi Rule, Dana Walrath, Cordelia Jensen, Mary Winn Heider, Amy Rose Capetta, Yamile Saied Mendez, and Jonathan Lenore Castin (and Elisabeth Castin), who among them read more drafts than I should probably admit publicly.

And then there are my writerly big sibs, who've always left a light shining on the route ahead. Marianna Baer, Varian Johnson, Alicia Potter, Bethany Hegedus, Kekla Magoon, Sarah Aronson, and Sara Zarr: THANK YOU. Thanks, too, to all of the VCFAers who've been my companions and confidants on the road, including my dearest Thunderbadgers (kek yeah!) and the Beverly Shores gang.

I landed in expert hands with Stacey Barney at Putnam Books for Young Readers. She and Kate Meltzer understood this story and helped make it the book it was meant to be. I'm amazed at their sharp minds and unflagging energy. Thanks, too, to Chandra Wohleber, Cindy Howle, Katharine McAnarney, and the rest of Putnam's oh-so-brilliant team. As for Erin Harris of Folio Literary: Where do I begin? You're the fiercest, smartest, and most committed ally I could have imagined. Thank you for navigating this road with me.

I'm lucky to know a small army of medicine women—including Marissa Bayerl, MSN, APRN, PMHNP-BC (woot!), and Drs. Alda Osinaga, Margaret Spencer Kepler, Jill Paulson, and Tamar Gur—who answered some truly bizarre questions along the way. Factual blunders are all mine, of course, as are any canonical quirks. (A dozen years of catechism classes should earn me a little poetic license, eh?) Andy Bayerl and Karen Schneider came to my rescue when I needed speedy readers. I took inspiration from the artwork of J Michael Walker, the music of Mariza and Ana Moura, Randall Sullivan's *The Miracle Detective*, Daniel B. Smith's *Muses, Madmen, and Prophets*, and countless pilgrimages to religious sites, art museums, botánicas, and other places where saints tend to hide.

Hearty thanks to everyone at GrubStreet, Patchwork Farm, the Writing Barn, Pine Manor's Summer Solstice, Boston KidLit Drink Night, Kindling Words, the Swanky 17s, and the PEN New England Children's Book Caucus. Everywhere I go: brilliant, generous writers.

I've left out many people I hold dear. So many friends and family members have kept encouraging, kept asking, kept cheering. Thanks to all of you for believing in me even when I faltered.

And last but definitely not least: My parents, Cynthia and Andy, are the real saints in this story. They got a kid who came into the world asking tough questions and veering off on unexpected paths—bless them, they went along for the ride and have remained my proudest champions.